What the readers said:

"It has all the explosive ing
everywhere in the world lo
romance, deception, traged

"Very compulsive reading. You simply have to know what's coming on the next page."

Stuart Carline, banker

"What a story! Beautiful love scene, and I really wanted the heroine to get her man."

Sharon White, secretary

"A good read for a long journey. It's written with such realism that you actually feel transported to those bygone days. There are so many interesting details."

Steven Ball, manager

"A very real, evocative book. I was fascinated by the people and the events leading up to the Russian Revolution."

Guy Sheridan, restaurateur

"Very moving. One of the most beautifully written death scenes I have ever read."

Sylvia Allan, nurse

"I was enthralled! I had a feeling that I was there, and I have learnt so much about those people and the way they lived."

Diana Downes, receptionist

"Brilliant! I couldn't put the whole book down!"

Tracey Gaunttett, hairdresser

JOANNA HORAIM ASHBOURN

THE AQUILINE INHERITANCE

VOLUME ONE

THE FAMILY SEAT

Sterling Eagle Books

First published in Great Britain
by Sterling Eagle Books 1991

Typeset by PR Reprographics, Berkhamsted

Made and printed in Great Britain by
BPCC Hazell Books
Aylesbury, Bucks, England
Member of BPCC Ltd.

Edited by
Jo Ashbourn
Samantha Ashbourn

To JULIAN, with love and thanks for all his encouragement and support.

To my daughters, Jo and Samantha – in the hope that this record of their ancestors may help them to uphold and maintain the high traditions of our family.

To Jane Irons with thanks for all her help and encouragement

"But man is not made for defeat', he said
'A man can be destroyed but not defeated."

E. Hemingway – The Old Man and the Sea

THE AQUILINE INHERITANCE

THIS IS A STORY OF ONE FAMILY'S FORTUNES BEGINNING IN THE 19TH CENTURY ON THE RUSSIAN PLAINS AND IN POLAND.
IT SPANS FIVE GENERATIONS AND ENDS IN CONTEMPORARY ENGLAND, WHERE THE DESCENDANTS LIVE NOW. IN THIS FAMILY, MEN FOUGHT AND DIED IN UPRISINGS, REVOLUTIONS, AND WORLD WARS.

IT WAS THE WOMEN WHO BROUGHT UP THE CHILDREN AND ENSURED THE FAMILY'S SURVIVAL AGAINST ALL ODDS.
IT WAS EASIER TO DIE FIGHTING, THAN TO STRUGGLE FOR YEARS TO ENSURE THAT THEIR SPIRITUAL HERITAGE WOULD BE HANDED OVER TO THE NEXT GENERATION.

TO THOSE STRONG, INVINCIBLE WOMEN I OWE THIS LEGACY AND DEDICATE THE TALE . . .

PREFACE

"We'd better make sure that you don't forget to take the book home with you", said my mother, setting aside the thick volume.

For the past hour, both she and I had been looking at the few bits and pieces left over from our family treasures:

Hand-painted china teacups, so translucent that you could almost see through them, the odd silver knife and fork with my great-great-grandmother's initials, a pair of bronze horses sparring playfully, a small figure of a pensive Napoleon standing beside his cannon, a sugar-bowl – all gold and silver with solid grapes cascading from the top down to the sides, a crystal mirror – almost two inches thick, a leather-bound volume of 19th century Russian fairy tales, and a frayed, old album full of sepia photographs of unsmiling women in high-necked dresses with their hair piled high, and men in stiff collars, looking away from the camera somewhere into the distance.

"This is all that is left," sighed my mother, "and it is a shame that you cannot take them all with you now – at least take the book."

I slowly turned the pages, thick and yellow-grey. I knew the stories, or rather the tales, by heart. I had heard them as a child every evening, read to me by my mother. She had remembered them from her childhood, and her mother had known them before her. They had been told and re-told in our family for four generations, the book having been bought by my great-grandmother for her children, sometime around 1880, and had been in use ever since. It was a remarkable book, having survived two uprisings, one revolution and two world wars, to finally arrive in England with me, to civilisation, stability and safety, as one hoped.

Its title, printed in large, ornate letters, read: "Tales of the Wise Cat."

Bound in dark-green leather, the thick volume had a beautiful outside sleeve: an ancient oak-tree standing gnarled, but powerful on a sandy shore. Tethered by a golden chain, the Wise Cat walked timelessly around it, day and night. Turning to the left, he would sing a song, while to the right, he would tell a story . . . Above the oak, travelling slowly across the firmament, the full moon silvered the Wise Cat, the tree and the shore, with its soft glow.

As far as I was concerned, this book was a real family heirloom.

Then there were the other stories, those about my family's past, which had been told to me many times over the years, as it had been my mother's wish to imprint them on my memory forever, because she knew only too well that world wars often destroyed whole towns and villages, and that old churches were burned to the ground, together with the parish books, containing entries of weddings, christenings and deaths.

Since then, I have passed them on to my daughters in the same way, by slowly recounting our family past, which is long gone . . .

"Is this story true?" I was often asked.

It is as true as our childhood memories are, when suddenly descending upon us in a missed heart-beat, they bring back the long-forgotten smell of rain-washed earth, the heady scent of summer nights, a place visited once before, or a sad song from a past which we thought we had left forever . . .

The feelings, experiences, and voices conjoin and merge with what we heard or saw in the dreams of our youth – they are still somewhere in the nostalgic yearning of our hearts . . .

Can you feel it?

Chapter One

The winterbound steppe stretched ahead of them interminably. Except for the purple shadows where their sledge-runners had passed, there was nothing for miles, but the blinding whiteness of the snow, against which the dark serpent of the convoy meandered sinuously towards the horizon, the iron-cast sky merging with the bound earth into the distant line.

From the east, at sunrise, the red circle hung from the steel sky in a rose-tinted, unearthly glow but the motionless steppe beneath lay freezing in sinister, utter silence.

The snow-storm was coming.

Sensing the ominous weather-change, the commanding officer shouted an order to the soldiers heading the convoy. One of these men turned his horse around and aligning with the commander, silently awaited his dispatch. Lieutenant Bobrov did not look at the man's darkened, frost-covered face. He knew that they needed to stay somewhere warm for the night, and the nearest village, according to his map and his memory, was no less than ten miles away.

Still not looking directly at the waiting soldier he curtly gave the order to move faster.

Any delays invariably made him feel bad tempered, and he impatiently waved the man away. They had to reach the outpost of the houtor* well before nightfall, or they would risk losing more prisoners, especially the wounded ones . . .

Following higher orders he had to take a contingent of prisoners from the Polish border, across the Russian plains to the depths of Siberia.

The men, all of whom were officers, had mostly been captured during the fierce battles in the Polish forests, in the recently quelled, latter part of the 1863 uprising.

He disliked this task, but being a true soldier he carried out his bidding unequivocally. The journey was arduous and aggravatingly lengthy during these severe winter months. Pulling the fur-lined cape tighter around him, he rode on with downcast, inwardly reflective eyes.

His thoughts turned to the serious problem of the wounded prisoners. They slowed down the wayfaring considerably and hence his own safe return home. Some of them would die during the tortuous journey and would have to be buried in the numb, frozen earth. Perhaps he could leave the dying few in the village – at least it would spare him both the delay and the inconvenience of the burials.

He shifted slightly in his saddle and although his features remained impassive the shadow of a smile crossed his face.

* *Houtor* – Cossack village

The sharp, piercing commands shouted from guard to guard along the convoy brought a response. Amid the crunching of the snow under the skidding sledges and the snorting of the nudged horses the convoy lurched forward.

The next few miles were covered in good time. Sensing that stables were near the horses were easy to ride, and the guardsmen's voices no longer carried urgent orders. Even the prisoners dragged themselves out from under the heaps of horse-blankets which they had been given to keep warm.

Feeling in slightly better spirits, Bobrov stretched himself up and scanned the desolate space ahead. In the far, far distance, down the valley, the blueish clouds of smoke above the greying roof-tops of the peasants' cottages, and the bulbous dome of the village church were now quite visible through the bare tree branches. As the convoy approached, he could hear the furious barking of the farm dogs. The remote, prosperous hamlet was known to Lieutenant Bobrov from his previous assignments, and – he smiled to himself – would serve his purpose well.

·

The stingingly frosty air forced Henryk back to consciousness. Weak and confused, he could barely distinguish between day and night. The throbbing pain in his left leg would not leave him – but mercifully, he drifted in and out of oblivion. Cocooned in his insensibility, he missed the arrival at the village, the ensuing commotion from the unharnessing of the horses and the division of the convoy among the peasants' abodes.

Somewhere through his woolly fog, distant voices rose and fell without meaning, however hard he strived to understand – and yet he was well aware of the people and changes around him. Without warning the pain soared, as he was lifted and moved onto a narrow stretcher before being jerkily carried away. A hot fustiness assaulted his nostrils used to the sharpness and clarity of fresh air, as the stretcher suddenly came to a halt. He was lifted up and lowered onto a bed, and then the men drifted silently away before he could ask them the question. What was it that he had wanted to ask – he could not remember. He sensed rather than saw someone moving slowly around the bed. An old woman brought him a tumbler of water, and moistening his feverish mouth, she muttered and chanted plaintively in Russian.

"Oh, those men, those men . . . fighting and fighting . . . such a young master, and now so sick. And what of your poor, dear mother, Hospodyn* help her, wherever she is. It's a shame, such a shame . . ."

Henryk listened to the woman's lament, and tried to focus his eyes on her face. She came in and out of his vision, old, dark and shrivelled, but wiry. Her grip on his arm was strong and he drank the water avidly, grateful for the support she gave him.

* *Hospodyn* – God

In the cottage belonging to the village elder, Lieutenant Bobrov sat at a table sorting out papers. There wasn't much he could do – the older man nodded in solemn agreement.

"I am glad you see it my way", Bobrov relaxed in his chair, and putting aside the papers of his four prisoners, added,

"The more badly wounded men are too sick to be carried with the rest of the convoy. They won't last more than a day or two."

The two men lapsed into silence. With the unfailing instinct of a veteran soldier, Bobrov knew for certain that the men were doomed. He gave a brisk order to bury them in the local churchyard. The elder bowed, and went out.

Lieutenant Bobrov wrote his report late into the night. The envelope, sealed with red wax and stamped with the lieutenant's signet ring, was left for the elder to despatch as soon as possible to the nearest garrison town, which was some fifty or so miles away.

With the first light of morning, the grey column of prisoners, soldiers and horses assembled hurriedly, and then, with order restored, wound out of the village onto the frostbound trail. By the time a few anaemic rays of winter sunshine had emerged, they had disappeared from the village's view for good.

Henryk woke up abruptly. The pain, sharp and intense, made him reluctantly open his eyes. Alarmed by the strangeness of the place, he tried to focus on the shadows slowly moving in front of the fire, burning strongly in the enormous black grate. The range extended on both sides of the squat chimney-breast into the seating places, large enough for people to sleep on during the coldest nights. This time, among the bright, hand-woven cushions sat three cats, looking at the stranger with curious, yellow eyes. With difficulty, in the dim light of the oil lamp, Henryk made out the old woman who had given him the water. She was standing with her back to him, stirring something in a black-bellied cauldron. He could hear her talking to the cats in a soft, muffled voice.

The room, low and oddly shaped, was full of bunches of dry herbs, hanging from the blackened beams. The old woman approached the bed holding a bowl of foul smelling liquid, and a bundle of cotton strips. Bending over the bed, she began cleaning his leg wound. He could smell the strong, bitter odour of the herb infusion and the coarse stench of unrefined spirit. It hurt as it burned his flesh, making him bite his lip in an effort to keep still. Meeting Henryk's pleading eyes with her faded, steady gaze, the old woman smiled, but continued. And all the time she worked, she talked to Henryk without waiting for him to reply.

"Don't mind the pain, young man. It will heal better, if it's cleaned properly, and there is still a good chance that we will all dance at your wedding! There is some life in you yet, but Hospodyn pomyluj*, you are a bag of bones, and no offence! You just try and get better, and we shall feed you up a bit . . . Kostucha † won't get you, no fear. You will get stronger in no time at all – I'll see to that!"

The woman's old voice rose and fell in the singing Ukrainian rhythm, but he understood her peasant dialect well, and wanted to thank her.

He stirred and moved his lips, but there came no sound of words, only a strangled moan.

The woman called softly:

"Katriona, get me more hot water here!"

Somewhere from the shadows of the far corner, a figure emerged. Tall and slender, the girl held a steaming wooden bowl in one hand, and a wide cotton towel in the other. As was the fashion for peasant girls, she was dressed in a thin cotton blouse, heavily embroidered and tied at the neck with a red ribbon. Her starched red skirts rustled faintly as she slowly approached the bed. She kept her head down and Henryk could only see the perfectly straight white parting of her shiny, black hair. Without a word she assisted the woman.

The old woman turned and walked back to the range. Henryk sank into the soft pillows with grateful relief. She had finished with him at last.

Washed and bandaged with strips of cotton soaked in herb potion, he hoped that now he would be left alone.

Instead a wooden spoon parted his lips, and a fiercely bitter herb-infusion washed out the sickly taste in his mouth, before trickling down his throat and forcing him to swallow.

Hospodyn pomyluj – God have mercy

† *Kostucha (folk)* – Death

He coughed, but the old woman made sure that most of the foul-smelling potion reached his stomach. The infusion must have been a powerful one, since before he could protest, however feebly, he was fast asleep.

The girl stole a covert glance at the man over her god-mother's shoulder. He lay with his eyes closed, and in the sombre light of the flickering oil-lamp his face had a deathly, grey pallor. He was terribly still.

Katriona dared not breathe. The sleeping man made no sound, and she looked at him again. She noticed with alarm that the bones of his face showed through his skin.

In her own confusion, she found it within herself to pity this stranger. It was wicked that a man so young had to die.

A strange feeling overwhelmed her. She could not find the words for it: an infinite pity or something else, something she could not even to begin to under-stand.

She felt a pang in her heart. Quickly, she glanced at him again.

The almost black hair, damp with fever, curled at his sunken temples. Above the pale cheeks lay in dark semi-circles the elongated shadows of his thick lashes. The strong mouth with full lips seemed set in an unnatural, straight line. Unshaven and sick, he was still a fine-looking man, and the girl suddenly blushed.

The old woman straightened the bed, and turning round said sternly.

"You can go now. I will stay and cook some chicken broth, just in case he comes round. If all is well, he will need something light and nourishing."

And with a glance at the man's now flushed face, she added quietly,

"Only God can help you, for whatever could be done here, I have done".

She picked up the cotton towels and turned to go, when suddenly her god-daughter hugged her, whispering hotly into her face,

"Please, please, Matushka, spasti eho!* Don't let him die, oh, please don't!"

Just as suddenly, she let go of Vassilisa and disappeared through the dark doorway.

Vassilisa shook her head and looked thoughtfully at the wounded man. He was restless, his thin hands clawing at the rough cover and was mumbling something over and over again in an urgent, hoarse voice . . .

It sounded like a name.

Whatever her thoughts were, the old woman said nothing aloud, but with troubled eyes, she turned towards the corner where the dark-faced Madonna's icon hung, and bowed low, before fervently crossing herself twice.

A few days passed, with the young man drifting in and out of a heavy sleep, unsure of reality, as in a hot, wet fog, where faces and voices appear from nowhere, only to fade away without a trace. The journey, endured over the last three weeks, left him confused and very weak.

* Mother, save him

As the old woman had said, his life hung in a precarious balance. As if to make matters worse, he would not, or could not, eat anything.

Katriona sat by the bed, alert and tense, despite her lack of sleep. From time to time, she rinsed a piece of cotton in a bowl filled with icy water, and wiped with the cold cloth the feverish face of the unconscious man.

Never in the whole of her secluded life, had she felt such a strong and unexpected emotion. Strangers seldom passed through the isolated stanitza*, bar the odd travelling old man or an army convoy. They would disappear as quickly as they had come, leaving an inexplicable feeling of wanting to go away too, of curiosity about the world behind and beyond the steppe, of being truly free.

She didn't know whether this man meant so much to her because he was part of that outside world or because there was something special in his face, something that she thought she had to know. And the only way that she could, would be by making him well, by saving his life, whatever the cost . . .

The old woman cleaned his wounds, and each day forced more of a different herb-infusion into the sick man's parched mouth. The look of desperation on Katriona's face stopped her from making any prognosis, but she was worried. The man had fought hard to live, but now he was losing his battle.

The days merged into nights, which dragged on, through his fever, delirium, ravings and the trem-

bling of his body . . .
On the surface he looked almost well, if it weren't for his eyes, bright but sensless, with the liquid irises almost merging into the oddly gleaming whites.
Katrina watched him constantly, more and more worried by the restlessness of his hands, clawing at the blankets.
She too knew it meant the end was near . . .

It was well after nightfall when Henryk's breath suddenly began to come very fast and then changed into a horrible ruckle. Katriona, who had been left on her own, panicked – he was dying, and all her efforts, all her prayers, had been in vain. Vassilisa had gone to see to a woman in labour at the other end of the village, and would not be back before morning.

She spun around the room, looking for something, anything. There was nothing, and no one to help her.
Now it was between her and the man alone . . .

. . . Henryk was swimming in the warm waters of the Mediterranean sea, just off the southern coast of Italy. They had come here for their honeymoon. Joanna, his bride, had stayed behind at the villa resting, while he went to explore the village and the rocky, little island, which was just minutes away.

Giant rocks rose out of the sea forming a narrow tunnel which led to the island. Swimming slowly, Henryk turned into the opening.

He felt tired, and curiously light. Floating on the water, he thought how wonderful it would be if he was a seal. He would be able to sleep, while drifting towards the sunny, green patch of land.

Suddenly, without warning, the giant rocks shook, and an avalanche of stones, large and small, gurgled down the slopes into the tunnel. A sharp pain made him realise that he had been hit. He tried to dive to avoid the stones, but perversely, the water brought him back to the surface, and in a panic, he realised that there was no way forward. He had to turn and swim back. Somewhere from the land, across the water, an unknown voice called to him, urgently and with anger. He could not understand the words, but knew it was he who was wanted.

Wearily, he turned around and let the water carry him softly back, the gentle waves splashing his face with a cool mist. He felt good, and raising his eyes he looked up at the sky. Instead, to his horror, he saw a pair of eyes, huge, dark and wild, boring straight into his. He shut his eyelids tight in the hope that it was just a bad dream, but suddenly the whirling current sucked him down, and then there was nothing but an impenetrable darkness around him . . .

. . . The man stopped ruckling, and lay still. Katriona ran to the bed. Desperation and anger made her reckless – with one fierce tug she split his shirt open, exposing his chest. Heaving and crying with anger, she scratched him with both hands. Her sharp nails drew blood.

The sight made her even angrier. Her voice breaking with terror and despair, she hissed through clenched teeth, "If you want to go, you can go, but in pain, not quietly, no!"

Her shaking hands clawed at his body again and again.

She hated him at that moment, and oh, how she wished that he could feel the pain!

Sobbing hysterically now, Katriona tugged at the motionless man. She grabbed his shoulders, and lifting him close to her, she shook him furiously; once, twice, and then again and again and again . . . but to no avail. Frightened and anguished, she kept on hitting at his chest with a clenched fist, and screamed at the slipping away man, still limp in her grip.

"Fight, damn you, fight! I won't let you die! Come back! Do you hear me, come back! You must live, you must, you must!"

Hot sweat and strands of wet hair almost blinded her; impatiently she threw her hair back, and looked down anxiously into the man's eyes, her face only an inch or so from his.

Henryk's vague, liquid eyes suddenly opened wide, and consciously focussed on her face. Their eyes locked together.

He stared at her in violent astonishment and terror.

With all her might, she willed him to come back, to life.

The strength of her young body, her burning warmth passed through to the dying man.

She held him tight in her arms, his face at her breast.

A minute or an eternity elapsed before Katriona, blinded by the tears streaming down her face, released the man and looked at him, expecting the worst. To her amazement he was now gently asleep, his breathing stable.

Exhausted, she covered him well and sat down by the bed to keep vigil.

Within minutes she was asleep.

By first light the fever had subsided. When Katriona awoke, startled by a dog's barking outside, the man was still asleep, his face relaxed and peaceful.

Vassilisa came back, late morning and she was crossing the yard just as Katriona bent over Henryk with the usual herb infusion. Suddenly he opened his eyes, and looking at her consciously, asked quietly:

"Where am I?"

He was left alone and without an answer as the girl dropped the bowl to the floor and then ran out, loudly calling her god-mother.

From that morning Henryk became visibly better, his body beginning the lengthy process of recovery. Katriona fed him at regular intervals with a light chicken broth, and tried to keep her emotions well-hidden. She was sure that the man remembered nothing about that night, and she was well pleased.

The dressing on his wounds was changed daily,

and if Vassilisa was surprised at Henryk's sudden recovery, or the deep weals on his body, she wisely asked no questions. But her thoughtful eyes often rested on the girl, and once or twice she stroked Katriona's smooth head with unexpected feeling.

Two weeks passed, and satisfied with Henryk's progress, the old woman announced:

"Well, young man you have cheated Death, eh? But all this sickening, all this fever has made you sweaty. You need something special though, to make you better – a good, hot bath! To warm the bones right through and clean the flesh, huh? Nothing is better for you than a bit of soaking, you know.
So what do you say?"

Henryk weakened by the fever didn't bother to argue.

And so, Katriona was despatched to fetch the two women, who usually washed the dead in the village. In the meantime, the old woman prepared the room. The big logs in the range burned noisily, throwing a red glow across the walls in long strips.

A wooden barrel stood filled with water, and alongside it, on the floor, lay a bed of fresh, golden straw.
Outside the house a strong bonfire, built by one of the lads, was heating a large rock. Vassilisa carefully diluted a small quantity of lye in a bucket, and bound the wisps of straw and phloem into a fragrant bundle.

The intense heat from the roaring range raised

the temperature of the room to such an extent that droplets of condensation formed on the beams, and fell down like warm rain.

The old woman's companions arrived and stood at the bottom of the bed, shifting from one foot to another, talking fast and looking at the stranger with an open, child like, curiosity. They must have been very old, their faces faded and aged, but their black, bird-like eyes, drowned in folds of wrinkles, appraised him sharply. Listening to their animated chatting, Henryk had the uneasy feeling that it was not often that they had the opportunity to wash a man who was still alive.

Embarrassed, he was just about to say something when two village lads, groaning under the strain, brought a red hot rock on a metal tray inside the room and tipped it into the barrel. Hissing, spitting hot steam rose up to the dark beams, and completely filled the room with opaque clouds. Through the fog Henryk could only feel but not quite see, the women's deft hands undressing and moving him onto the straw bed. The straw bundle soaked in grey, oily lye mercilessly pummelled and massaged his painfully thin body, squeaking at each bony joint it met, while they turned him from one side to another.

In between each turn, buckets of hot water almost drowned him.

Finally washed and dried, he was dressed in a long peasant's nightshirt, and lifted onto the clean bed. The soft shirt, which had been washed many times before, smelled comfortably of straw and

wood shavings. From the sheepskin folded at the end of the bed drifted a peculiar, sour smell of old leather and stale bread.
He felt incredibly fresh, light and well.
Exhausted, he fell into a deep sleep, and, for the first time in months, without any dreams.
Silently, the women returned the room to order.

Henryk slept soundly for several hours after his ordeal but the bath had made him feel much better, and when he woke up during the evening of the next day, he was ravenously hungry.

The smell of tasty, rich chicken broth cooking on the stove made his stomach contract and rumble loudly. Vassilisa turned round with a smile,
"You can only have a little bit. We don't want to kill you now, do we?"

He felt gratitude to these simple but warm people, and ate slowly, savouring each spoonful for the first time in weeks. After he had satisfied the first hunger, Vassilisa took the bowl and wooden spoon away, and he sank back with a sigh of relief, in blissful repose, happy to receive all the attention.

He had a strange feeling, as if his body contained no bones, but was only stuffed with cotton wool, through which hot blood pulsated in spasms . . .

The low, dark ceiling reflected the moving red glow from the half open oven door, and somewhere behind the whitewashed chimney-breast, over the warm range, a cricket played his jerky, sweet song.

It seemed to him that it would be wonderful to

stay like this forever – warm, safe and comfortably weary, listening to the cricket's playing and unconcerned about anything more important than the next meal. He smiled, amused. It was only a dream, and a short one at that.

He slept, he awoke, and then slept again. In a half-dream, half-reality, he observed life in the peasant's cottage in unconnected fragments, as if it weren't a real life at all, but the cut up pieces of strange, fast moving, oscillating pictures.

During the next few days, he slowly made an effort to reconstruct recent events in his mind, but could not remember much of the past few weeks; the time before his imprisonment was clear by contrast, and sombrely, he sought to consider his situation.

A clenched fist came down on top of the gnarled, wooden table with a crash. A jar of gorzalka and thick-glass mugs angrily clattered against the stained planks.

"Nu, wy staroy, tak durakom ostanyosh! Vy shto, uma potieriali?"*

Mikhail stood bent forward, his narrow, rodent-like face white in anger. His small, dark eyes, set close to the long, twitching nose gave an impression of permanent annoyance. Menacingly, he looked at the stunned faces around him.

He could not stand their stupidity any longer, why the whole village was in danger as long as this man was alive. And yet through their greed, they could not see it, the damn fools.

The men stirred, uncertain again. They had gathered together in a side room of the village inn to discuss the future of the prisoner. It wasn't fair. He should have died with the others and then there would have been no trouble. As it happened, he was getting better each day, and it was obvious that he was not going to oblige them.

The men had been arguing for over an hour now as to what to do next. The heavy smell of tobacco and the odour of the vodka hung above their heads among the clouds of smoke.

Most of the elders wanted to keep the prisoner as there was always a shortage of working lads.

The Czar's decree had robbed many Cossack's settlements of their young men, taken "v soldaty"†, usually for a full 25 years. They would come back middle aged and tired, dissimilar to the dashing

* You are old but still stupid! Have you lost your mind?

† *"v soldaty"* – into army

youths who had left all those years ago – and that was only if they came back at all.

Nikita slowly counted the good points of the proposal, broadly gesticulating with his rough, stubby hands:

"He is tall and muscular – also as a nobleman, he has been well fed all his life. Must have plenty of stamina to have survived this far . . . As we saved his life, he owes it to us to work hard. As it happens, there is that far corner field, you know, the big one behind the woods, which was Alexey's before his conscription . . ."

He was interrupted by Vasyl who wasn't too sure whether Henryk would recover enough to do heavy work.

Only Mikhail saw the danger at once. He got up again. What if the soldiers ever came back and found him here, unreported to the authorities? They were only safe if he was dead or in Siberia, wasn't that obvious?

Mikhail's high falsetto voice penetrated the spirit and tobacco fumes, and disconcerted, the men turned to Fiodor, the most respected man among them, who was sitting at the head of the table.

He was looking into space, drumming his fingers impatiently.

Vassilisa had made him promise to keep the man in the village.

She was a wise woman, who could see beyond and into the future. He guessed that she was puzzled, concerned, and perhaps even frightened.

He had a strong feeling that she knew more than she said.

There was something about this man, he sensed, that was very special indeed. It was important that he stayed, or there would be misfortune for the village, that she knew for sure.

"I have done the wild fern runes twice, and there is no doubt that we must keep him. He has to stay." That is what she had said last night and he believed her.

Fiodor came back to reality.

The men around the table waited patiently for his words. He looked at them silently.

In the dim, flickering light of the wooden tapers, stuck high on the blackened beams, the men's faces were red and sweating from the heavy heat of too many bodies gathered together in a small room, and too much drinking.

He coughed to clear his throat, and then stood up. He addressed the men, speaking solemnly, and with the authority of a village leader.

"The man has arrived at our village for a special reason.

I know this and it's my belief that we must make sure he says here to fulfil his mission. The whole village – all of us – will benefit. I will deal with Lieutenant Bobrov myself if the need arises. If necessary, we could easily hide him. At this moment I cannot give you more details, but I need your trust, support and full cooperation."

Fiodor paused and looked around the table at the suddenly alert faces, all eyes fixed on him.

He spoke to the men directly,

"Who says that the prisoner should stay?"

Apart from Mikhail's, all hands went up.

It was agreed that until he was fully recovered Henryk would stay in Vassilisa's house. His fate would later be decided by the elders, who would have learned all the facts by then.
The men walked home in small groups, still discussing the unexpected news.

The snow was thawing with the approaching spring.
Across the wet, soggy fields Mikhail furtively made his way to the house of his old friend, Gregory.
If they thought that he had accepted defeat, they were bigger fools than they knew.
His dislike of Fiodor had never been stronger, and he grudgingly mumbled under his breath,

"You had better beware, Fiodor, it is me, not one of these prattle-heads, against whom you think you are running."

Slowly a plan formed in his mind, and he instantly felt better, his small, black eyes shining with mischief.
Gregory's house was just behind that cluster of trees, and it should not be too difficult to ensure his help in taking Fiodor down a peg or two . . .

Anyhow the village could do with a new, younger leader, and he was ready for it.

Chapter Two

All day long, the low sky was overcast and grey. The previous night, a strong easterly wind swept the barren fields and the estate's orchards, whirling up and up the last of the dirty leaves, bending the poplars' tops in the deserted drive, and whistling hauntingly in the Lodge's vast chimneys, before disappearing, loose and roaring, into the distant woods.

"It's going to snow tonight, that's for sure", said Prakseda, putting more logs onto the burning fire. The two young girls sitting on a large sofa looked up from their embroidery, and the taller of the two exclaimed,

"We can have a kulig* on Sunday then!"

The thought made them drop their work and start chattering excitedly. The picture conjured up was so colourful! The racing of the sleighs, the jangling bells, the jubilant coachmen shouting, "Who-ha!", the snorting of the horses, the flurry of the snow under the sleighs' runners, which would settle in a delicate mist on the girls' glowing faces and the air, so clear, fresh and invigorating.

As Prakseda sat on her heels stoking the fire, the girls collapsed in another fit of giggles. They

* *kulig* – sledging cavalcade

just remembered a neighbour's dashing young sons, who would jump from their sleigh to that of the girls. This was a real challenge as the sleighs would be moving at full speed and more often than not the young man would fall off into the deep snow amidst everyone else's shouts and shrieks of laughter. In the last sleigh just behind this assembly, would sit the kapela* from the village inn. The musicians always played lively folk dances with such passionate abandon that most of them would be half lying in the folds of the sheep-skins, which lavishly lined all the sleighs. Except, for Big Peter, of course, who always played the double-bass, standing at the back of the speeding sledge, with his powerful legs widely spread for balance.

In a small clearing somwhere in the middle of the forest, a few stable lads would be waiting beside a huge bonfire. A trestle table, which stood nearby, bore a cauldron of bigos, sauerkraut baked with pieces of meat and spiced with dry mush-rooms, juniper berries, peppercorns and a gen-erous helping of red wine, this having been very slowly cooked for a few days before the event. On another table would stand a well-blackened dish filled with hot sausages, roasted over the bonfire. A large round loaf of bread, the size of a coach-wheel, sliced thinly with a sword serving as a knife, rested on the wooden board, while on the other side of the table, a handsome gathering of black bottles boldly held various home-made vod-kas – strong and straight for the men, light and herbal for the women. Nothing could taste better

* *kapela* – Folk band

than the aromatic amber coloured concoction, which would be icy cold to start with, but then liquid fire as it reached the stomach. And, of course, there was the real treat: those scorched and cracked smoked sausages, fragrant with juniper berries, served wrapped in a slice of bread . . .

Coming back to reality Prakesda turned back from rousing the fire, and standing there unnoticed, she watched the laughing girls. How they had changed from the time when they had arrived, barely three years ago. Two bewildered unhappy orphans. She was a kind-natured girl and felt so sorry for them. The old Duchess, who was mistress of the lodge, had been a widow for some time now, and being childless, welcomed the newcomers. She made it quite clear to the servants that she wanted the best for the girls, they were her dead sister's children after all.

It was whispered in the kitchen that the girls' father had been wounded and then taken prisoner, while fighting in the 1863 Uprising against Russia. He had been sent on a fatal journey to Siberia in a convoy of other ill or wounded prisoners. He never got there.

His wife, the Duchess's sister Joanna, was not in the best of health. A shy and gentle woman, left without her beloved husband and without the estate – the Russians had confiscated everything in retaliation – she expired shortly after the official confirmation of his death. Some said that she had died of a broken heart.

According to the official documents, Captain Henryk Horaim died of his injuries while in transit.

His place of rest was unspecified, and further enquiries were left unanswered.

The duchess took the girls into her home and her heart. They were to be looked after and educated properly, as befitted young girls of their status. A French maître was engaged to improve their French and their dancing, while a governess was to teach the girls literature and history, which were considered to be the most important subjects at that time in Poland. They were also to learn deportment, drawing and needlepoint. Horse-riding was obligatory as it was considered to be the best exercise for young ladies.

Both girls responded gratefully to the simple kindness of the servants and the gentle nature of their aunt.

The duchess wasn't a disciplinarian and so after finishing their lessons, the girls would have plenty of time to ride or roam the vast grounds.

"There is nothing wrong with those two children, which can't be cured by my cooking," Martha the cook used to say.

The girls, Theophila and Josephine, who had been named after the French fashion, couldn't agree more. They would burst into the kitchen at any time, quite often by coincidence of course, at the very moment that the trays of bread or cakes came out of the enormous, black oven.

The smell of freshly baked bread usually proved to be irresistible to Thea and Josy, as everyone called them. Prakseda would hand each of them large chunks of crunchy bread-ends, spread thickly with creamy butter, sprinkled with coarse salt. The butter was made almost daily and still bore the imprint of the horseradish leaves in which it was kept. The girls would skip away, licking the crystals dissolving on top of the hot bread.

Martha would often make little pasties from the remainder of the bread-dough, which was enriched with milk and eggs. These she would fill with gently fried onions and spices, before glazing them with egg yolk and baking the whole batch in the oven, next to the bread. The pampushki, as the cakes were called, would disappear with the speed of lightning, to Martha's obvious pleasure.

But then, Martha knew how to bake the bread.

"Well", she would explain when asked, "First, what you need is a special wooden bowl in which to prove the dough.

That bowl holds the secret to everything!"

"How come?", exclaimed the new kitchen girl, Ula.

"It's really quite simple. Gradually, you will come to know its likes and dislikes – they all have personalities, you know. Do close your mouth, girl! What I mean is that some might like warmth; if so, you must place it for proving next to the range, and don't forget to tuck a pillow or two round it well.

Or, perhaps, it would like to be christened with feathers as custom requires. Others prefer to be seasoned, always with the nut oil and onion, of course. Some don't like any noise at all, not even a tiny sneeze, others won't work without people milling about the kitchen. Oh, there are many things which you need to learn about the proving-bowl . .

They all have the needs like us, people, you know. That how it's . . .

Then, after you have humoured your bowl, there is the question of flour, and one more thing, it helps if the baking can be done on a sunny day . . ."

"Don't say!"

"I promise you it's true! You see, the hot loaves should be put carefully on a bench outside so that they will soak up the sun. The aroma will be trapped under the crispy crust, and only then will the bread become a real daily bread, blessed by God. And don't you forget to always treat bread with utmost respect: if you drop a loaf, pick it up instantly, kiss it and apologise."

Bemused kitchen girls went about their chores thinking how strange and mysterious the world was. Thinking bread bowl! Whatever next?

The girls' very favourite snack, however, was discovered by chance, when Josy sat down one evening with some village girls sewing their trousseaux. It consisted of large slices of soft black bread spread with an inch of thick, well set soured cream, and then topped up with thick acacia honey.

Food apart, the two sisters couldn't have been more different in their likes, dislikes, and even their looks. While blonde, petite Thea favoured reading and embroidery, Josy, who was darker and tall, felt more in her element out of doors.

She loved wandering around the estate, and always started her walk at the stables where the horses would lift their heads and snort at her in friendly greeting, and where the sweet smell of fresh hay sharpened and defined the pleasure of being alive, well and young.

Not far from the stables glistened the ponds. Covered in algae, and half-choked by rushes and canes, they made an ideal home for the ducks, who would splash and dive almost to the muddy bottom.

Fat sleepy frogs sat on warm stones among the rushes, lazily watching her walk past.

Just to the right, in front of the Lodge, an orderly row of continuously leaves-trembling, silvery poplars led from the house to the driveway, twisting through the sandy fields, up to the edge of the darkened woods. On warm, summer days the hazy sunlight, which filtered through the poplar leaves, laid intricate, quivering shadows on to the dusty track.

Josy would walk down the lane as far as the eye could see. The humming fields, the old trees, and the ever present dogs trailing behind her, were good companions to her yearning for peace and tranquillity. She thought a lot about her dead parents and their lost family home, Vronovo. In her mind, she would talk to her sweet, gentle mother who could not cope with a world she hadn't been bred for, and her father who was rarely home, but whom she adored. Silently she vowed to get Vronovo back some day. Her grief had to be very private as she felt so obliged to Aunt Cornelia for her kindness. And Aunt Cornelia wanted her to be happy.

Despite her good intentions, Josy's rebellious nature would often land her in trouble with her strict governess. She hated being controlled and trained by the caustic, sour spinster. Mature beyond her years and born with the rare quality of common-sense, Josy defied nonsensical restriction.

"Why do I have to walk with a heavy book on my head for hours?", she wailed

"I'm not a hunchback, am I?"

Miss Apolonia didn't condescend to argue, but raising her stern eyes upwards, silently asked God to be a witness to her suffering.

Josy longed to be grown-up and to finally be in charge of her own destiny. But as it was, her future was clouded, making her stamp her foot impatiently at the very thought of it.

Two more years passed, with mornings unwillingly spent over the books with Miss Apolonia, and afternoons on free-spirited escapades around the estate.

As the girls approached their third Christmas at the Lodge, the duchess decided to give them as a special treat – a ball.

It was the first winter during which they were allowed to attend the string of carnival balls, held during January on various neighbouring estates. The duchess felt Josy and Thea should be introduced to the world first at the Lodge ball. Even Miss Apolonia caught some of the excitement and kept drilling both girls in the art of looking suitably demure:

"Straighten your back, Thea", she would admonish, "Josy, don't forget the routine: twist your ear-lobes and slap your cheeks, then moisten your lips, cast your eyes down, and straighten your back, girl – and only then walk into a room."

Both girls sighed but while their bodies went through the routine of the entree once more, their thoughts were already at the ball, endlessly dancing and dancing . . .

This was just the beginning! At last Christmas passed and the carnival began. The first ball was to be held at the Lodge two days after New Year's Day. On the day, a whirl of activity started just after dawn. Martha busied herself in the kitchen, preparing various meat dishes and puddings. The very favourites with the guests were her roast goose with buckwheat and apples, and her wild boar pot-roast. The hare pate gained so many compliments that she prepared some small ceramic pots filled with it, for the guests to take home. The kitchen girls were sent, in a frenzied flutter of starched skirts to fetch, scrub or polish, and it seemed that the whole Lodge shook with excitement, thought Josy.

Prakseda unfolded the girls' dresses on the large bed and checked that not one lacy flounce was crumpled.

Both dresses had been made from white organza, which had then been dyed in different, subtle colours. Dusky pink for Josy and sea-green for Thea. Frothy lace pettit-coats plumped up the skirts, softening the otherwise sombre design.

Prakseda brushed the girls' hair, and arranged Thea's blond strands into a mass of ringlets.

Josy only had one alternative: to either put her

plait up or to let it down.

"This is my best feature", she thought, looking at her image in the silver framed mirror. Well defined by the black, thick lashes, large grey eyes looked seriously back at her from a finely chiselled face. Her pale skin was simply dazzling. She had a straight nose and full lips, but it was her hair which seemed to have a life of its own. It grew past her waist, and its thickness and dark, honey colour drew everyone's attention.

Josy coiled the thick plait twice round her head, securing the ends with diamante pins.

Moistened finger-tips smoothed and straightened her dark brows. She looked at herself again, and smiled with pleasure. Tall and slim, she was fresh and good looking rather than pretty.

In contrast Thea, who was petite and fair, doe-eyed and dimpled, appeared soft and helpless. She had an endearing habit of looking up shyly from under her very long lashes, in a manner which would make most men ready to go to any lengths to protect her.

Alas, she wasn't aware of her powers yet.

Meanwhile, conscious of her fame among the neighbours, Martha summoned every servant-girl she could find who was not already working in the kitchen. The oak table, which had been pushed against one wall, was covered with a snow-white, damask cloth, with garlands of pine-twigs hanging at the front.

Martha stood back, and carefully supervised the platters which were being brought from the kitchen in rapid succession.

"Look out, Annie! Your thumb's in the jelly! Not that way, Tonia, put that platter sideways, next to the ham. I said 'sideways' – oh! What a shtourmack* you are!"

Under Martha's stern eye the girls ran even faster, suddenly awkward and clumsy.

Finally the cold starters had been arranged to Martha's satisfaction on the left-hand side of the long table. There were platters of pickled herrings, rolled around gherkin sticks with slivers of onion rings. Stuffed with a savoury mixture, the eggs lay under a velvety lemon sauce, next to a platter with hare pate which was cut into small squares and served on the thin pieces of bread. This year's smoked ham, cut into wafer-thin slices, was spread in a wide circle like a giant fan. Piled high, various pastries formed miniature pyramids. But the enormous, blue carp in aspic took pride of place. The magnificent fish seemed to be swimming in the diamond- cut sea of jelly and accompaniments.

When all the cold platters and puddings were in place, Martha surveyed the table once more, and satisfied, returned to the kitchen to check the hot dishes,

"Hurry up girls, the guests could be here anytime now!"

Just after dusk, the driveway became busy with the arrival of the first coaches and the stable lads rushing to and fro, unharnessing the horses.

Hidden by the heavy curtain, Josy stood at the window, watching the guests arrive. She could

* *shtourmack* – clumsy idiot

hardly wait. At last Thea, was ready and both girls could go down to the Grand Hall.

The duchess, busy kissing ladies and exchanging New Year's greetings with her neighbours, turned round just as they came down. She looked at her nieces, her eyes suddenly misty. To see them now, having been little orphans not so long ago, so transformed, curiously different and grown up, gave her a catch at the heart. She gave a little sigh, and then composing herself, she proudly presented the girls to all the guests.

The evening had begun.

While the older generation ate and loudly complimented Martha's talents, the youngsters were already dancing in a large side-room, which had been specially adapted for the occasion. The musicians, brought from the nearby garrison town and fortified by a few drinks, played vigorously.

Josy found herself opposite a tall young man, who whirled her around the room. She thought that somewhere in the crowd she glimpsed golden locks and Thea's frothy dress, but she wasn't sure.

All she wanted was to keep dancing and dancing till dawn!

It was not until sometime later that evening that Josy began to see the individual faces around her, instead of a hazy blur. From that moment on, she really began to enjoy the evening. She felt confident and grown up at last.

Suddenly, Josy found herself dancing again with the tall young man who had been her first partner that evening. This time she was able to notice that he had dark-grey eyes, a slightly lopsided, wolfish smile, and angular, lively face. His eyes were smiling too, and his gaze was fixed on her face, holding her in an appraising scrutiny. Curiously enough, she didn't feel embarrassed, only pleased. He was amusing, and this time Josy listened to him with intent interest.

He took charge of the conversation with ease.

"I came on an impulse, you know. Nobody warned me how beautiful the Horaim girls are!"

He said "girls", but it was obvious from the way he looked at Josy, that he really only meant her.

"In that case, perhaps you wouldn't mind telling me your name?"

"But I already told you, during the first dance, remember?"

"I don't think I was paying attention properly. I was so nervous!"

"If I tell you my name now, will you promise to remember it?"

"Oh, but I shall remember your name forever – it's my first ball!"

A flicker of a smile passed his lips.

"Andrew Dobrohovsky, at your service".

She felt instantly at ease with this stranger and his comments made her laugh.

Somehow, without really wanting to, she told him all about her past as if they had long known each other. Andrew listened, and looked down at her with kind, concerned eyes, willing her to say more.

" . . . and here we are, as happy as we can be, under the circumstances, but still waiting for something . . . And . . . and don't know what it is as yet . . ."

She broke off, suddenly embarrassed, but Andrew squeezed her hand reassuringly,

"I do understand. My mother died just a few years back . . . it has never been the same since. I don't get on with my father", he added, his face set hard.

Instinctively, Josy knew what he really meant. She too missed the warmth of a real family life. However kind she was, Aunt Cornelia could not be a substitute for her parents.

The rest of the evening was spent together. They danced and talked as if they have been close friends for years. They both shared a love of horses, solitude and long country walks. They both wanted something different than what life had dealt them so far, and both were impatient for it. His easy assured manner sparked an encouraging confidence in her, and she loved the new feeling.

Around the illuminated, buzzing Lodge, the night grew dark and frosty. The older guests started to leave, afraid that the roads would become treacherous later.

The dining room, untidy with platters of left-over bits and with crumbs littering the stained table cloth, stood empty with both doors ajar.

To the young couple standing at the hall window, the loud laughter and farewells of the departing guests, the coachmen's calls and the barking of the dogs were all distant, muted sounds. At last, they had to say goodbye and Andrew asked:

"I hope . . . May I see you again . . . soon?"

Josy smiled. She could not help but know that she had made an impression on him.

"We do have the most wonderful tea served on Wednesdays."

Andrew looked at her with warm admiration. Her ease was so delightful. He bowed to kiss her hand.

"Goodbye till Wednesday then."

Josy watched him mount his horse. Glimpsing her silhouette at the window he raised his hand in a last salute, before turning his horse, and in a moment the rider and the horse merged into the darkness of the driveway.

Running up the stairs, two steps at a time, Josy burst into her bedroom just as Prakseda was bending over the bed, folding back the covers. In an instant, the astonished servant girl found herself waltzing around the room with Josy laughing and hugging her at the same time. Her eyes sparkling, Josy gave a happy, little laugh of triumph.

"You did like him then?", was all Prakseda could ask, before she freed herself, hot and breathless. Josy did not answer, but planted a kiss on the servant girl's cheek, and then pirouetted across the room.

Prakseda looked up at the ceiling in mock horror, "Good God, help us, if Auntie were to find out!"

During the next few days the weather worsened, and Josy worried whether Andrew would be able to keep their assignation. The snow, falling thick and fast, cocooned the whole Lodge in a soft, white cover. The driveway had disappeared and only the black silhouettes of the poplar trees marked the way out.

On Wednesday, Josy did her lessons at double speed. Miss Apolonia eyed her suspiciously but for once decided to say nothing.

Throwing her books onto her desk Josy only stopped long enough to wash her face and run a comb through her hair. She fled down the wide staircase and entered the summer-room, taking care not to be seen. Unused during the winter months, the room was Josy's favourite place when she wanted to be alone.

She closed the door, and stood at the window for a while, gently blowing on the opaque glass pane, which was covered with frost flowers. She looked intently through a clear spot, and then turned away disappointed. There seemed to be no sign of life on the track between the snowy fields. She sat down in one of the large armchairs, and pulled its wolf-skin cover around her for warmth, thinking about Andrew. They were both so much alike – impatient to live and ready for anything . . . And he made her laugh so much . . .

Her heart beat faster at the thought of meeting him again.

She would not even admit it to herself, but she was falling in love.

Two riders emerged wearily from the far side of the darkened forest. Sensing the stables, the horses hurried along the poplar track. The wind, which was now blowing in their faces, covered their eyebrows, hats, clothes and even the horses with a stiff, white frost.

They finally reached the courtyard, and Andrew dismounted stiffly, leaving his horse to his groom,

Vassyl.

Hearing the crunch of snow under the horses' hooves, Josy threw the rug aside. Her heart beating wildly, she ran to the main door, and sliding the heavy bolt aside, Josy pulled the door open to stand face-to-face with Andrew.

Neither spoke. Miss Apolonia who was descending the stairs in measured steps, called icily,

"Aren't you going to ask your guest in?"

They both smiled absentmindedly, and with unseeing eyes they walked past the governess into the dining room, where Prakseda was busy setting the table for tea.

"My God, you are almost frozen", exclaimed Martha, who had walked in with a laden tea-tray. She hurried back to the kitchen to fetch her never-failing antidote, remedy for everything from chills to a stomach upset. She brought back a large glass of a clear, amber-coloured tincture, and handed it to Andrew.

"Drink this in one go", she ordered.

"Your lad got his portion in the kitchen and is just tucking into a plate of stew", she watched Andrew drinking the concoction without protest.

"And now lots of hot tea", commanded Martha, leaving Prakseda to pour the hot, strong tea. Miss Apolonia sat at the table, distant and apprehensive. To her mind, Josy's behaviour was absolutely scandalous, but she could not voice her opinion in front of a stranger, especially since he . . . She remained lost in thought for a moment.

Thea and Josy sat on either side of Andrew, and Prakseda served huge slices of smoked ham, hot savoury pies filled with a mixture of onions and wild mushrooms, and freshly baked bread. Small bowls of various pickles stood in front of each place-setting. Andrew ate with such gusto that he made both girls laugh. While they ate and talked, Prakseda noiselessly exchanged the plates and brought from the kitchen warm cakes, fluted glass bowls with ruby-glistening confitures and another pot of freshly brewed tea.

"How happy and young they are", thought Prakseda, looking at their faces, glowing in the pool of light, from a lamp which hung low over the table. What Miss Apolonia thought was anyone's guess. She sat with her eyes downcast and ate very little.

The time passed by unnoticed, and after Prakseda had cleared the table and Thea had excused herself, the young couple were left almost on their own, except for the governess, who sat some distance away, engrossed in a book, and was soon forgotten.

They spoke in low voices and then in whispers, at times holding hands. Miss Apolonia looked at the clock with alarm. Hours had passed and night was falling fast.

"Would you like me to send Prakseda to prepare your room for the night?", she asked Andrew at last.

From the expression on his face, she could see that Andrew had lost all sense of time. He leapt to his feet, apologising profusely.

"I am dreadfully sorry, I'm afraid my father doesn't know that I've ridden this far, and I had better go home at once."

Surprised, Josy could only sense how intense his anxiety was, and then she remembered Andrew's guarded remarks about his formidable father, and it rent her heart with foreboding.

"I shall come back as soon, as I can." Andrew was already putting on his vast sheepskin coat, but his again smiling eyes gave his words a meaning which she could not fail to understand.

Josy watched Andrew and his groom hurriedly depart. By then deep night had fallen and the cold moon shone brightly above the ghostly-white courtyard. At last the riders disappeared from sight, and Josy slowly closed the door.

She took the warm shawl from her shoulders and hung it on a hook next to the hat stand. A sudden noise stopped her from going upstairs. She wasn't sure what it was – a stifled sob? She opened the door of the summer-room and therein saw Miss Apolonia, sitting alone, her head bowed low, and crying her eyes out.

Stupefied, Josy stood there for a split second. She could not have imagined the governess being able to cry. Wasn't she always so cool, capable, and even sarcastic?

"Why are you crying?", she managed to ask stiffly at last, trying not to look at the thin, shaking shoulders.

The older woman sat upright and wiped her eyes. Without looking at Josy, she said slowly,

"My brother was killed in the fighting of 1849 . . . I am afraid that young Andrew reminded me of him very strongly."

Her reply disconcerted Josy.

"I never knew that you had a brother", she said, thinking that she knew nothing at all about her governess. Suddenly, she felt ashamed that she did not try and like her more.

The governess sat silently, her eyes and her nose red from crying. She found her handkerchief and tried to restore her composure. On impulse, Josy embraced her.

Andrew and Vassyl rode steadily for a good four miles, before heading westwards, to join the road leading to Andrew's father's estate. The weather had stabilized, but the frost began biting severely again and hot steam whirled around the horses' heads. The track was now covered by snowdrifts, and they rode blindly on, trying to keep to the right direction. Apart from the horses' neighing and the occasional cracking of the low, naked tree branches, there was an oppressive silence. Both young men rode on, deep in their thoughts: Andrew reliving each moment at the Lodge and Vassyl enviously remembering the excellent food which the Lodge servants evidently had every day.

"Good for some", thought Vassyl grudgingly, remembering how rarely his master's cook was generous or favourably disposed towards the ever-hungry stable lads. Vassyl liked the Lodge – the atmosphere was so relaxed and informal. Martha had even given him a glass of her concoction, and he could still feel the warming effect of the fiery liquid in his body, making him feel comfortable and a little sleepy.

For some time now, they had been followed by shadows which slunk close to the ground and sneaked in-between the black trees. The horses were the first to sense danger and suddenly hurried forwards. Having been engrossed in his reverie, Andrew turned round in his saddle surprised and with a chilling horror saw sleek bodies – thin, dark shapes with coldly burning eyes, moving against the snow.

He shouted to Vassyl,

"Quicker, for God's sake quicker, boy!"

The terrified horses blindly dived forward through the thick undergrowth, with the riders holding the reins short and lying close to the horses' necks, having to duck everytime they passed under low branches in a flurry of snow. Behind, the silent wolves pursued them relentlessly.

Somewhere in the distance, Andrew could see the light of a clearing, a road-track perhaps . . .

He leant close to his horse's ear and shouted in desperation:

"Come on, you can make it, come on, boy!"

The wolves were closing in.

The leader of the pack suddenly came up on the left of Andrew's horse and ferociously attacked it. A second later, they were surrounded by a group of at least ten wolves, snapping and snarling with such force and rapidity that Andrew almost fell to the ground. This was a matter of life or death, and both master and horse knew it. Andrew hung onto the horse's neck with all his strength. Out of the corner of his eye he could see Vassyl and his horse disappearing through the trees somewhere towards the right.

He understood and approved of Vassyl's tactics, this might split the pack and weaken the onslaught. But the black shapes began to come closer again. They let off the other rider and his horse, and determined not to lose their main prey, they were on both sides of Andrew now. Their eyes shone with cold, green light, as they rapidly moved ahead in darkness.

The horse whinnied as one of the wolves sprang and sunk his teeth into its side, hanging on with all his might and then, sliding under its weight, ripped the flesh open. The others, smelling the hot blood, followed the leader like crazed demons. In an instant they had formed a mountain of wriggling bodies, with the man and horse underneath. Above the wolves' snarling, came the eerie sound of the horse whinnying in agony. It only lasted a few seconds, but it seemed like an eternity.

Andrew could almost feel the teeth sinking into his body next, were it not for his long, heavy sheepskin coat and long boots. He fought his way out of the convulsed pile of stinking, bloodied and snarling bodies.

The wolves were busy ripping the dead horse open.

Andrew moved backwards slowly until he felt a tree-trunk against his rigid back. He looked up to check the branches, before turning to climb the tree as fast as he could, despite the hot sweat which stung and blinded his eyes. Some of the wolves had left the carcass, and now tried to reach Andrew's legs, which were still dangerously close to the hideous jaws and savage eyes looking up.

He was soaking wet inside his heavy coat and he trembled uncontrollably in every limb. He clung to the tree as his head swam, and suddenly he felt violently sick. He hoped that the dreadful stench of animals and blood would lessen at a higher level, and so he slowly climbed up some more branches. If only he could stay there till daytime, since the wolves would have to go away sooner or later.

Andrew hoped that Vassyl had arrived home safely and would come back with help. The fresh air had cleared his head, and he began to feel shame, guilt and fear.

Dawn seeped through the misty windows while the whole Lodge lay silent and asleep. Josy didn't know what had awakened her, and she sat for a minute, listening. Suddenly she heard shuffling footsteps outside and a voice calling out. Without hesitating, Josy pushed her feet into thick, sheepskin slippers, and grabbing a shawl, she tiptoed down the stairs. It was almost impossible to lift the heavy bars, and she struggled fiercely before the door finally opened. In the pale light of the dawn, a figure emerged from the shadows.

Josy's eyes widened in horror at the terrifying apparition – Andrew moved in her direction, and sensing his utter exhaustion, she reached out and helped him inside. Even in the dim light, she could see that his coat was covered in blood and patches of dirt. Torn pieces of sheepskin hung loosely from the sleeves. His face, bloodless and aged, had a look of such desperation that Josy wasted no time asking questions, but sat him down and ran to the servants' quarters to wake Prakseda and Martha. Between them, they organised as quickly as possible hot bath, a change of dry clothing and a stiff drink.

A spare room was always ready, prepared for any unexpected guest, and Andrew fell fast asleep as soon as he lay down. It was not until late afternoon that he came downstairs, and was able to relate the previous night's events. The violent death of his beloved horse had distressed him far more than the danger which he had encountered, or any fear of facing his father.

Unfortunately, it was not his first youthful incident and Andrew was certain that the reprisals would be severe, and that he would probably be sent away to one of his father's army friends in another part of the country.

Josy listened apprehensively and with mounting foreboding. She knew nothing about Andrew's father, and these predictions greatly frightened her.

A sudden feeling of fear made sweat start out in the palms of her hands. She was frightened and at the same time angry – angry with Andrew's father. What right had he to treat his son like this, to separate them . . . ?

The search-party arrived shortly afterwards, and a sombre-faced Vassyl took Andrew to one side. The old master was beside himself with rage and Vassyl had orders to accompany Andrew home at once.

The young couple were left alone for a few short minutes and vowed to wait for each other forever. They arranged to write each other letters and to exchange notes through the trusted stable lad. With that, Andrew and his party left hurriedly.

The next few months passed uneventfully except for the occasional letter from Andrew, which was brought secretly to the Lodge. He was staying with Colonel Suchy, a friend of his father's on an estate near Kiev, and hoped to be allowed to return in a few months time – in the meantime, he led an exemplary life and had mended his wicked ways. Josy smiled through her tears, as she read Andrew's letter – she missed him so much. His words inspired her with new courage, and she was more determined than ever to wait for her happiness. Sooner or later, Andrew would come home and she knew that they were destined to be together.

Josy fell into the comfortable routine of her everyday life once more, and engrossed in her day-dreams, she hardly noticed the tense current of apprehension around her. The Duchess lived alone in her part of the Lodge, only attended by her maid and her old butler. Sometimes she would have mysterious visitors, but since she never invited confidences these days, Josy was unaware of the oncoming unrest.

Then one day, a messenger arrived with news for the Duchess. That evening everyone was summoned to the Grand Hall and dressed in black, the Duchess addressed them all.

"As you are all aware, we are on the brink of very important events. There are large groups of men already gathered to fight for our freedom, and some have already started the fight. It is up to us to support them with money and food as well as in any other way they may need, but above all, with our prayers and love. From the list brought by the messenger I know that many young men in the neighbourhood have already joined. I don't have a son, but, if any of my stable lads or farm men wish to join, they will be given provisions and anything else that they need."

The atmosphere in the hall was charged with emotion, the servant girls crying, and the men gathered together deciding who should go. Having appeared reclusive and remote for the previous few months, the Duchess now came back to life with an amazing enthusiasm. Even Josy, who was normally lost in her dreams, looked at her with admiration. There wasn't much time to organise the horses, provisions and medical supplies for the underground army, so everyone was expected to help, the spirit of love and common interest their tragic country making all barriers disappear. The farm boys would freely walk into the Duchess's study to discuss any arising problems, and even Miss Apolonia was seen sitting arm-in-arm with a servant-girl, together preparing bandages or embroidering flags. The flurry of excitement was such that Josy hardly had time to read the letter, which was brought a week later by Andrew's groom. When she at last sat down to open it, the news which he wrote was not such a surprise:-

"My Dearest", wrote Andrew briefly, "Just a few words to tell you that I have joined a group of young men in my district. I hope to God that I will be able to rehabilitate myself in my father's eyes and also fight for the freedom of our country. Take heart, Dearest, I know that we are going to win and I shall be able to come back and rightfully claim you as mine forever. I love you more and more every day. Andrew."

The letter was scribbled on a piece of notepaper and had obviously been written in a great hurry, just before he left to join the others. Vassyl did not know where they had gone or where they would be during the next few weeks. In the meantime, she had so much to do that there was no time to mope or daydream. If anything, she felt even more compelled to do whatever was necessary for Andrew's sake as well as for the others.

Messengers would come during the night and collect the ready supplies, eating hurriedly under Martha's watchful eye. She tried to compensate for their lost youth, the hardship of marching in ferocious weather and the precariousness of their future, with huge, well-cooked meals. Many of the youngsters were to fondly remember Martha and these meals, when standing on guard in the bitter cold or marching for miles. Some, of course, would not return. That was the reality, and the women tried hard not to dwell on this tragic aspect.

The winter that year was particularly bad. The temperature dropped to -30 C, and the snow drifts stood as high as horses' necks. Sometime in February, a lone rider rode up to the Lodge. On seeing Vassyl's face, darkened by frost and drawn after his long journey, Josy almost dragged him into the drawing room, calling for hot drink and food on the way. She did not notice his strange stiffness and looked up at him impatiently, expecting a letter. Nothing was forthcoming. Vassyl stood awkwardly, holding his fur cap, and barely feeling alive.

Numbly, he was at last able to say,

"I'm sorry, Miss, I really am sorry . . ."

Josy did not remember much afterwards. Miss Apolonia led her away, while Prakseda feverishly tried to find out what exactly had happened. Vassyl did not know much himself.

A messenger from the underground movement had formally informed Andrew's father of his death during an attack on a Russian garrison.

Josy was shattered. Her pain was so great that had she been left alone, she would have screamed. For days she sat dry-eyed and numb. Nobody could get through to her, and extremely worried, the Duchess decided to hold a conference with Miss Apolonia. The governess advised total rest and promised to talk to the girl at an appropriate moment.

"It cannot be done now. She must be allowed sometime to grieve. If only she could cry . . . She was so fond of Andrew. We all were . . .", Miss Apolonia's voice lost its icy tone, and Cornelia looked up at her companion with concern.

"I know, I know . . . He was only a boy, no more than nineteen, wasn't he? It's a tragedy that people so young are dying defending their country."

It was almost impossible, in that comfortable, quiet room, listening to the sounds of everyday life at the Lodge, to even imagine the horror of underground war raging outside, not far away from their estate.

Miss Apolonia looked down. She was very pale. For a fleeting moment she saw in her mind Andrew's laughing grey eyes and angular, animated face, when he sat to tea with Josy. Just a few months ago . . . just like her brother . . .

Rising stiffly, the Duchess put her arms around the governess and kissed her lightly on both cheeks, her pale lips quivering a little.

It was so unexpected that Miss Apolonia blushed and turned her face away, fighting the welling tears.

Cornelia hesitated for a moment, but watching the governess, she could see that the spinster, who was normally so reserved, was visibly moved.

There was a brief silence and then the Duchess, assuming a lighter manner, said,

"Spring will be here soon, and thankfully, we are going to be too busy to dwell on the past. Only the future really matters, you know. We must think of the girls".

Miss Apolonia nodded placidly, smiling bravely through her tears.

The loud peal of the ave-bell soared above the village, sending the cold-puffed sparrows, sitting humped and shivering in the hedgerow, up into the icy-blue sky.

It was Sunday morning and small groups of villages, obedient to the persistent ringing, walked towards the stone-strew hill, on which their church had stood for a good hundred years.

Rosy, the plump wife of the village carpenter, held for support the elbow of her best friend, Thercka. They were engrossed in exchanging the latest of the village gossip. The next Sunday, there was to be a wedding and Rosy felt compelled to mention the scandalous liasion between the young groom and a girl from the neighbouring village. Thercka nodded in solemn agreement,

"It had to end, and no mistake. Marcia's father has got a heavy hand and wouldn't have his daughter being upset."

"I know my dear, I know. This is what happens when a young man isn't allowed to follow his heart."

"How can he? A rich farmer's son cannot marry a girl without even one cow's tail to her name! What would the world come to if . . ."

Thercka leaned closer, whispering urgently,

"They say that the girl is threathening to throw herself in the river if he marries Marcia next Sunday!"

"Lord, have mercy!", Rosy hastily crossed herself.

"I've always said . . ."

She didn't manage to finish her remark since

they both had to jump aside, pressing themselves well into the hedgerows.

From behind the old barns, a huge black horse emerged at a furious gallop. Astride the foaming animal sat a barefoot girl, her enormous, long hair loose and tangled. She didn't seem to even notice the startled women, and within seconds, she and the horse, both had disappeared in a flurry of dust and chippings.

Thercka pulled indignant and mumbling Rosy back onto the road. They dusted themselves down.

"That spoilt brat of a girl!"

"Now, now, Rosy. It's Sunday, mind." Thercka pushed the crooked headscarf back from her forehead.

"That girl will flatten someone one day, mark my word."

"Well, they say she's got so unruly like, since young Andrew was killed . . ."

"But that's no reason to trample over folk." Rosy was not to be pacified.

"The Duchess is far too soft, bless her. I would know how to deal with such a wilful child, and no mistake."

The bell's tone became more urgent, and so they turned, onto the hill path and followed the others.

In the oncoming spring news of the downfall of the uprising became more frequent and real. The whole country was in mourning and the feeling of dejection and despair had never been as prevalent as it was now.

The churches, full of prostrate bodies, stood silent while grieving women wept miserably, sobbed and shouted for God's mercy upon their dead fathers and sons.

From the wooden pew at the estate's little church, Josy gazed at the sweet-faced Madonna at the main altar, and thought with detachment that God had either abandoned them or was indeed in need of help Himself. Her own grief turned into a cold determination to remember Andrew and be faithful to him forever. It would mean being a spinster of course, but she did not mind that a bit. So many women around her had lost their menfolk, and would stay in mourning and widowhood until their deaths.

Their happy, gentle self-contained world was falling apart, but they had to go on living and making the best of what was left.

The governess observed the girls with a serious concern. Thea was too young to grieve for long, and would soon recover, given a chance. But Josy, headstrong and rebellious, would not accept her fate so easily. She was not to know the financial situation which worried the Duchess more and more. The Russian reprisals for helping the uprising were now imminent.

Miss Apolonia decided to take matters into her own hands. She waited till Josy had left for her daily walk around the farm and estate, and then carefully choosing her path, walked down the green lane.

They met in the farthest part of the orchard. The tree's branches already swollen with sticky green buds hung low. The first flowers appeared in the meadow here and there, and the ploughed fields around them smelled of freshly-furrowed, rich earth. In a clear blue sky, a nightingale hung above the edge of the woods, and without even waiting for the evening, sang his first song of spring.

Along the vegetable patch, in the garden, the last year's butterflies, awaked by the warmth, danced upon the golden air, reflecting in their delicate wings the radiant light of the sun.

Miss Apolonia evened her step with Josy. They walked together for a while, talking about the farm and what was to be done at home, what with Easter coming soon.

The girl listened but, as usual she seemed distant, her face stern and unsmiling.

"Dear Josy", started Miss Apolonia haltingly, "I know how you feel, I too lost my family in the uprising. I've seen you grow up, and I can't bear to just stand by and watch you destroy your future. If anyone has the right to talk to you, it is I, for you are looking at yourself, child, only older, and as you will be, if you don't abandon your vows."

Josy looked at her sharply, but continued to walk silently, and so Miss Apolonia continued.

"I was once like you, pretty, well-brought-up and carefree. The death of my father and brother left my mother and myself without any means of support. Our small estate was confiscated by the Russians, and I had to work to support my mother. Do you have any idea what it's like to live in somebody's house forever, sleep in a room which is not yours and eat at someone's table? All that I will ever be able to call mine is my travelling trunk."

She paused and looked at Josy, still slowly walking beside, her profile pale in the sharp light of the morning.

Something like bitterness crossed Miss Apolonia's face.

"And then there are the children to teach – often rebellious and unwilling, often rude and ungrateful – are you going to accept that? You who always wanted to be the head of your own house and your own destiny?"

Josy gave a little shudder.

"Dear, dear Miss Apolonia, you are forgetting that Aunt promised to equip Thea and myself well. And then there is the Lodge and estates . . ."

The governess stepped in front of Josy and held her shoulders affectionately.

She had to stop herself from shaking the dreaming girl.

"My dear Josy, this is sad news but Aunt Cornelia has almost nothing left. Has it never occurred to you why she lives in the Lodge while her palace in Lvov belongs to someone else? Many noblemen were ruined in the last uprising, and this is the most obvious way for the Russians to ensure that there won't be any more. If you and Thea don't marry well, all that you will be able to do will be a governess like myself! Is that what Andrew would have wanted to happen to you? What about your father's lost estate? You wanted to recover the house so much, and to live there with your children. Are you going to abandon everything for the sake of a dream which was never anything more than a dream?

Please Josy, I beseech you, at least think about it, for Aunt Cornelia and Thea's sakes, if not for your own!"

Exhausted, and with trembling lips, Miss Apolonia turned and walked back to the Lodge. Josy felt like someone awaking from a long sleep. The enormity of her situation, and the grim prospects lying ahead both hit her – she could not bear to leave this place to go and work among strangers. Her thoughts floated upon the surface of her mind, and she stopped abruptly under the old apple tree to gather her senses. It was singular that, although so much had happened to her, she was now back at the same point that she had started from several months ago.

She gave a little sigh – perhaps it had all only been a dream, and reality was now. And as for the future? There was only one thing to do, and it was her duty to do it. She felt tired and oddly indifferent to her own fate. The only thing that mattered were Vronovo and Thea's happiness.

The depth of her emotion made her determined to succeed, if not in her personal life which she feared was finished, then at least in securing the future of her family and her father's estate.

How strange, she thought looking at the orchard

with here new found feeling, I do believe, I have grown up at last.
Slowly she followed the governess back to the Lodge.

The sun was setting down and grey shadows climbed the white-washed walls. Josy stood in the middle of the summer-room and looked around her.
It would not be in use until after Easter, and the calico covers hung loosely over the furniture. The drapes half pulled over the tall windows and dusty mirrors added to the strange feeling of detachment and isolation.
She sunk into a large leather armchair, which had been nicknamed "Conrad" by Thea, and thought about the future for a while.
For the first time in months she saw things as they really were, clearly and calmly; gone were her impulsive and impatient outbursts.
I shall never be so hot-tempered or romantic again. From now on, I must remember what I need rather than what I want.
She sat thinking and planning.

The shadows grew longer, and the room stood still in grey silence. The last mottled sunrays moved along the wall onto the massive mirror and beyond . . . The shadows fused and trembled on the silvery surface, specks of gold dancing and disappearing into the clouded glass.

Josy looked up at these strange patterns wide-eyed and suddenly alert.

"It can't be", she thought. Leaning forward, she strained to see better. Could she really recognise the shadowy faces, pale and distorted, deep inside the glass?

They were there, distant but real enough in the twilight. Was it her mother's face, beautiful and fine-boned, that she could see? Was Andrew's face there too, so young and sad? They seemed to silently plead with her. She did not understand how, but she could hear their voices now, faint and far away, coming closer and then fading away . . .

"You must continue, dear, you must. We cannot help you much, but . . . will always watch over you, always . . ."

Josy cried out tearfully,

"Where are you? Mother! Andrew! Why can't I be with you?"

"Not yet, dearest, not yet. There is so much for you to do, and so much time left. You must continue, you must . . . We shall wait for you . . . Prepare the path for others, those who are waiting to come after you; Hurry . . . "

"Who? Who are they? When? Tell me . . . don't go yet!"

A sudden flash of light disturbed the darkness. A bright triangle swept the floor to lie flat at Josy's feet. Thea stood in the doorway, trying to see into the darkened room.

"Josy, are you there?" -

She saw her sister, and visibly relieved, stepped forward, "I have been looking for you everywhere, and here you are, daydreaming in 'Conrad', and missing Martha's special pre-Easter supper!"

Josy made an effort to look and talk as usual. Surely she could not have imagined any of the occurrences in the summer room. But she wouldn't tell anyone about her experience until she had had time to calmly think out the whole incident.

A nagging thought kept passing through her mind – why hadn't her adored father's face been there?

She wondered whether her sensibility was abnormally acute. Perhaps it was . . . It did not seem to matter, the encounter at least if nothing else, had calmed her and rested her tired spirit.

The sisters wound their arms around each other's waists and went back into the light and warmth of the hall.

This particular year Martha had decided to make the Easter celebrations very special.

"Poor girls", she muttered to herself, "I must cheer them up a bit, dear little lambs." She wiped her eyes and decided to bring out all the silver which had been put away during the national mourning.

"Nonsense, all this nonsense, such a waste of all those young lives!", she grumbled angrily under her breath, arranging the silver on the polished sideboard. The starched, buttercup-yellow cloth lay neatly folded on the top of the oak dresser, waiting to be spread over the table.

An array of tall and small clay vases, full of early, velvety catkins, stood on one side of the sideboard, grouped together for effect.

Josy came down to the kitchen with the sudden

thought that she should perhaps help with the preparations, and be of some use, at least to Martha. Through the half-open pantry door, she could see pashas*, hanging from the beam, suspended in muslin. Moulded into different shapes and decorated, just before being served, with angelica, sugar flowers and confitured summer fruits, they were her very favourite puddings.

The original, Russian version had to be in the shape of a pyramid and embossed with Christian symbols such as X.B., which stood for 'Christ is risen', or with the Russian Orthodox cross. They used special wooden moulds for making Pasha, and the word meant Easter in Russian. To distinguish her pasha from the Russian's Martha used rounded moulds and plenty of rich toppings.

On impulse, Josy came up behind Martha and put her arms around the cook's substantial girth.

"What would we do without you?"

She held on to the protesting, but obviously well-pleased, woman.

"Now look here, Josy, stop this nonsense. Anyone would think that I am soft or something . . . It is Easter after all – the Resurrection. No point in moping forever, if one can do something . . ."

She stopped startled. Josy stood in the middle of the kitchen, with her arms clasped, unable to hold back the sobs that choked her.

Martha stroked Josy's head, and the girl seized her hand as though it were a hold upon life itself.

"Cry if you want, my child, it will ease your sorrow."

Her calm, reassuring kindness brought her com-

* *pashas* – Easter sweet

fort, and Josy tried desperately hard to compose herself.

"I thought . . . I had got over the worst . . ."

Martha's round, good-natured face bore an expression of real concern.

"Here, let's sit down and have a nice cup of tea together, eh?"

Without waiting for an answer, she put the blackened kettle onto the hot stove.

"It'll be ready in a minute . . . Have a look in the pantry – you might find something that you fancy right now."

Knowing how proud Martha was of the pantry's contents, Josy walked in.

Surprised, she gasped. Martha, just behind her, stood beaming.

The pantry shelves, already groaning under the weight of meats and pasties, sagged even further with the bulk of shiny, thick coils of smoked sausages, which were piled high next to terrines of pates and a whole ham. Marinated, and then slowly smoked, the ham was studded with cloves and juniper berries. Covered in honey and apricot glaze, it smelled just wonderful. Mazurki occupied a whole shelf by themselves. Fashioned like shortbread 'trays', they were filled either with almonds, dates, toffee, or marzipan, while others had a praline filling, but they were all decorated with candied nuts and fruits in elegant, intricate designs.

Josy's eyes opened wide at such riches.

"That's nothing, look here!" Martha pointed to the other side of the pantry.

On the wide bench covered by a freshly starched

tea-cloth, stood imposing babas, the royal cakes for the Easter table.

Every Easter, Martha had baked them at night to avoid the slightest noise or draught, which might have been caused during the day by talking or the opening and closing of doors; this might easily have made the capricious dough collapse! The baking of these cakes involved much ritual and was regarded as the ultimate measure of a cook's ability. Once the baking had been safely completed, the kitchen girls would place the hot babas on pillows and then rock them very gently, just like babies, until the cakes had cooled down evenly. The slightest jerky movement meant that the baba could end up lop-sided – the greatest shame !

How truly magnificent they looked – at least a foot high and shaped like a pyramid with its top flatly cut, they had a dark amber colour, which was due to a spoonful of saffron and the dozens of eggs used. They would stand as the centre-piece on the table, surrounded by a wreath of shiny, dark green blueberry twigs.

Josy looked around with misty eyes. She had a lump in her throat, Martha's unexpected kindness had affected her so much. Life was indeed beautiful. She did not want to cry – she wanted to live and be happy so much and . . .

The kettle hissed and spluttered on the stove, breaking the spell, and so, picking up one of the praline and confiture shortbread trays, they went back companionably into the warmth of the kitchen.

Easter arrived. That Sunday Martha got up at dawn. Everything was ready but she wanted to add the final touches herself. She set the table first, and then standing back, looked on with pleasure at the lively contrast between the buttercup yellow of the table cloth and the vernal green of the mustard-and-cress hill in the centre of it.

It would always be about three weeks before Easter when she started to sow the mustard-and-cress on to an upturned, empty flower pot, covered with cotton wool. This was placed upside down on a large plate filled with water, so that the cotton wool would soak up the moisture rapidly. The seeds, scattered thickly over the cotton wool, produced within days, a dense cover. It would form symbolically the green hill of Golgotha.

On Easter Sunday a sugar lamb, carrying a red flag with a cross, was placed upon the hill, which was then surrounded by hand painted eggs. These were real works of art and Martha smiled, remembering how many hours Thea and Josy had spent each year preparing them for Easter.

They would also prepare special eggs (goose eggs would usually be used) which immersed in hot wax, would then be covered with pearls and colourful beads to form exquisite patterns of flowers or other shapes. The gifts were finished with a ribbon attached to one end, and because of their beauty often became treasured family heirlooms.

Martha turned away. Ah, the past and its memories . . .

They would all have to learn to look to the future.

Everything having been completed in the kitchen, Martha decided it was time to ensure that the dining room was ready for her splendid fare. The whole of the previous morning the servant-girls had waxed and polished the parquet floor until it shone like the surface of a lake on a sunny morning. Built-up high in the grate, the fire hissed and roared. The smell of wax was suspended in the hot and dry air, pervading the house and mingling with the aromas of the dishes arranged on the sideboards. Armfuls of catkins stood in vases on every free surface.

Satisfied at last, Martha left the room. She could hear the girls' voices upstairs; it was time to wash and change into her best dress before they all drove to the church.

Easter Sunday brought mild weather for good. Scores of birds flew high above the Lodge in a jet-black pattern, sharp against the iridescent-blue sky. The ponds stood covered in frothy algae and shimmering with life, and the first posies of buttercups emerging from the tangle of dark leaves, looked up with envy and wonder to the sky and the birds passing above. Among the pale green rushes last year's young frogs chorused without a break, and the tall poplar trees shivered in the fresh breeze despite their new green jackets.

From the gently rolling coach Josy gazed with admiration at the already silvery fields on both sides of the poplar track. They swayed in rippling circles, rocked gently by the wind spreading across the young wheat, as if it were the disturbed surface of a waterpool.

Full of both gentry and peasants, the village church called the faithful with a joyous, high- pitched peal of bells.

Josy and Thea, dressed in light coats and matching bonnets, sat in the pew, happy and calm. Miss Apolonia looked her usual efficient self as she supported an ailing Aunt Cornelia, who had felt unwell for the past few months.

Both women prayed for their beloved country to be free, for the boys who had died so young and the men who had been taken so many thousands of miles away.

While Thea discreetly surveyed the church, Josy stared straight ahead, lost in her thoughts. The incident in the summer room had left her convinced that she hadn't been dreaming that day. Perhaps the unhappiness which she had suffered had not been entirely in vain, now that she had a goal. She devoutly prayed to God for guidance, help and the determination which she would need to do what her loved ones wanted her to accomplish.

"Halleluja, Halleluja, Jesus is alive", sang the congregation.

Peasants from the neighbouring villages crowded the church. The women knelt at the front of the church, dressed in bright, hand-woven woollens, and holding baskets containing hard-boiled eggs and freshly smoked sausages; the men, red-faced from a thorough shave stood behind solemnly, in oversized Sunday best suits and dazzling, starched shirts. The elderly priest stepped forward and gave the blessing to the food and the crowd. By ancient tradition, the egg would be divided into small portions at the Sunday breakfast table, and everyone would share a small piece with other members of the family to bring them luck, prosperity and health, or so they believed.

After Mass, Aunt Cornelia, Miss Apolonia and the girls, with Martha and Prąkseda some distance behind them, joined the stream of people leaving the church.

As was customary, they solemnly greeted those they met on their way,

"Christ is risen!"

"Truly he is!", the others would reply.

The Duchess's groom impatiently waited for everyone to climb up into the open coach. The Easter breakfast feast was ready and waiting, and even the horses seemed to sense that.

A few more weeks elapsed before Josy could bring herself to tell Thea about the incident in the summer room. Her sudden revelation made Thea's eyes widen in excitment, but all that she understood was that they should do something to recover the family home and fortunes, although what this could be, wasn't too clear in her mind. Slightly embarrassed, Josy explained their financial position and the need to marry adequate suitors. Thea listened intently to her sister with parted lips.

"Does this mean that I can't fall in love?", she finally asked.

"It would help if you took care to fall for the right

man!", giggled Josy with soft affection.
It was all proving to be more fun than she had at first thought possible, and relieved, she looked forward to the future with a light and buoyant spirit.

Chapter Three

The months which followed were crammed with visits to and from the neighbouring estates. Miss Apolonia made delicate enquiries and let it be known that the two Horaim girls were of suitable age for any interested suitors. Visits were exchanged and many young men paid their respects in the company of their mothers or sisters. Unfortunately however, further enquiries usually revealed financial problems and each would-be-suitor soon disappeared without a trace.

As the girls were pretty and also very young, the Duchess felt that they could afford time, and so she did not worry too much. Neither of the girls was in love, and they both regarded the whole process of finding a husband as hilarious.

During one of the gatherings at the Lodge, Josy danced all the time and by mid-evening felt ravenous. One of the strict rules was that the girls should not eat much in public. This was partly because they were tightly laced into their corsets and partly because " . . . young girls should eat like little birds", in Miss Apolonia's own words. She made sure that the girls only had small amounts of food on the plates in front of them. But this time the vigorous dancing made Josy even hungrier than usual. She stalked Prakseda, who had come from the kitchen, and in a loud whisper, asked her for something to eat.

"There is nothing left in the kitchen, my angel – all dishes have been sent here", said the servant girl.

"But I'm famished! You must have cooked something for the kitchen girls!", wailed Josy.

"Well . . . there's only a pot of baked buckwheat for the stable lads, but you wouldn't want that, surely, would you?"

"Bring some here! Please! Please, dearest!", Josy hugged the maid, lightly pushing her towards the kitchen.

Prakseda hurried out, and after a short while discreetly set down the low, wide-necked dish with piping hot buckwheat on a table which stood in one of the side-rooms.

"Do be careful! It's very hot – straight from the oven", she warned before departing.

Josy ate a few spoonfuls of the coarse, brown grains, which were oozing with melted butter, and instantly feeling better, she carefully wiped her mouth with a napkin before sneaking out to resume her dancing. She was well-pleased with her ingenuity.

All went well until one of the eager young men decided to follow her during one of the breaks. Looking above people's heads, he was intrigued to see Josy entering one of the side-rooms.

On hearing the door being opened, Josy blew out the table-lamp and sat still in the darkness on the sofa which stood behind the table. The young man took this for an invitation and moved forward but unfortunately on his way he encountered the table, and tripped over, stretching out his arms to steady himself only to place his hands in something devilishly hot.

He screamed loudly.

Terrified, Josy dived under the table just as the door burst open with the other guests anxiously peering in. Someone brought a lamp, and the bright light displayed to everyone the unfortunate young man standing in the middle of the room holding out red and sticky, grain-coated hands. In the confusion which followed, Josy managed to leave her hiding place, but the Duchess guessed who had been behind the incident and bluntly told her she was not amused.

The young man left hastily and was never seen again.

A few more suitors also departed hurriedly, but for different reasons.

Weeks later, having fully recovered from the experience, the girls laughed together, remembering two of them in particular. The first one was their distant, widowed neighbour, aged and balding, but still amorous. On the pretext of being an old friend of the Duchess's, he began arriving at least once a week, without invitation, but always with a gift for Josy.

"He obviously had honest intentions!", laughed Thea loudly,

" . . . And those gifts! The jewellery! How could you be so cruel! We could buy Vronovo back just like that!"

She snapped her fingers.

"Vronovo or no, I just couldn't. Why, he's old enough to be my grandfather. And I didn't accept his awful presents, remember!" Josy sounded quite indignant.

"Oh, I do, I do!" Thea burst out laughing again, " . . . And do you remember his face when . . . when you wouldn't take any of the riches that he was showering you with?"

"Dear old fool, I felt quite sorry to do that, but he just could not understand why not! And you know I couldn't say anything. Aunt would have had a fit, and I would have been reprimanded again!"

"I watched him while you were sitting at the piano and singing that little love-duet to him. I thought that he was going to have apoplexy, you wicked girl!"

Thea ran to the piano, and mimicking the man's elderly voice, sang a well-known song, exaggerating the endings:

"I am asking you kindly,
Please don't be mischievous,
But look at me more tenderlyyy,
And I shall buy you
A large diamond riiiing!"

Josy, standing by the piano in demure pose, her hands neatly folded, joined in:

"I don't like diamonds, Sir,
Don't buy them, don't buy them,
Don't buy them, for me . . . .

My dearest angel,
Your eyes are more
Precious than goooold,
Please let me give youuu
This string of pearls.

I don't wear pearls, Sir,
Don't buy them, don't buy them,
Don't buy them, for me . . .

You are my happiness,
Why are you rejecting my gifts?
Why are you breaking my heart?
Oh, tell me, please tell me,
Please tell me at leeaast.

I don't want your gifts,
Dear Sir, the reason
Is clear enough,
You are too old, too old
And too ugly by far,
For me . . ."

Suddenly the door opened and Miss Apolonia stood on the threshhold.

"What on earth is going on in here?"

Both girls stifled their giggles.

"Oh, it's nothing really, we were only having a game!"

Miss Apolonia eyed them suspiciously for a second, but then departed, closing the door.

Thea turned to her sister. "You are lucky – if only she or Auntie knew!"

Josy sighed – it could not be helped. Just as well that Auntie hadn't been there to see how the highly embarrassed suitor had smiled politely after her rendition, and praised her voice, but had refused to stay to dinner and no one ever saw him at the Lodge again.

Exhausted, the girls sat on the sofa, talking in whispers and still giggling as they remembered the other shameful incident.

This time, the suitor had also been quite old but he seemed to be mostly interested in the girls' titles and their ancestors. Josy swiftly got rid of him too by singing a very rude folk-song, which depicted "her ancestors" in very dubious terms.

Some time afterwards, visitors arrived, quite unexpectedly, at the Lodge. Aunt Cornelia warmly greeted her long-unseen cousin, Robert. He was regarded by the family as a clever, jovial man with various interests, and a dedicated traveller. Thea and Josy came down to find Aunt Cornelia in his company together with another stranger. As the girls entered the drawing-room, cousin Robert broke off from recounting the latest news, and introduced the stranger as his friend, Anthony Kaschinsky, a businessman from Warsaw.

Josy looked at him in sudden interest. Never before had she seen a more remarkable looking man.

He was tall and dressed with the nonchalant elegance of a true gentleman. His hair, raven-black and slightly wavy, framed a straight forehead and piercing dark eyes.

To her utter surprise and annoyance, Josy found the man's calm, penetrating gaze strangely compelling.

She discreetly watched him from under her thick lashes, feeling her heart beating unevenly within her.

The stranger had the fairly dark complexion, so often found in men with such black hair, and a generous, sensuous mouth. Without any doubt, he had presence, thought Josy, and was obviously a man of authority.

It gave her a curious pang in her heart to notice that when he was introduced to them he bowed with the utmost politeness but did not extend his hand, and that his eyes rested for a fraction longer on Thea.

The resumed conversation touched on many subjects. Both men had travelled extensively abroad, and the Duchess and both girls listened spellbound to their accounts of the latest theatre productions, the Summer Exhibition in Paris, and the music written by the marvellous, tragic Mr Chopin . . . They talked for a few minutes longer and then the conversation turned, inevitably, to local problems and the sad happenings of the previous winter.

The Duchess expressed her belief that as long as there was even only one man alive in Poland, they should fight for freedom. Cousin Robert exchanged glances with Anthony and gently interrupted,

"Dear Cornelia, so caring and yet so misguided! We have had two uprisings, both complete fiascos, and you want a third one? What we need to do is to build a strong, industrial country. That would be our best weapon. Only then could we win against the Russians."

Anthony nodded in agreement.

"We need an industrial background and we must unite. By that I mean all the people – peasants and noblemen, landowners and industrialists . . . Do you realise why we lost the last uprising? We lost because we were divided. The majority of peasants didn't trust us, and the Russians used the land laws to wedge an even wider gap between the common soldiers and their officers."

Alarmed, Josy looked at her aunt. She seemed so frail and at a loss. If only they knew what the real truth was . . .

Robert began to outline French foreign policy and France's promises of help for Poland.

"But", he finished, "they only seem to be promises, with no real action."

The mood changed. Their hopes and disappointments, the tragedies . . . Each of these people had had some experience of the country's downfall and for a moment they sat lost in thought.

The door opened and a servant-girl brought in a laden tea tray. Robert stood up and courteously helped her with it to the table. In a low voice he murmured something to the girl, making her blush, and even Aunt Cornelia could not help smiling at his easy chuckle reverberating around the room.

"There really is no point in giving in to black moods," exclaimed Robert, who was evidently unable to remain depressed for long.

“Let me tell you a heartening, if slightly roguish, story!” He said, bowing in the directon of the Duchess and the girls, and then continued,

“Every estate doctor in this country could tell many similar stories, but this one has become a folk tale now.

Everybody claims it happened on their estate, so listen carefully and cheer up. With people as resilient as our peasants, we won’t remain defeated for long!

This is what, I am told, happened two summers back around harvest-time.

The day was hot and humid and, after lunch, the estate doctor had his usual nap at home. When he awoke he found one of the farm workers sitting outside, patiently waiting for him.

On seeing the doctor the man got up and clasped him round the knees according to the customary humble peasant greeting.

“What do you want?” asked the doctor.

“Beggin’ yer pardon, sir, would you come and take a look at the missus? The bull messed her up a bit in the field.”

“My good man! Why didn’t you wake me up? Where is she?”

“Why sir, I didn’t dare . . . I reckon she’s had it this time. If you could only tidy her up a bit – it ain’t Christian to bury her with all her innards hanging out,” said the farm man.

The doctor grabbed his bag, being led by the peasant to the field where a woman lay, covered by a cloth. A small child, a girl, sat next to her, flicking a long twig against the flies. The doctor lifted the cloth, only to find to his horror that the farmer had been right – her belly was cut open with all her guts hanging out onto her wide cotton skirt. She was conscious but said nothing.

The doctor bathed the wound with medical spirit, re-positioned the guts and sewed her up. Apart from her alert wide-open eyes, the woman appeared to be already gone.

She still uttered not a word.

"You'd better take her to the nearest hospital," the doctor instructed the man, who had stood watching him intently.

Three weeks passed before the doctor had a chance to find out whether the woman was getting any better in hospital. He had not heard of any funeral in the village and concluded that she must have survived.

That afternoon he called at the farm cottages and asked the little girl playing outside,

"Is your mum in?"

"No, she's in the field, digging potatoes," said the child.

The doctor thought that he had either got the wrong woman or the wrong cottage, but the girl seemed familiar. He ran to the field, and sure enough, the woman was there, bent over a potato-sack.

On seeing the doctor, she dropped everything and running to him, thanked him loudly for saving her life.

"Have you been in hospital?"

"No, sir, me old man could not leave everything at harvest- time so I lay down at home for a week, and, thank God, now I've never felt better."

"The doctor ordered her to lie down on the grass and lifting her skirts, he examined her there and then. A fresh scar was still very visible, but apart from that, his pushing and prodding at her stomach only made her giggle.

He wrote about the case to a medical journal but I believe that he has not recovered from the shock himself yet!"

Both Thea and Josy laughed unashamedly at the story and Robert's excellent rendition of the broad peasant dialect. The Duchess looked fondly at Robert.

"I wish you could be here more often – you make life seem so carefree!"

Anthony laughed along with the others but his eyes often strayed to Thea's radiant face.

The next few days were busy with excitement. Robert wanted to show his friend the neighbourhood and they also intended to visit some cotton mills. Anthony was interested in making contacts which might prove useful to his cloth production business.

Full of visitors, the Lodge resounded with laughter and discussions. Robert was obviously proving to be the most popular man in the county by far, thought Aunt Cornelia, smiling with indulgence. Miss Apolonia, standing close, followed her gaze. The Duchess turned to her,

"Dear Robert – always ready to be of service – such a charming man. It's so delightful having him here, even only for a short time."

The governess moved uneasily. Perhaps she

didn't know Robert very well, to appreciate him as much, but then she knew even less about Anthony.

Had anyone noticed his interest in Thea?

She decided to say nothing for now. Robert was delightful, it was true, but she could not help a slight feeling of impatience that Cornelia should be so easily taken by his charm, and charm alone.

Taking her usual daily walk down the twisting lane, Josy examined her disturbed feelings. She felt in such turmoil, and yet she could not think why. She sat on a large stone, which marked the end of the field, to enjoy the freshness of the early morning before the heat of the day could begin to hang over the estate like a closed net, forcing her indoors.

Why didn't she feel at ease with Anthony? Was it because he was so cool, polite and inscrutable? By contrast, Cousin Robert talked so much, making them all laugh. For some inexplicable reason, she yearned to know what was in Anthony's mind. Yet she had no illusion as to where his interest lay. Her abstracted gaze rested on the smoothness of the swaying wheat. It was heart-breaking to know, as she did, that everything in her life lasted such a short time, and she had to accept that she had little chance of ever knowing Anthony really well.

The time came for Robert and his friend to depart and everyone was sorry to see them go; Martha – because they ate as if they had never seen such good food, often loudly saying so; the

Duchess, because they made her feel less of a recluse, and had made her laugh for the first time in months; and the girls, because they had suddenly been shown glimpses of exciting, unknown worlds and different outlooks, the existence of which they had not suspected before.

Even Prakseda seemed to regret Anthony's departure, when, while combing Josy's hair, she suddenly remarked,

"He seemed to be a proper gentleman, no nonsense with the kitchen maids or suchlike . . ."

She stopped halfway through the sentence remembering Josy's age.

The evening before the departure, during dinner, Cousin Robert seemed to gather his thoughts from afar. Anthony also sat somewhat preoccupied, and in a more serious mood than usual.

Josy gave the two guests a rapid glance, but there was nothing obvious amiss which she could see. She could not quite understand the deep emotion which this stranger evoked within her, and she seriously asked herself whether it was a dream.

After dinner the girls expected to stay in the drawing room as usual, but instead they were sent to have an early night, since the departing guests would be leaving at dawn in order to catch the Post-coach in town.

Disappointed Josy gathered up her book and was on the point of leaving, when she heard Robert asking Aunt Cornelia for a few minutes in her office.

She was not normally curious about other peoples' affairs, but today her instinct made her do something completely out of character. Instead of ascending the stairs she quietly opened the door of the room, which adjoined her Aunt's office. Thankfully, it was empty. Josy stood still to accustom her eyes to the darkness before tiptoeing to a door on her right which linked the room with the office. In a short while, a light outlined the contour of the door and the keyhole, and she recognised the voices in the next room.

Robert sat heavily in a vast armchair, facing Aunt Cornelia's desk. He said in a cordial, breezy way,

"Dear Cornelia, I feel so refreshed. It's a shame we could only stay two weeks; what with your Martha's cooking, it's felt like the best vacation that I've had for years."

Aunt Cornelia laughed lightly.

"You know very well, Robert, that as far as your visits are concerned, the pleasure is all mine!"

Robert continued,

"Before we depart, I'd like to ask you a favour, Cornelia. Would it be possible for Anthony to come and stay with you next month? He still has some unfinished business to attend to . . ."

"But Robert, dear, need you ask? Of course, he is welcome here anytime!"

There was a pause and sensing Robert's unease, Aunt Cornelia asked.

"What is it, dear?"

Stiffly and with strange formality, Robert said,

"I think I should tell you that he is quite taken

with Thea."

"But Robert", interrupted Aunt Cornelia, "that is splendid news!"

"I think you should hear me out, my dear," Robert's detached voice sounded so odd that Josy, her heart beating wildly, bent down trying to see through the keyhole into the room.

"But of course, . . . I don't think I understand . . ." faltered Aunt Cornelia.

"Anthony asked me to speak to you in confidence. I am to tell you who he really is and all about his business, before he and I expect your answer on this matter."

Josy's heart skipped a beat. She guessed from the familiar sound of tinkling glasses and the unhurried movements that the guest was being offered her aunt's favourite evening tipple.

She put her eye again to the circle of light.

Robert looked at the amber liquid, which was floating to and fro in crescents within the glass, seeming to search for the right words. Aunt Cornelia fondly gazed at him across the desk, her open face relaxed and encouraging, if a little bit curious.

"Good God, Robert, I have known you practically all your life – nothing can shock me. Anyhow you would not have brought Anthony here if he were an escaped villain!"

Her confidence and trust were so sincere that Robert got up and stood at the window, his face clearly showing his turmoil.

He seemed to have some difficulty in starting.

Suddenly he put down his glass and looked fully at her. Because he had averted his eyes for so long, his sudden direct gaze gave her such a feeling of fright that unable to stand it any longer, she cried out,

"For God's sake, Robert, what is it?"

"As you can see, it's a difficult task for me," Robert spoke gravely.

"Because Anthony comes from such a different world from ours, I wonder whether you could possibly accept him without prejudice for what he is – an honest, thinking, outstanding man."

He paused, gazing at his aunt questioningly.

Cornelia looked at him quickly. She thought that she had heard amiss for a second. What was he talking about? What different world?

Robert watched her without any gesture, his face immobile.

His strange manner made her a trifle uneasy, making her unsure of what to say.

On the other side of the door, Josy steeled herself for the revelation, her knees a little shaky.

Finally, Robert seemed to have come to a decision.

He said boldly, in a steady voice,

"Anthony is a con . . ."

To Josy's despair, the loud noise of a slammed door, somewhere down the hall drowned out the rest of the sentence. A shudder passed through her.

She could only read the full impact of the news from Aunt Cornelia's shocked and pale face.

Why was she staring so fixedly? What had he said? Oh!, what on earth had he said?

Robert's face remained impassive. He seemed to be

waiting for her reply.

"This is indeed a surprise to me. I hope you understand that I must gather my senses and ask you some more questions before I shall be able to give you my answer." She looked at Robert with, what seemed to Josy, an air of desperation.

"He certainly behaves like a well-bred and educated gentleman."

"But as you have probably observed, it has been a long time since I have . . . Well, I don't know the outside world well enough to see the differences if there are any . . ."

"In Anthony's case there aren't any," interrupted Robert hastily.

Someone was approaching the office door and Josy lingered for a moment longer, before turning and quietly leaving the room.

She hurried up the stairs. What had he meant? She just had to know."Why?" she mocked herself, "he only wants Thea, doesn't he?"

Robert and Anthony's early morning departure left the Lodge unusually quiet. Aunt Cornelia stayed in her office poring over the accounts with the administrator, a small balding man. Thea sank back into the comfort of the sofa and opened a new French romance with joyful relief. Her face lit up with intense interest and her lips parted a little as the tangled love story of the dashing young lieutenant and the beautiful heroine unfolded with each page.

"How silly of her to read such nonsense," thought

Josy passing through the hall on her way out, and catching a glimpse of her sister through the open drawing-room door.

She felt a great need to be alone. Wandering around the estate she tried to solve the puzzle, but halfway through the woods she had to admit defeat. He might be an escaped convict . . . Maybe it had happened in America and that was why he was safe here. It must have been a crime of passion, of course; perhaps, he had nobly defended his honour . . . Oh, what nonsense! Annoyed with herself she considered the other options.

Perhaps if she were to ask Miss Apolonia . . . But then she would have to own up to eavesdropping behind the door . . . No, she could not do that.

And, of course, the immediate future had to be faced. It was just as well that Aunt and Miss Apolonia seemed preoccupied, possibly even planning Thea's wedding; this would serve perfectly as an effective disguise to her unexpected feelings.

She could not understand herself. It was so unexpected.

What was it that had seized her, so that, not even knowing, not even liking him, she passionately yearned for his embrace? She despised herself for having already forgotten Andrew's face – instead now every time she closed her eyes to recall it, it was Anthony whom she saw in her mind.

"What is happening to me?", she asked herself aloud in desperation. "Am I going mad?"

Whatever happened in the future, however lonely and difficult it might be, no one but no one must know how she felt. Perhaps it was once again nothing but a dream from which she would suddenly awake . . . and then all would be well?

One day passed after another, and Aunt Cornelia spent considerable time discussing something, which was obviously important, with Miss Apolonia behind closed doors. Josy tried to stay close by to hear at least fragments of their conversation and once she thought she caught Miss Apolonia's raised, enraged voice saying,

" . . . but such a scandalous marriage! What will everyone say?"

She heard her Aunt replying in low, soothing tones, but she was unable to distinguish the words.

Lost in reflection, Josy stood there for a little while, but since she could not hear anything more, she went away disappointed.

Two or three weeks later, a familiar carriage pulled up in front of the Lodge. Josy heard Thea's excited voice calling Aunt Cornelia from somewhere in the house.

She didn't run to the door but instead, went up to the summer-room, and looked down into the courtyard, unobserved. Anthony stepped down from the dusty coach, his attention fully on Thea's up-turned, smiling face.

Josy grew pale, and quietly leaving her position, she took care not to be seen as she made her way to the back door.

The stables were close enough to be reached

safely, before the tears, veiling her eyes, spilled onto her burning-hot face.

Since Anthony was busy from morning till night with his business meetings at the Old Mill, Josy saw little of him; but one evening, a week or so after his arrival, Aunt Cornelia summoned the girls to the drawing-room, where Miss Apolonia and Anthony were already sitting.

Josy and Thea sat at opposite ends of the sofa. Looking very discreetly at him, Josy noticed how the bright lamp-light displayed Anthony's profile in clear-cut, immobile lines – yet he seemed anxious. Josy was somehow sure that the mystery which had fascinated her for the past few weeks would now be solved, and this realisation made her feel unaccountably nervous.

The door opened softly, and Anthony stood up and bowed as Aunt Cornelia walked in with the easy dignity of a woman of her good-breeding. She took her place directly opposite the sofa on which the girls were sitting demurely, hands folded in their laps. Miss Apolonia, pleased for once, could claim full credit for their faultless deportment. Aunt Cornelia looked at Josy first as though delving into the secrets of her heart, but when she noticed Josy's anxiety, she gave her a little reassuring smile, before slowly turning her gaze on Thea. She seemed to reflect.

Once more, she gave Josy a long and searching sagacious look, and then unexpectedly addressed Thea in a crisp clear voice.

"Anthony has just asked my permission to formally court you, my dear. This pleases us for many reasons, but, of course, you must do exactly as you choose. I would never force either of you into marriage nor must you think it necessary for you to marry the first man who declares himself, unless you wish to, of course . . ."

Thea said nothing, making no gesture, but her lips outlined a little smile, while her eyes remained downcast under her long lashes.

"Are you agreeable to his courtship, my child?"

This time Thea gave a little gasp, and then blushing deeply, she nodded her bowed head.
Anthony rose and took Thea's hands into his:
"My dear, my dear . . ."
There was just a shadow of a tremor in his voice.

Josy sat shattered. She felt an urgent need for sympathy and shot a rapid, sideways glance at Miss Apolonia. But the governess looked away, distant and unsmiling. There still had been no explanation, nothing. Why had Aunt agreed to what the governess called "a scandalous marriage"? And then there was Thea agreeing to marry him just because he was so wealthy – why, she hardly knew him. She certainly wasn't in love, that Josy knew. She would not be able to appreciate him, help him and console him. Thea behaved really like a spoiled child with an expensive toy. It was just a game to her, and Anthony would be the one who would get hurt, which troubled Josy a great deal.

As though through a fog she heard Aunt Cornelia speaking again. The words seemed to be issued from her lips with difficulty.

"I . . . we have decided to have a respectable period of engagement, in order to allow Thea and

Anthony to get to know each other better, and with a proviso for a wedding in the spring. This will permit Anthony to prepare a suitable home for you in Warsaw."

A flash of anger passed through Josy. She wanted to disagree, to stand up and say something. He had chosen the wrong girl, but he seemed unaware of his mistake. Aunt Cornelia should make him see sense. Why had she looked at her with an unspoken question before? Could she suspect the truth?

She forced herself to look Anthony full in the face; his eyes rested adoringly on Thea. She smiled with ironic resignation: it wasn't Thea whom she would have to fight, it was Anthony, and this would be as hopeless as it was ridiculous. Quite ridiculous. Her thoughts wandered strangely. In the end she said nothing.

As it was expected of her, she congratulated Thea and Anthony, but a few days later she asked Thea straight out,

"Do you think that you love him?"

Thea could not prevent the smile which crossed her face.

"I don't know why you should be so anxious about my happiness. I thought that you said we should marry well without any dreams of love. Wasn't that what you said?"

Josy did not quite know why, but suddenly she felt afraid for Thea. She sounded so different from the naive little girl that she had been just a short while ago.

"I think Anthony deserves better than what you can offer," she said stiffly at last.

"And I think it's none of your business!" Thea's eyes flashed angrily.

"I dare say that he is old enough to know his own mind, and so am I."

Josy turned to her sister gravely.

"I don't think that you know what love is. I can only pray that you won't find out too late."

Thea smiled, but said nothing, and then rose ready to go. Josy's serious eyes followed her as she walked from the room with measured steps.

Winter approached slowly. The first frost set the pale grass-blades rigid. The ponds stood silent, with only the bedraggled rushes rustling gently over the numb frogs sleeping among the muddy stones. In the deserted drive the poplars, stripped of their leafy coats, stood dark in their intricate outline, every branch and every twig sharply distinct against the iron-grey sky. The absence of birds suggested imminent first snow, and in the village inn the old farmers sat over their hot beer drinks and solemnly predicted a severe winter.

Fearing that he would be unable to return in time for Christmas, Anthony decided to leave the girls' Christmas gifts with Cornelia. The Duchess exclaimed with admiration on seeing the beautiful delicate porcelain souvenirs, which had been bought on Anthony's visit to fashionable Dresden.

To her unexpected surprise, her fondness for Anthony grew. She liked him and she was sure that he was kindly disposed towards her. Because of her, so he called, unparalleled tolerance and perception she had already gained his profound respect. He had told her this himself.

She shrugged her shoulders lightly and closed her eyes for a moment. The past few unhappy years spread before her and she remembered all the suffering, which had preyed on her family for the past decade. How could she despise a man whose only crime had been to be born into a different world to hers? It was all so petty, so insignificant. And yet were the truth made known to her friends or neighbours, not one of them would understand or approve of her decision. She smiled and there was a hint of bitter amusement in her eyes.

"At least for now, no one, not even Thea, must know the truth," she thought.

His business completed at the Old Mill, Anthony had to return to his factories and prepare a house for his young bride. With everything settled and sealed, he finally departed, reluctantly leaving a bemused and contented, if slightly triumphant, Thea. Nobody noticed in the general excitement of his departure, how strangely silent Josy was.

This was to be Thea's last Christmas at the Lodge, and Martha was determined to make it an unforgettable one. With the first frost, a huge ham was being smoked slowly over oak leaves in the smoking house, having first been marinated for several days in spicy brine, and then hung to dry in aromatic wood-smoke, one of the stable-boys being posted to turn it every so often in a sombre ritual. It would be quite a few days before the colour settled into a rusty-red, and the smell became strong and mature.

The next to be made were the traditional spice-and-honey loaves, which needed at least five weeks to become just right for Christmas. Made with many spices, including cloves, cinnamon and nutmeg, together with butter and lots of honey, the loaf started as a dry sort of cake, but by the end of the fourth week of its rest in an air-tight tin, it would have become soft, highly fragrant and more-ish. As a last touch, Martha would always cut the loaf horizontally twice and then sandwich the cake with thick, smoky tasting, plum jam. The top of the cake would then be iced and decorated with candied fruit and nuts.

The most important Christmas cake, however, was Makowiec, which was a poppy seed cake, similar to Stollen, but of a different texture. While Stollen was dry, Makowiec, which was made with yeast, dozens of eggs, butter and plump, brandy-soaked sultanas, ended up as a soft, moist Swiss roll of very large proportions, a slice about 5-6 inches across in diameter. The filling was traditionally made of poppy seeds and baked within the roll. Pounds of poppy seeds, soaked in milk and then minced at least three times, were creamed with sugar, vanilla and spices, before the addition of the brandied sultanas.

A slice of Makowiec with freshly brewed coffee after the Christmas breakfast constituted one of the most delightful moments of the festivities!

The appearance of the first star on the evening of Christmas Eve would end the lengthy period of semi-fasting and the Christmas excitement would reach its pinnacle. On the morning of that day, everyone who lived away would travel hurriedly home to reach it before night-fall:

" . . . that safe harbour of happy childhood memories among the turbulent waves of life," as Miss Apolonia had said once in an unguarded moment of lyricism. The family reunion over the Wigilia table was as much a part of the Christmas enchantment as Christmas itself.

Wigilia, the Christmas Eve supper, consisted of a dozen courses to represent the twelve Apostles. Nothing was more traditionally prepared than this particular dinner – from the setting of the table to the number of courses and the ingredients in each dish. The meal had to be Lenten, as the Church dictated, but every household used two ingredients without exception, which were centuries-old symbols of fertility and harvest – honey and poppy seeds. The diners were expected to at least try a little of each of the twelve dishes to ensure a happy and prosperous New Year. The number of table settings had to be even and, for that reason, an empty place setting would be added for those who were unavoidably absent or even dead. These traditions were rigidly handed down from one generation to another and were unwittingly designed to ensure the continuity of attitudes and beliefs.

For most of these people, the ways of the past, which had been trodden by the steps of generations of their ancestors, were never-failing and God-abiding, and therefore the best.

Martha's soul was steeped in tradition, and in her own, unique way, she was determined to pass on some of her knowledge to the girls.

"It is unseemly for the girls to be so ignorant of their heritage", she declared. "The old mistress hasn't got a head for such things, bless her heart, and those poor girls don't have a mother to make sure that they would learn it all naturally... Well, it's down to me then..."

Thea's apparent unwillingness to learn anything in the kitchen sorely vexed her, whereas by contrast, Josy had love and enthusiasm for anything that was ancient, ritual, or mysterious, and she found her lessons with Martha greatly refreshing to her spirit.

In addition, Josy was also learning to cook well, since to Martha's mind as far as cooking was concerned, there was always a one and only way of doing things properly.

Once, when Josy had accomplished a complicated recipe well, Martha had given her a sidelong glance and said,

"You are old enough now to know something, which, I'm sure, your mother would have told you, had she been alive."

Josy listened smilingly.

"Great passion in marriage only lasts a short time, my girl, but a man will always be hungry."

"Oh, Martha! You are quite impossible", cried Josy, blushing to the roots of her hair.

"My dear girl, I promise you, that it's true! And don't you forget it!"

Christmas was approaching, and heavy snowfall covered the sloping roofs of the Lodge and the boughs of the trees with plump snow pillows. One of the grooms brought a tall bushy tree from the forest and amongst laughter and shouts of delight, set it down in the drawing-room as far as possible from the burning fire.

Both Thea and Josy, and even Miss Apolonia succumbed to the gay mood of the day, and forgetting all their past differences, they joined forces in getting out the large boxes of Christmas tree decorations from the back cloakroom. With giggles and exclamations, they pulled out colourful paper chains, small glass and china ornaments, paper angels with golden hair, and sets of miniature candles together with their tiny holders – all of these saved from year to year, from one Christmas to the next . . .

The girls argued lightly about who should hang what and where.

"Look! The star, the star!"

"Careful! Oh, do be careful!"

"Do you remember these little angels?"

"Of course, we made them three years ago with Martha's golden silk thread."

Miss Apolonia sat on the sofa cutting thin strips of glossy paper to join the broken chains' ends, shortening the candle wicks and replacing the damaged red ribbons on the honey hearts, her face soft and relaxed for once.

The door swung open and Martha rushed in with a whole tray of specially baked honey-dough shapes – stars, hearts and various funny faces. The smell of cinnamon and cloves filled the room.

Drawn by the joyful din, Aunt Cornelia came in

and stood unobserved in the open door of the drawing-room, her eyes moist at the sight of such an enchanting scene. The girls stood on tiptoe, trying to reach the topmost branches of the tree, their flushed faces and sparkling eyes radiating innocent, child-like merriment.

"This is what Christmas is all about," thought the Duchess, her eyes taking in the animated conversation between the governess and the cook. She left quietly, her smile full of a profound sweetness.

With the decorating finished, the spruce tree, bright and luminous, was placed on a low table. For a moment everyone looked at it with wonder, united by the magical Christmas spirit. Thea began to sing in her breathless, melodic voice,

"Silent night, Holiest night,"

"Darkness flies, all is light . . ."

Strangely moved Josy joined in and both sisters sang their favourite carol to an enthralled audience.

The impromptu concert over, the presents were brought in and placed under the tree. Most of these had been made during the long autumn evenings, and included beautiful embroidery or lace, and pressed flowers or intricate designs of beads and pearls in wax, set in elaborate oval frames. On one side, in the space reserved for the servants' presents, Miss Apolonia placed individually wrapped shawls, inexpensive jewellery and, for the men, fur hats, gloves or neckerchiefs. The presents for the servants were usually bought in the nearby town and delivered each year by a local inn keeper, Mendel.

The following day was Christmas Eve. From early morning Martha shuffled noisily the pots and pans on the vast freshly blackened range. The kitchen resembled a buzzing beehive with the servant girls constantly fetching, mixing, chopping and mopping under Martha's watchful eyes.

In the drawing-room Prakseda, down on her knees, was trying desperately to erase all traces of the previous day's merriment from the formerly highly polished parquet floor. The large table, brought in for that night's supper, already stood in place. In the very centre, Prakseda placed a nest of straw under a white damask cloth to symbolise Jesus's humble bed, as was the custom. On top of the straw lay a little gold rimmed plate bearing a few pale wafers previously blessed in the church. The wafers were to be shared among everyone, just before supper, together with good wishes for the next year. The family silver, which had been polished laboriously by the kitchen-girls, sparkled and flickered with every movement of the flames burning noisily in the low grate. Full of majestic splendour the Christmas tree stood proudly, surrounded by stacks of presents.

The fresh, strong smell of warmed spruce needles and apple logs on the fire gently scented the air. The huge gilded mirror reflected far into its depths the luminous tree, the swirling lights of the silver and the festive table. Prakseda finished her task at last, and straightening her aching back, she looked across the room, her eyes catching the magical reflection in the mirror.

"Christmas truly isn't only for children," she murmured to herself, her face softening with unexpected emotion.

It snowed all day and by the early afternoon, the sky had grown dark and the drift leaned high against the windows. The lamps were lit, and Aunt Cornelia, Miss Apolonia and the girls sat in the drawing-room awaiting the guests. As in previous years, they had invited for Christmas two elderly neighbours, who had no close family nearby, and also the administrator and his wife. They all arrived in a short time with more parcels to be placed under the tree.

Thea stood at the window trying to spot the first star, without paying too much attention to the conversation going on behind her. One of their neighbours, a tall grey-haired man, was telling Cornelia in an indignant voice the latest news from the nearby town.

"I assure you, my dear, they are going to move them to the garrison on the west side, the one, which was rebuilt after the fire. Everyone around here is quite alarmed, since it will mean bumping into them in town, at various functions, and, God forbid, even in some people's homes. You know how aggressive they are . . ."

Relaxed and happy, Cornelia smiled.

"Aren't you being a little too morbid?"

"I shouldn't worry too much – no one would ever dream of acknowledging those people. If our paths ever cross, I shall cut them dead; it's as simple as that!"

The elderly gentleman did not argue, but looked unconvinced. He knew that it would be impossible to refuse an invitation when pressed to accept or to deny hospitality when faced with uninvited guests. Josy, listening closely, understood his uneasiness – moving a whole regiment to their town, only a year after the failure of the Uprising, was an insensitive move. She thought about Andrew and could almost hear his easy, cheerful laughter and soft voice. A sudden chill made her shudder, and she pulled the lacy shawl tighter around her shoulders. She felt an inexplicable foreboding. Why should she be afraid?

Of whom? Of what?

Prakseda's joyful calling brought her back to reality.

"Look! The first star! The first star!"

The first bright evening star had evidently been spotted by the groom, who had been posted outside the stables, and every kitchen maid rushed to help with the serving of the supper. Prakseda and one of the grooms, dressed in their finery, started serving the twelve course Christmas Eve supper. After everyone at the table had shared a small piece of wafer and exchanged good wishes for Christmas and the New Year, the steaming first course was brought in – Borshch with Ushka, which was a strong extract of beetroots, dry wild mushrooms and some vegetables. A dash of red wine added during the cooking and some beetroot kvas, ensured a deep crimson colour. The rich, aromatic liquid would then be strained and served as a clear soup with tiny dumplings of a peculiar shape (hence the name – "little ears"), full of sauted, chopped mushrooms, onions and spices.

The second course followed very quickly, consisting of a large platter of pasta shapes, similar to diagonally-cut ravioli but twice their size, called Pierogi. These were stuffed with a special concoction of sauerkraut, onions, mushrooms and herbs, which had been cooked in a little oil beforehand, and would always be accompanied by a sauce-boat of melted butter.

The third course, regarded as the principal one, was traditionally fish – Carp in Grey Sauce. The large, silvery-blue fish, often over 4 kilograms in weight, would first be slowly fried as thick steaks, before being reassembled into a fish shape on an enormous platter. A thick sauce, full of sultanas, almonds and spices, and tasting creamy, sweet and sour, was then poured around the fish in elegant swirls to resemble the waves of a lake.

Large potatoes were cut thinly into game-chips and cooked crisp in butter with fresh rosemary, and then served sprinkled with salt crystals. This course also included a bowl of winter salad made with celeriac to balance the rich taste of the fish and to add a sharp tang to the meal.

The diners ate and complimented Martha's culinary feats. The platters began to be brought in at a slower pace and the interrupted conversation was resumed over the sweet dishes. There were platters and dishes with Kutia, Lamaniec and a compote of dry fruits. Kutia, the most popular of the dishes, was made of softly cooked wheat-grain mixed with honey, poppy seeds and sultanas, and represented everyone's idea of a satisfying, gooey pudding. Suszemina, a dry fruit compote, would be served after Kutia to refresh the palate. It had a wonderful tangy flavour and looked very grand when poured into a sparkling bowl, raised high on a crystal fruit stand. In the event of anyone still feeling peckish, the sideboard was crammed with platters and stands of sweetened almonds, candied fruits, and slices of honey cake.

When supper was over, Aunt Cornelia and the guests moved nearer to the Christmas tree to watch the girls handing out the presents and unwrapping their own. Prakseda quietly lit the multitude of candles on the tree, taking great care to leave the holders in their correct positions.

Replete and sitting comfortably on a large sofa, surrounded by presents, the diners sat watching the glowing tree. The holy evening carols were softly sung in voices charged with emotion. All of them wished for something personal and important – their freed country, a secure future, good health or even great love . . .

Deepest night descended low over the Lodge. The logs in the grate suddenly crackled in a cloudburst of red sparks as an icy wind whirled and rushed down the chimney and back, before disappearing among the white roofs and the treetops of the darkened orchard.

The Duchess was the first to break the enchantment.

"Time to get ready, everyone, the hour is very late and we must leave soon, if we want to be on time for Midnight Mass."

She rose, and pausing at the door, she said with a sweet smile,

"A very Happy Christmas to you all."

"Merry Christmas," answered all voices in unison.

The crisp, clear night air refreshed everyone and the colourful and joyful Mass, so different to the weekly solemn Sunday service, raised their spirits. They headed home slowly, and once back at the Lodge, elated and fully awake, Josy followed Martha into the stables. Martha firmly believed that the Holy Night extended its magic over the animals, and on that night alone, man and beast could worship together, united in their wonder for the baby Jesus' humble birth in the stables.

Martha stopped at every pen and gave each horse and cow a slice of blessed bread. Patting their heads, she softly murmured either good wishes or gentle admonishments:

"Sandy, good wishes to you, old girl. Make sure you present us with a youngster next spring! You have been a bit idle lately, haven't you?"

She stroked the silky soft ears, and while silently chewing the bread, the cow turned her large, liquid eyes on Martha. Catching Josy's amused gaze, Martha smiled.

"She understands everything today, and as sure as day follows night she will produce a calf in the spring, you'll see."

Carnival time began with the arrival of invitations for the girls to various social functions in the neighbourhood. Josy and Thea were allowed to go to as many balls as they liked but only on the condition that Miss Apolonia accompanied them each time. The governess did not mind the task and would patiently sit aside during the dance evenings, content to wryly observe her pupils' unexpected change of fortune.

"Especially Thea," she thought , "How she's changed in the last two months."

The sweet-mannered girl had given way to a confident, beautiful young woman, suddenly conscious of her power. Now that she was engaged and wearing a magnificent ring, she seemed to be very attractive to all the young men, who constantly surrounded her.

Thea enjoyed the limelight, but she well remembered all the previous suitors, who had vanished at the first indication of her lack of large dowry. She knew they would have been less attentive, were it not for her ring and Anthony's wealth. Nevertheless, she was determined to enjoy her last season as a free girl. And after that? She could not clearly envisage her future but at least Anthony seemed to love her; as for herself she wasn't even sure what love was, which worried her a little, but she had learned to brush the thought aside and to go on dancing and smiling.

It was just too bad that Josy didn't seem to be pleased for her. The only thing she knew was that she wanted to be free from any financial worries, and free to do as she pleased, and this was all that

Anthony meant to her – freedom.

Shortly afterwards occurred an incident, which was to change the lives of both girls completely. At one of the gatherings held on the neighbouring estates, they were faced with an awkward situation, which arose when a small group of young Russian officers arrived at the ball, apparently at the host's invitation. How this had happened was not clear and became unimportant in view of the consequences which turned out to be far more serious than one could ever have imagined. The officers behaved impeccably if somewhat boldly. Everyone present discreetly observed them, the men's faces grim and the women's full of indignation at such impudence. Thea turned her head slowly in her newly-found, confident way and looked across the room at the group of young men. Josy, engaged in conversation, had missed their entry, and now, seeing her companion's alarmed face, she too looked in the direction of the door. Suddenly she understood – these were the officers from the new garrison. Her face darkened with anger and she whispered to Miss Apolonia before they both beckoned to Thea and motioned her to follow them out. The governess and Josy were already in their wraps standing in the main hall when Thea, who was following slowly, passed the group of officers. Her striking blue eyes scanned fleetingly the forlorn group of young men, who all hastily bowed. Without acknowledgment and in a dignified swish of her blue gown Thea left the room. One of the officers asked in a low voice the embarrassed host:-

"And who was that divine creature?"

"Why, that is Thea Horaim. Younger of the two Horaim sisters. She was just engaged last month to a Warsaw industrialist. They say the man is very wealthy . . ."

The host broke off at seeing other guests leaving. His hand went up, involuntarily tugging at his limp moustache.

The officer exchanged a sharp look with his companions. It was obvious their group was not an object of sympathetic interest.

Among the clamour of spurs and swords they left abruptly, their faces bearing a look of grim amusement.

The next Sunday Josy and Thea were leaving the Church after the service, when a young lieutenant standing on one side stepped forward and bowed to Thea. To Josy's dismay her sister blushed profusely under the persistent stare of his brilliant blue eyes and seemed to hesitate before moving on.

The governess walking behind the girls passed the officer without giving the slightest indication that she had noticed him. The silence during the drive home was quite ominous. However, once back home Josy threw her coat and hat into the arms of a passing maid and almost dragged Thea into the study She was startled at herself for feeling as angry as she did. Pausing only for a second to suppress her temper Josy said firmly:

"There will be no more of this behaviour Thea. Anthony trusts you and I intend to make sure he is not betrayed. What's even more incredible, how can you encourage a Russian officer of all people ?"

She stopped frightened by the enormity of her accusation and waited for Thea's denial, explanation, anything, but the silence.

Thea stood at the window gazing vacantly at the bleak, snow -covered drive. If she felt any emotion she certainly did not show it.

It was the first real quarrel between the sisters and they both sensed the odd strangeness. From that day, they avoided any open confrontation and for a while life appeared to be back to normal. To Miss Apolonia's delight Thea started riding again.

"It will help her to think everything over. Fresh air should clear her head of that French nonsense she keeps reading!"

Josy, eager to make amends, offered to accompany her but Thea declined the offer vehemently, she wanted to be alone.

That Josy could understand easily; hadn't she often found, in her yearning for solitude, the need to walk or ride on her own?

Thea rode between the snow-capped, dazzling fields, her eyes narrowed from the glare, towards the faintly blue line of trees on the horizon. The day was sunny, dry and the frosty air reflected the crisp snow grinding under her mare's hooves. She had intended to ride through the woods and onto the main track that led to the town. There was no need for her to be back before tea, and her mood altered for the better. She had felt lately irritable and could not think why.

It might be something to do with Josy's odd behaviour. She made her feel guilty and on the defensive, as if it were her fault that men found her irresistible.

And Miss Apolonia's stern gaze . . . perhaps she would prefer to see her less in demand, and more willing to stay in and wait for Anthony.

Well, she wasn't going to, and that was that!

From the opposite direction a lonely rider emerged from behind the trees. The enormous black horse danced under the man in the smart uniform of an officer. Even at a distance Thea had recognised the upright figure of the lieutenant, and embarrassed she lowered her eyes. She was a little frightened, but she was also elated, and despite trying hard not to look at him, for some inexplicable reason she was conscious of his appearance.

She had seen him twice already, and now riding so close to him on the narrow path, she couldn't help noticing how devastatingly handsome he really was. He passed, his eyes openly on her face, his head bowed in a courteous greeting.

He gave her a strange, piercing look and she felt her eyes drawn to his. She was amazed to see that there was a longing and tenderness in them, something she had never expected from this outwardly bold, if not even arrogant, looking young man, and her heart began to beat a little more quickly.

Her face must have betrayed her feelings because the lieutenant turned his horse round in an instant and aligning with Thea said in a low, deep voice,

"May I ask your permission to introduce myself?"

Before he spoke she was ready to rebuke his impudence, but it was the hidden desperation, the slight tremor in his voice that changed her mind and she did not know why she hesitated, instead of refusing him at once.

The lieutenant put his hand out and stopped her horse.

"But I don't know you, I don't know you at all", Thea cried in sudden panic.

"If you will only allow me I can remedy that . . . Lieutenant Alexander Rogov, at your service, Madam".

Thea looked at him quickly and she saw that in the smiling face his eyes were filled with painful anxiety.

Oddly touched, her heart beating wildly, she smiled at the young man.

"I am Thea Horaim"

"I know who you are. Are you angry with me?"

"Oh, I should be, but I am not, I am not! But now if you will excuse me . . ."

"I hope I shall see you again soon", he said casually, but his eyes, warm with admiration, betrayed him.

"I often ride this way", said Thea calmly, but in her heart she was already afraid of her own inexplicable feelings.

Josy busy helping Martha in running the Lodge, did not notice the regular pattern of Thea's excursions. Miss Apolonia felt uneasy but kept her thoughts to herself, waiting for the right moment to talk with Thea.

It was the beginning of March.

Slowly, reluctantly Winter gave way to the first signs of Spring. Under the pale sun, the snow melted and the thaw set in. The river swelled rapidly with icy trickles of snow water coming down the hills. The sticky, shining brown buds covered the naked tree branches and the green mist on the uneven patches in the fields stood out against the dark earth. In the mornings, despite the still greyish-dun of the sky, the birds' chorus started earlier each day.

Enthralled, Josy absorbed the changes and breathed avidly the clear air on her daily walks. Unsurprisingly she felt herself to be part of the timeless cycle. The surge of energy made her light and breathless, and quickened her step. It was just impossible to be unhappy at this time of year.

She looked wide-eyed around the orchard and on impulse bent down the nearest heavy branch and kissing the pale, fat buds, whispered softly, "Grow quickly, Spring is here!" Kuba, one of the dogs forever trailing behind her, observed the procedure with amazement and just to make sure that he didn't miss anything, he too sniffed at the lower branches, but found not a trace of anything tasty. Disappointed he followed Josy home.

"Even - Josy thought, slowly walking back to the Lodge - if I never marry, there's so much I could do!"

These days Josy wore, for comfort and convenience, thick cotton dresses and laced up boots. She spent her days with horses, dogs, lambs. in the kitchen with Martha, and on her walks. Gradually her heart rested and she thought herself cured of dark moods, wild dreams and impossible yearnings.

"Who ever said – Time is a great healer – knew human nature well", she thought with wry self mocking amusement, "I bet if Anthony stood in front of me right now I would not even flush".

One day sometime towards the end of March an unexpected visitor arrived. It was a market day and when the dusty coach appeared in the driveway it was a minute or two before the solitary groom surfaced from the stables. Anthony stepped out tired but happy. He had managed to prepare the new town house for his bride earlier than expected, and once that had been accomplished he rushed back to the Lodge in half the time needed to cover the almost 1000 miles distance.

Anxiously he looked around for a sign of Thea, but it was a flustered Miss Apolonia who came out to welcome him.Taking charge she sent the groom with Anthony's bags to the guest's room, and Prakseda to arrange for tea to be served shortly in the drawing room.

To the governess's relief Anthony decided to refresh himself and change before the tea. He was ascending the stairs when he turned and asked suddenly,"By the way, where is Thea?"

Miss Apolonia felt herself blush and, annoyed, she answered with a dignified affability,

"She is presently taking riding exercises. She should be back in a short while. Perhaps in time for tea."

As soon as Anthony had disappeared from sight Miss Apolonia ran for help. Prakseda hurriedly summoned Josy from the orchard and the groom was despatched on horseback to look out for Thea.

Alerted by the governess Aunt Cornelia came down to the drawing room to keep Anthony company. There was so much she wanted to tell him and so much to ask. She sat herself down and waited for him impatiently.

Shaved and changed Anthony felt much refreshed after the long journey. He entered the room and held both Cornelia's hands warmly, looking at her with affectionate appraisal,

"My dear duchess, it is a great pleasure for me to see you again".

"I am delighted too. This place does seem quiet without Richard's and your company".

Pausing only to inquire about everyone's welfare, Anthony told her the important news:- The house was ready and he would dearly like to set a date for the wedding as soon as possible.

Josy stole past the open doors, up the stairs to her bedroom, to change her gardening clothes. The loose hair escaped from the plait and tumbled around her face, wild and untidy. She smoothed the clean dress and pinned her hair up without taking much care. It didn't matter much what she looked like, only that Anthony wasn't unduly alarmed at Thea's absense. She looked around her room but found no guidance in old familiar objects.

Steadying her thumping heart Josy entered the drawing room trying hard to look inconspicuous. Aunt Cornelia, relieved to see at least one of the girls, smiled and in her low, controlled voice, relayed to Josy the good news.

With some unease Josy felt that Aunt Cornelia's eyes held her in a long, questioning look.

She hardly dared to lift her eyes to the guest and her answers were somewhat subdued.

They talked of commonplace things and Josy was thankful that between Miss Apolonia and Aunt Cornelia, Anthony didn't seem aware of her strained behaviour.

Suddenly the door opened with such force that only the hinges kept it in places, and Thea walked in. Her beautiful face looked unusually troubled and Josy involuntarily shivered a little.

Anthony looked at her with surprise – was she much taller and somehow different than three months ago? He wanted to greet her with affection but Thea looked at him so coolly, that confused, he hesitated before firmly putting his hands behind his back. It was obvious that Thea had come back from her ride agitated by something or someone and in a temper. She didn't seem to pay any attention to Miss Apolonia's warning signs behind Anthony's back. Thea ignored her and with her eyes downcast listened to Anthony enthusing about the house, the wedding and how very anxious he was to take her to Warsaw soon.

For the first time Thea smiled at her fiance but there was a hint of malice in her grave eyes.

Her indifferent reception began to affect Anthony's rapport and in desperation he glanced at Aunt Cornelia for an explanation.

But Cornelia looked interrogatively at Josy and then turning to Thea said in her placid tones,

"Isn't that splendid news, my dear?"

Thea, her face still and sullen, faltered a mufled affirmative.

The sudden gap in the conversation seemed to be the prompting she needed. Hesitating only to take a deep breath she straightened herself up to her full height and looking Anthony in the face she said clear and loud:- "I am not going to marry you, Anthony, not now or ever, and I am not sorry either. I have been happy, very happy for the first time in my life and I won't let anyone try to take it from me."

Josy sitting on the sofa just behind standing Anthony didn't see his face but she felt him stiffen, and from the tone of his voice understood how shocked and angry he was:-

"You agreed freely without any pressure on my part . . . you promised . . ."

He didn't have a chance to finish.

Thea, her face contorted with emotion, erupted:

"You thought you had bought me, didn't you? I can tell you now, I love another, and I will marry him soon, very soon!"

Suddenly she remembered:

"You better have your ring." – she wrenched the

ring from her finger and shaking with fear at her own reckless courage she threw the ring at Anthony. It missed him and rolled somewhere near the sofa. Miss Apolonia, with horrified eyes looked at white-faced Aunt Cornelia. Both women sat rigid as if struck by lightning.

Relieved at the incident that gave them time to compose themselves, and both highly embarrassed, Josy and Anthony bent down simultaneously. In their haste their hands touched over the ring. Suddenly shaken, they experienced an electrifying sensation of a current passing through their fingers. The feeling was so intense, that they both lifted their eyes and looked at each other, as if to make sure that they both felt it. Their eyes locked together. For a split second the world around them ceased to exist. It was as if she were the only woman, and he the only man left on Earth and now they had found each other. A depth of emotion and a physical desire were so intense that they both felt strangely moved yet calm and certain. Quite certain.

"I will marry you," Josy said slowly, hardly knowing that she had spoken, and so casually as though she were continuing an earlier conversation.

Anthony helped her to the sofa, his eyes still holding her in his scrutiny. He seemed to gather his thoughts from a remote distance. Without letting go of Josy's hand, he asked, "Do you really mean it? Why?"

Seemingly unaware of other peoples' startled presence Josy said breathlessly,

"Oh I do, I really do! And why? Because I love you, and . . . . . . and I think I know you love me!"

Miss Apolonia gasped aloud in exasperation. How she wished to God that Josy would not show such uncontrollable emotion.

Anthony took both Josy's hands and kissed them,

"If you really mean that you would have me, than I can only say that I am very, very happy."

His laughing eyes looked down at her with such tenderness that her face grew hot, and she didn't know any more what he was saying, only that the pressure and warmth of his hands were still on hers, and in her heart she finally felt without any doubt infinitely safe and secure.

The same evening Miss Apolonia and Aunt Cornelia held an emergency meeting. Thea summoned from her bedroom stood facing her aunt. Her eyes were red and swollen with tears and her face was stained. It gave Aunt Cornelia a little pang. She sat lost in reflection. It was all so . . . so unbearable, and yet . . .

With a sigh she asked Thea for an explanation.

Nervously, her face slightly turned from her Aunt, Thea started to recall events. It transpired that for the past two months she had been secretly meeting the young Russian lieutenant from the nearby garrison.

They were desperately in love and both would die rather than be parted. They had arranged to marry in secret, but now Aunt knew, Thea hoped

Alexander could come and ask for her hand directly.

She paused and looked at her Aunt. She seemed older and thinner, and Thea felt genuinely sorry for her. But it could not be helped. She had to marry Alexander or she would die, that's how devastating their passion was. She didn't expect the duchess to understand that, and so she had to prepare herself for the worst. If necessary they would have to elope. Anything, just to be with him.

The duchess sat with her eyes closed for a moment and Miss Apolonia thought with alarm that she was going to cry. Her face bore an expression of such misery.

After all those unhappy years she stupidly thought their fortunes had changed for the better.

What irony! Her niece in love with a Russian officer! For all she knew he or his comrades might have killed Thea's father. In this wretched world those two had no hope of ever living happily together. If only there was a way of explaining this to Thea. And what about the officer?

"I suppose nothing I say will change your mind?", her voice was weary.

"Nothing", Thea said vehemently, "absolutely nothing!"

"Then go to your room, my dear. I don't feel we could resolve anything tonight. Perhaps morning will bring new answers . . ."

After Thea left the room Cornelia turned to Miss Apolonia who had sat through the entire conversation frowning silently.

"What are we to do with Thea? I think I am at

my wits' end . . ."

"Nothing hasty, that's for sure. Perhaps we should speak to the man himself . . ."

"What, and invite him here! To this house! A Russian officer in the Lodge! My late husband, my dearest sister and her poor husband would come back from beyond to haunt me. Oh, no I could not consent to his visit."

A little shiver ran through her at the very idea.

Miss Apolonia looked at her with sad eyes,

"We don't have much choice, Cornelia. Thea is wilful and if we don't assume control now, she will disgrace this house forever by running off with lieutenant Rogov."

"Perhaps we could discuss the whole thing with Anthony, after all he is practically family now, and so worldly wise a man . . ."

"But Anthony? How could we, after yesterday? It wouldn't be seemly to involve him, really most embarrassing . . ."

"Never mind that, Cornelia. The man is well travelled, nothing will shock him. Anyway he seems so happy to escape making such a dreadful mistake, and marrying the wrong girl. What if it had happened after he married Thea!"

"Well if you think . . . then perhaps you could ask him to talk to us tomorrow morning in my office . . . it is more private there."

Silence fell upon them and then the duchess rose slowly,

"I shall go and pray for guidance. I am afraid right now I don't have any strength of my own to decide a great deal in this awful matter . . ."

Next morning Cornelia sat in her office long before anyone else at the Lodge was awake. When Martha sometime later walked in with the morning tea tray, the duchess raised her eyes from the pile of papers on her desk:

"Thank Goodness, Martha, at least you are up, I am already frozen in here!"

"You shouldn't be working that early. I will send Tonia with hot logs right away.Nothing like a good blazing fire in the grate to brighten a dull morning, eh?"

She poured the steaming tea into a wide cup.

"The breakfast is almost ready, are you having yours here?"

"Perhaps you could ask Anthony to share it with me?"

The door closed behind Martha and Cornelia looked down at the papers in front of her. The sums stared at her in black, stark numbers.

She frowned a little.

If she was to be very frugal she could manage to run the Lodge for a few more years. Thank goodness Josy at least would be safe in marrying Anthony. But what about Thea?

Before she had the chance to think more of the solution the kitchen girl brought the burning logs in a tin bucket, and then proceeded to start the fire in the cold grate of a green – tile covered, chimney-breast.

The door opened quietly and Miss Apolonia came in, followed by a smiling Anthony.

Tonia was sent to fetch the breakfast tray and the duchess motioned the guests to sit down with somewhat affable formality. She tried hard to smile, but her lips were stiff and she felt nervous.

Miss Apolonia watched her anxiously. Smiling, Anthony turned towards Cornelia,

"Try not to upset yourself, You can count on my absolute support in any decision you will make . . ."

"This is exactly where the problem lies. The decision! What am I to do? How are we to stop Thea from ruining hers and my life?"

For a moment Anthony was silent. Then he took Cornelias hand and pressed it gently.

"Are you sure this is the best course of action?

If, and I stress, if you manage to break this dangerous liaison, what then?

Thea, as I see it, has two options only. Either to marry without love, someone suitable and with money; that assuming all the time she is lucky, or lead the wretched life of an inpoverished spinster.

The question I am asking is: has anyone the moral right to condemn her to a life of misery?"

The duchess flushed and then grew pale. Anthony's unexpected question hung in the air more like an accusation.

Annoyed, she looked at her guest with a cold gaze,

"And what may I ask would be your solution?"

"If you'll allow me to say so, I think you should let her choose for herself, Cornelia. After all, what does it matter that Rogov is Russian? Life is so very short and to spend it constantly fighting seems to me faintly absurd, if not disproportionate." Cornelia's steady eyes rested on him and he thought with sadness that she did not like a word he had said.

"Surely, you couldn't expect me to do that", she said with cool irony.

Anthony did not answer. He looked at her for a moment, then put his hand on her arm.

"I'm sorry you don't like what I advise. But to prove that I am serious, I promise in the event of Thea marrying Lieutenant Rogov to settle on her five thousend roubles, to ensure that she starts her married life on an even footing with her husband."

Miss Apolonia straightened up in her chair.

"I am sorry if I sound very stupid, but I can't make head or tail out of what you're saying. Why do you wish to help Thea so much, when you are supposed to be . . ." She broke off uncertain.

"When I am supposed to be in love with Josy? Is that what you wanted to say? It is very simple: I am a very, very happy man, my own wedding is near, and I would like to spread a little of my happiness. Perhaps for good luck! Is that so bad?"

He spoke lightly but there was in his voice just a sort of catch. He continued,

"I will ask for one condition only; Thea must never know about the source of her bequest".

The duchess smiled grimly, her eyes met Anthony's in a reflective gaze.

He never ceased to astound her. It was just as well she wasn't thirty years younger, he really was something else . . .

"Well, certainly I will have to think this over. Perhaps I should also meet Lieutenant Rogov to see what his thoughts are . . ."

"I think, Cornelia, that this is a very good decision", Miss Apolonia's trembling voice and moist eyes betrayed that she was overwrought and oddly moved.

Cornelia gave her a sweet smile.

Dear Apolonia, had she felt for this remarkable man too?

The very next morning brought an unexpected end to Cornelia's perplexity. Lieutenant Rogov arrived and requested to see the duchess. Grim-faced Miss Apolonia left him unceremoniously in the hall and went to summon Cornelia.

Lieutenant Rogov stood rigid where the governess had left him, his cap under his arm. His immobile face did not show that he noticed or indeed cared about the contemptuous manner in which he was being received.

Somewhere, from the the side corridor leading to the servants' quarters came the muffled noise of whispers and giggles. The kitchen girls tried to steal a glance at the handsome Russian officer.

At last the governess returned and motioned to the young man to follow her. They entered the office.

Never having seen Lieutenant Rogov before, the duchess held him in a long and unembarrassed look of cool appraisal. It was almost to the point of rudeness, but then social graces did not seem to matter anymore. They had to get acquainted and time was short.

She had to admit that he was the most handsome man she had ever seen. Grudginly she took in his well-shaped head of thick black hair, the dark clasp of his smooth brows, magnificently set above a straight, proud nose, the brilliant blue of his eyes fringed by dreamy lashes and the fresh, cherry-red lips, half-hidden under the silky moustache. His complexion could have been the envy of any young maiden. She looked at his wide shoulders which tapered down to a narrow waist, tailored to perfection by the expert cut of the officer's uniform, while his legs, strong and muscular seemed endless . . .

"Won't you sit down?" Cornelia asked amiably, but the officer, with a small bow towards her, silently declined.

Cornelia sat herself and looked up questioningly at the young man:

"To what purpose do I owe this . . . pleasure . . .?"

Lieutenant Rogov's shining blue eyes rested on her coldly, and then he spoke in a deep voice,

"In other circumstances I would not intrude on you. As it is I am here to ask your permission to marry your ward, Thea Horaim."

The duchess was watching his face and it was obvious from his grim eyes and the controlled tone of his voice that the question was purely a rhetorical one. He seemed to say in fact that whatever the outcome of their conversation he would marry Thea anyway.

She looked at him again. His enormous eyes were directed at her, steady and unblinking, his face set and stern.

She felt a shudder running through her body and quickly averted her eyes.

"Perhaps, perhaps you would be so kind as to

allow us two days to think your offer over."

She hoped her voice didn't falter too much.

Lieutenant Rogov bowed again.

"I shall come back for your answer the day after tomorrow.

Same time."

Without waiting for her to speak he left the room, and for a short while she could hear his measured steps receding down the corridor.

Sometime later Cornelia asked Thea to come and see her.

The girl walked into her Aunt's office with a defiant face and sullen mouth. Her eyes wandered restlessly about the room.

"Like a caged bird", thought Cornelia with terrible sadness.

Thea suddenly looked at her Aunt with such desperation that Cornelia grew pale and quickly said,

"I wanted to talk to you about Lietenant Rogov, and his proposal."

"You saw him? He was here?"

"Yes, but this is not the issue, What is important, to me anyway, is whether you realise fully what would be the implications in the event of you marrying Lieutenant . . ."

"Oh, but I don't care, I really don't! Please, please allow us to marry!"

The duchess looked down at the sheet of blotting paper in front of her.

"Do calm down, Thea, and sit quietly, or I won't proceed". Cornelia paused for a moment.

"If you really want to marry Lieutenant Rogov, you'd better listen carefully.

It is very difficult for me to say this, but if you marry this man you will never, never be happy."

"Why not?" Thea's voice was barely a whisper.

"Because you will have to renounce your whole life.

To start with you would have to marry secretly. Nobody, but nobody will accept you around here socially. You will be forced to move away. You will have to forego your family, your home, your friends and your way of life. Even your religion. Are you really prepared for this?"

Thea, her hands folded at her breast turned to her Aunt, her voice breaking with emotion,

"I don't think you can even imagine what love is.

You don't understand at all how desperately in love Alexander and I are with one another. Nothing really matters to us except being together, nothing! I will sacrifice everything, all you have mentioned gladly, for life with him."

She trembled in every limb and tears were now rolling down her pale cheeks.

Cornelia stood up and held her close in her comforting arms.

"Don't cry, my child, perhaps there is a way . . . perhaps it can be done . . ."

The night before Lieutenant Rogov's return for an answer Cornelia was tortured with terrible dreams. Her late husband came back to the Lodge, but was silent and angry. Her sister Joanna, pale and ethereal stood in the distance with her arms outstretched pleadingly.

Cornelia tried to explain that she was helpless and old, that it would be morally wrong to condemn a girl so young to a life of misery, and that she had not the heart or courage to distress Thea any further. What if the girl in her confusion and desperation decided to do something stupid?

But they didn't seem to understand. Fading into the shrouded past, their faces were still reproachful and sad.

She awoke with tears streaming from her eyes. The morning drew on and the cool sunshine of an early Spring dispersed the night's fears.

By the time Lieutenant Rogov arrived Cornelia was calm and composed again. It was about time to come to a decision before the uncertainty of it all drove them to madness.

In a short while Thea, her lieutenant and Cornelia sat in the office facing each other.

Ignoring Thea's feverish, pleading eyes the duchess turned to the young officer.

"I have decided to allow my niece to marry you on cond . . ."

Thea in one jump threw herself at Cornelia, almost strangling her in her hot grasp.

"Oh, Auntie, Auntie!"

"Now, now, Thea, do sit down, or we won't finish this business . . ." She gently disentangled herself. "As I have said, on condition that you obtain the transfer of your commission to elsewhere. Preferably as far as possible."

Lieutenant Rogov rose and bowed.

"I will arrange for transfer straight away".

The duchess' lips moved, but her smile was a trifle forced.

"That's that then. I have something else to tell you. On your wedding I shall be able to settle on Thea five thousand roubles and I would appreciate if the money would remain Thea's property, Lieutenant Rogov."

The young man sprang to his feet.

"I assure you that the sum will be Miss Horaim's for her disposal entirely."

Satisfied, the duchess turned her gaze to Thea and gasped. The transformation was quite remarkable. The pale, tear stained girl of the past few days had been replaced by a raving beauty. Her eyes had gained a starry, ecstatic expression, her face glowed with boundless happiness, and her gaze was entirely on the young lieutenant.

Chapter Four

"At the first moment I could quite believe it was a great shock, but when your Aunt came to look at the facts calmly she saw that this was the most, if only, acceptable thing to do."

Josy shot a rapid glance at Anthony walking beside her.

A sudden thought struck her and it took her breath away.

"You don't still feel something for Thea, do you?"

Anthony stopped abruptly and turning her round to face him, held her firmly in his arms.

"Never, never doubt me again! My infatuation with Thea was short and most regrettable. It is you I love and want more than anything else in the world.

Surely you know that?"

Reassured, she nestled up to him like a child, and when she looked up, she saw that his eyes gazed down at her with infinite tenderness and love.

They walked on. The orchard was now in the first bloom of Spring and the bees hummed amongst the half open pale buds. The morning mist coloured the grass in pearly shades of green, and

the steaming earth in the newly dug flower beds filled the air with a fresh, intoxicating and wholesome scent. Down, by the meadow joining the end of the orchard, the bushes of silver- gleaming catkins reflected their gently swaying branches in the clear waters of the fast running stream.The first swallows swooped in jet pattern across the brilliant sky and over the stream. It was magic.
Anthony held Josy's hand.

"We haven't had a chance to talk of something very important. Something you should know."

"Should I?"

In an instant she had a picture before her mind of Aunt's Cornelia's shocked face and the partly heard news she didn't understand. Yet at this moment she trusted him completely and she wanted to prove it.

"I don't want to know!"

"But you must! I can't go on letting you think that I am someone else. If we are to marry soon, you must know or it could be dreadful for you . . ."
Josy turned away and putting her hands firmly over her ears stamped her foot.

"No, no and no! I trust you and don't want to know your secret until after we are married. Take it as my wedding present to you."

Anthony began to kiss her. She wound her arms around him and closed her eyes. The same sensation shot through her body as when they first touched and she moaned softly in ecstasy.
Between kisses she heard his rapid, breaking up voice saying crazy, adoring words, words she wanted him to say again and again. Forever . . .

The date for Anthony's and Josy wedding was set for the end of April, just after early Easter.Richard summoned by Cornelia arrived to give Josy away. The duchess smiled at his dandyish appearance of a man about town. He wore a jacket that was a little bit longer than usual, with velvet collar and cuffs. His blond hair swept elegantly from his high forehead was kept raffishly long at the back. He was delightfully talkative and made everyone laugh.

How different to him was quietly clever, thoughtful Anthony, with his powerful body, and masterful, conservative style in clothes. And yet she liked them both so much.

The big day arrived. The wedding party drove on the track twisting among the already green fields. Josy looked with misty eyes at the young wheat and rye fields swaying towards the coach as if they were sea waves of brilliant colours, merging and moving in the light breeze, as far as the eye could see.

Her heart was beating fast. It was her wedding! If only her parents could be here today. It would make everything just perfect!

The church was drowned in flowers and fragrance. Cut up green rushes were strewn , like chinese letters of good luck messages, over the red carpet leading from the church door to the altar.

The crowd packed the church. Everyone wanted to see the beautiful bride and the unknown, wealthy groom.

To Anthony, waiting at the altar, Josy seemed like an ethereal vision, the silvery clouds of the

dress and the veil floating around her with every step.
He watched her coming towards him strangely moved and in fear. Somehow he could not believe that she would not disappear like in a dream.
The elderly priest spoke ancient words. They repeated them solemnly after him, their eyes locked together.
Aunt Cornelia and Miss Apolonia, both sat in the pew, elated and tearful. Behind them Martha cried softly, her face florid under the tightly laced ribbons of her large bonnet. Next to her, Thea stared ahead, oblivious to the whispers and curious looks from the neigbours. Outside the church the peasants and the Lodge's farm workers lined the path, shouting good wishes for the newlyweds.
At the Lodge the sumptuous lunch was ready and waiting.
The young couple sat amongst the revelling guests. The tinkling of the glasses and plates, and the noise of voices, talking, making speeches, laughing, seemed to them distant and detached.
Anthony's eyes didn't leave Josy's face for a moment, he neither understood what was said to him, or answered correctly. Still unable to believe his good fortune he was certain of one thing only – had he needed to fight for his love he would rather die fighting than lose his bride.
The duchess observed reflectively the newlywed couple. It made her happy to see so plainly the evidence of the truth she had always believed in, that no difference of birth, religion or family really mattered in the path of true love.

For a second she wondered whether Anthony had a chance to tell Josy about his past and his dead parents. It didn't seemed to matter anyhow, judgeing from the way they looked at each other. She knew that Anthony was going to keep his word and present Josy soon with the biggest surprise and joy of her life. But for now that too was to be kept secret. The toasts and the speeches over, Josy came down changed into her plain travelling clothes.

It was time to say goodbye.

Miss Apolonia looked suspiciously red-eyed and drawn. Both Anthony and Josy hugged and kissed Aunt Cornelia, and thanked her once again. She felt so moved that all she could say to Josy was:-

"As my only return, I want you to be happy."

Thea stood behind her, already lonely and waited her turn to hug her sister. They kissed and looked into each other's eyes without a word. They both had chosen what they wanted most and at this very moment their paths diverged forever. The sudden realisation, that this was the end of her carefree, familiar life here, that she would not see those she loved for many months, perhaps forever, that she was on the threshold of the great unknown, made her burst out crying too.

Among the loud sobbing Josy climbed into the coach. Embarrassed, Anthony followed her quickly. Martha looked up sharply from the side of the carriage into Josy's tear stained face -

"You did want to go?" – she asked in a quiet whisper.

"I did" – agreed Josy, sobbing.

"Then stop crying." she hissed.

Josy laughed through the tears and calmed down at once, to Anthony's visible relief.
The last trunk hoisted onto the roof and the door was closed. Among the good luck wishes, cries, and grinding of the huge wheels on the gravel, the coach moved on. The horses well rested, stretched high their necks and galloped along the sunstrewn drive. Within minutes the coach disappeared from sight, and only clouds of dust were left drifting slowly into the distance.

The journey was uneventful if not tedious. The coach stopped at various Inns to change the horses and Anthony and Josy refreshed themselves hurriedly at the long wooden bars with hot soups or occasional rabbit stew. They ate little.
The food was not a patch on Martha's cooking, and anyway they still seemed to feel the effects of the euphoria surrounding the wedding.
They were arriving at their destination at last.
It took them two weeks to reach the dusty sprawl of outskirts of Warsaw and Josy looked curiously out of the open coach window at the new world.
Anthony instructed the coachman to drive slowly right through the main streets and squares, to show Josy at least the glimpses of the capital.
Warsaw struck Josy as a very grand city. The centre with elegant white buildings standing under colonnades, the monuments and the parks, the old churches and the crowds of people, walking, riding or standing, seemingly without anything to do - made her look around with wonder.

Why, in the country there was always something to be done according to the time of year.
Anthony gazed at her reflectively, that thoughtful, kind look in his dark eyes, but mixed with it, a shadow of regret, as if he knew already that she would always be a country child at heart, lost and bewildered in the big city he himself loved so much.
"As soon as we are unpacked, clean and well rested I will take you shopping, and then . . . to the theatre."
"Oh, good, good!" Her eyes shinning, Josy flung herself into his arms and kissed him with such boundless passion that Anthony caught unaware almost lost the balance on the narrow seat. They both laughed. Anthony held her close, his whole body growing tender and passionate. Without letting go of Josy, he called the coachman:
"Hey, Mathew, take us straight home. I think we saw enough for the first time."
The coach moved instantly faster, just as Anthony sought and then found Josy's lips and his arms encircled more closely her tiny waist.

When Prakseda arrived ladden with provisions, Martha insisted she must take with her, Josy could hardly believe that it was almost a month since they had seen each other last.
The time seemed to fly by. What with the shopping for the fashionable dresses more suitable for the city, and in theshops which looked to her like the elegant salons rather than places of business, meeting Anthony's friends and learning her way

around the centre of Warsaw, there hardly was any time left.That of course was during the days. And then there were the nights. She had no idea how it was going to be, except that it would be special.Nothing however prepared her for the passion, the wanting and the ecstasy of the nights. She was sure everyone could read it in her face and she felt embarrassed, but alas she was completely helpless against the force of her emotions.

She hoped that Prakseda's sharp eyes hasn't noticed anything unusual. Carefully they unpacked the oblong baskets onto the long kitchen table, with Prakseda anxiously checking that the jars of honey were not broken, the ham and smoked sausages weren't crushed and the cakes didn't dry out during the journay

"You shouldn't really . . ." Josy felt overwhelmed.

"Have you ever tried to persuade Martha to change her mind?"

Prakseda put the food away and satisfied sat at the table with glass of cool drink.

"Oh, it is so hot in the city. How do you survive here?"

"Well, it isn't easy, but I have Anthony and I am very happy!"

Prakseda looked at Josy , a smile enlighting her kind face.

"I am glad for you, I wish Aunt Cornelia could see you now".

"I wrote a letter home, it must be a week ago, to Aunt Cornelia and of course everybody else, but it will be another week or two before it reaches the Lodge. I am simply dying for any news!"

"Everything as usual, you know. Except Martha misses your help, and I suspect your company in the kitchen. Miss Apolonia spends most of her time with your Aunt . . . now that Thea has left."

"Thea has left? What do you mean?"

For a moment Prakseda was silent. It seemed she could hardly find her voice.

Josy was beginning to feel a trifle impatient with her.

"For God's sake, what happened! Do tell me!"

"It was awful!" She blurted it out in one breath finally.

"There was the wedding, yes, but they were married secretly in the Russian Church. They left immediately for his family home in Kiev, and after that they were going to his new posting, somewhere in . . . , oh, I don't even know how to pronounce it. It didn't sound to me like a Christian name of a place any how . . . And now your poor Aunt is quite unwell."

Her voice trembled dangerously and she swallowed hard trying to stop the tears.

Prakseda never cried easily, and to see her anguish upset Josy more than anything else. She felt guilty for being so happy, for forgeting the problems at home . . .

She put her arms around her and tried desperately to find the right words, but what on earth could she say to lessen the tragedy. Prakseda's handsome face was distorted by the grief and by the effort to restrain the tears welling up her eyes.

Josy hugged her silently. But in her heart she knew already that they had lost Thea for ever.

The next few days brought the consolation for Prakseda. If she could make Josy's and her new husband's life more comfortable, more homely it would be something worthwhile at least. There was not much sense in dwelling on bad incidents in life if you couldn't alter them for the better.

One late morning, after Anthony left for the office, she walked into their bedroom with the breakfast on a tray. It was nice to have again the opportunity to spoil Josy a little. Slowly, she opened the door expecting her to be still asleep, but hearing Prakseda's steps Josy must have jumped out of bed, because she was standing in the middle of the room anxiously looking for her negligee.

On seeing her like this Prakseda stifled a cry and stood stupefied. Josy's long hair tumbled loose around her bare shoulders. The usually grey eyes, now huge in her small, pale face, seemed almost black. Her still swollen mouth bore the sign of a passionate night. The crumpled nightdress, nothing like the high-necked cotton ones used at the Lodge, revealed the beautiful, young body.

Avoiding Prakseda's eyes, Josy wrapped herself in Anthony's bedroom gown. A little, wilful smile of satisfied love lingered on her lips.

Embarrassed, Prakseda turned away. Not ever having been married, she suddenly felt curious yet shy, unused to such an open display of passion and happiness.

She knew not why, but for the first time in her life she was filled with awe.

Their life settled into a pleasant routine: the social rounds, the theatre, the walks in the park and the companionable evenings at home.
Josy wrote to her Aunt long letters with minute details of her excursions around Warsaw, her trips to the theatre and her amusing observations of the city fashion and the people she met.
In between the lines Cornelia could detect that Josy was often homesick, and she wished aloud that Anthony would hurry the proce . . . She stopped just in time at seeing two pairs of alerted eyes. Miss Apolonia and Martha usually read the letters with her in the office, and now they were looking at her with an unspoken question.
Cornelia's kind, tired eyes rested on them for a moment.
"Oh, it isn't anything important. Just like Josy, you will have to wait and see."
She continued reading: "How is my beloved orchard? Is the harvest going to be good this summer?
From where I sit and write I can see over the rooftops for maybe a mile; there is not a single field to be seen or smell . . . How I miss my daily walks with Kuba. Is he missing me too?"
She never ended a letter without adding in her large, bold hand writing:-
"But the most important thing, dear Aunt – I am gloriously happy!"
Cornelia sat smiling, the letter on her lap.
With somewhat detached curiosity she wondered whether God would spare her for a while yet, so that she could see that everything was settled pro-

perly before she was gone.

One day, around the middle of September, Anthony came home earlier and announced:
"I am taking you today somewhere special. Get ready quickly, but do wear something comfortable."
Josy jumped to her feet and gave a little laugh. She simply loved surprises.
"Well, what is it? Where are we going?"
Anthony did not answer, but smiled at her with roguish eyes.
"You are simply wonderful. I shall be ready in five minutes!"
She put her arms lovingly around Anthony's neck and kissed him on the lips.
Anthony drew her very closely to him.
"I only hope you are ready for this."
"Whatever it is you want me to see, you won't find me disappointed."

Within minutes they were walking towards the main Avenue. She had noticed that at some point they had abandoned the known route and turned into the side street. They kept on turning into the little alleyways and slowly she realised that they were in a different world to the one she knew.
The terraces of narrow town houses were old and shabby. Their dilapidated fronts had patches of dirty plaster flaking everywhere. At regular intervals the dark arched doorways lead into the bowels

of the back buildings surounding the stone yards. To Josy's unaccustomed eyes they looked like giant empty wells. Strange and soulless, they couldn't possibly be inhabited. But looking up at the row of blank windows shrouded in dirty scraps of net curtains she realised with a shock that the houses were occupied.

They hastened along the narrow, cobbled streets until they came to one, which seemed at last to have a shadow of a commercial life about their dusty shop fronts, rusted shutters and crumbling stone steps. In some of the shop windows black-robed men sat sewing. The tailors wore the flat caps and Josy recognised the Jewish way of dressing, similar to the Jewish innkeepers on her Aunt's estate.

From time to time they saw a solitary passer-by, or the small groups of dark haired children, who on seeing the strangers stopped playing and stood huddled together, staring at them with mature, old eyes.

Josy turned to her husband, but her smile vanished at the sign of his solemn face.

"You did not tell me where we are heading?"

He gave her quick sidelong glance, but did not answer.

Instead he asked her a question.

"If you are tired we could go back?"

She smiled and shrugged her shoulders.

"Of course not, but perhaps you could tell me why are we here."

"We are almost there. You will understand soon."

He seemed pale and strangly serious.

They stopped in front of one of the shops. It didn't seem to be any different from the others, except that instead of the drab coloured bales of cloth or tailors' dummies, this particular shop window had been filled with brown boxes of leather gloves, belts and wallets.

Anthony held the door open. Josy walked inside and stood for a second uncertain looking around. It was a dusty little shop with the same brown boxes lining the dark walls, and a wooden counter alongside one wall. The musty smell of leather pervaded the whole place. Behind the counter, on the high stool, a man sat poring over what looked like a book of accounts. He was wearing in the same Jewish custom a long, black coat and a skull-cap.
On seeing the well dressed customers he rushed to the front and bowed low his gaunt figure, at the same time loudly exclaiming the greetings and his delight at such honor.

"Ay, what a lucky day this is, such a lady, such a gentleman, in my little humble shop! I couldn't wish for a better day, it makes my tired eyes better, and my poor hands better, and my wife , she is going to be so happy too . . ."

His darting eyes appraised expertly Anthony's country gentleman suit and Josy's dress. Today she wore for comfort an old dress from the Lodge. It looked slightly provincial, not at all like the latest fashion dresses she bought recently.

Anthony requested to see a pair of riding gloves. The merchant nodded and then turning into the dark doorway leading to the back room, called something in a harsh sounding foreign language.

Josy gave Anthony a quick, sidelong look, but his face was impassive and calm.

From the darkness a small woman emerged holding a box of gloves. A tightly curled wig was perched slightly askew to one side of her shorn head. Dark, red rimmed eyes glanced furtively towards Josy. She put the box onto the counter and then stepped back behind her husband.

Anthony tried a pair of gloves. He checked other pairs carefully, and then replaced the last pair and pushed the box away. Turning to the merchant he spoke fast and angrily in the same guttural language.

Josy looked at him blankly and her heart began to beat a little more quickly. The mystery of all this fascinated and horrified her. What did it all mean?

The merchant flushed and grabbed the box in such a hurry, that some of the gloves scattered to the floor. He didn't bother to pick them up but thrust the box at his wife and then turned to Anthony apologising and bowing feverishly.

"Ay! Ay! How could a stupid man like me know? I couldn't have recognised! Oh, let me make all amends right now!

Here are the latest, the best gloves ever made. And what do they cost? They cost a fortune, but not to you, oh no! The price for you shall be a pittance, less than the price I have paid myself. I shall rather rob my poor wife and steal from my hungry children, but I would not risk again the wrath of such a noble man, such a special man . . ." Anthony waved away the merchant impatiently.

"Wrap this pair for me, will you? And charge a normal price. I would hate your family to go without. I am not angry with you, merely disappointed at your way of running the business, that's all."
Among the loud thanks and more bowing Anthony led Josy out.
They walked for a few minutes but did not speak. Josy felt her heart beat fast against her ribs. She had no inkling of what was in Anthony's mind. Only that she loved him so desperately, and that nothing really mattered as long as he loved her too. She knew what love was now and she remembered his passionate, tender ways of pleasing her. How could he doubt her love? Did you cease to love someone just because they have a secret past?
They turned sharply into a side street and suddenly Anthony asked quietly.
"I suppose you want to know the meaning of all this, this . . .
for the need of a better word, pantomime?"
"At the first moment, when you spoke his language, it was a shock, and then, and then. . . .", she hesitated, searching for the way to formulate her thoughts.
"I think it's time for you to know. I am a converted Jew."
"I should have guessed!"
She was watching his face and knew at once that her flippancy angered him.
Quickly she took his arm.
"I think you're attaching too much importance to something completely insignificant, at least to me."

"You mean you don't find this dreadful news?"
"You know very well that I wouldn't! It isn't as if you were really different. In a way you are as foreign to them as I am, and that's the reality."
"Yes, you are right. Money and education are great social levellers."
"What did he say anyway? You seemed quite angry."
"He thought we were a pair of country bumpkins on a shopping trip to Warsaw, and ready for a rip-off. He wanted to sell me old rejects for the price of the best ones. It did not even cross his mind that someone who looks as I do, could be one of them and understand his remarks to the woman."
"I am not surprised. I've never thought of you in that way" Josy chuckled. She was glad to have an opportunity to laugh a little, for Anthony still seemed to be frowning.
"It goes deeper than you think", he said slowly at last.
"I never wanted to be explained away in a category. Pidgeon-holed for life, the way people are, on both sides, as you have seen just now. There aren't any real differences between us, you know, just the stupid, superficial ones. If we could only make an effort, take time to understand, and learn about each other, damn it, together we could turn the world around!"
Josy felt herself colour, and saw by the shadow in his eyes that he was angry. She took Anthony's hand and pressed it without saying anything. She had a lump in her throat. She remembered with

embarrassment that she too had been guilty on occasion, of the judgemental remarks about people she knew nothing about, just because they did not belong . . .
Anthony took her arm, his eyes calm again,
"I have always believed in being a human being first and a Jew second. If people could be reconciled, one to another, all the cruelty, all the ugliness would disappear, but perhaps . . . I don't know if I am making any sense to you?"
He gave her a look and she felt her eyes drawn to his.
"Of course you do! I don't care about those things anyway. Perhaps, perhaps because I love you more than anything in the world!"
"You are not unhappy with me then?
There was a caressing sound in his voice and at last his eyes looked down at her smiling.
Josy stretched herself to reach his lips.
"I adore you", she whispered, "don't you think you were very foolish to think otherwise, even for a second?"
"A complete fool, I willingly admit."

That evening, after they had retired to the drawing-room, Anthony raised the subject again. Josy looked up at him and a sudden chill passed through her limbs. It saddened her that he felt the need to explain his life-decision and that he was evidently uncertain of her approval. It wasn't a logical feeling, since she had already married him, but stemmed from his need for total understanding from the only person he loved and trusted. She got up and walked to where Anthony was sitting in an armchair. Without a word she sat quietly at his feet, her arms resting on his knees. He smiled when she asked in a soft, low voice,

"Now what's troubling you ?

He took her face in his hands and kissed her.

"There is no real trouble, and it makes me feel better just to hold you."

They sat in silence for a minute or two before he spoke again.

"I must explain. It is very important to me that you understand why I had to choose the way I did . . . I am not a coward or traitor . . ."

The words seemed to be issued from his lips with difficulty, as if his throat was dry.

"I have never laid bare my innermost thoughts before, to put it plainly, but you are . . .", he paused and Josy looked up at him, smiling reassuringly.

"You needn't be nervous. You know that I will always stand by you."

"It is difficult to put into words . . . it might sound somewhat pompous to say this aloud, but . . ." he hesitated. "But I simply abhor this human stupidity, which allows one group of people to claim superiority over another. Even the oppressed are often the oppressers. There is so much suffering caused because most people are conditioned to only feel secure and superior within their own race, religion, class or country. The fools cannot see that, when the frontiers are down, everyone IS like everyone else!

I . . . I wanted, perhaps in the folly of youth, to prove as much to myself as to them that it is only an accident of birth that one is born in England or in Poland, or in . . . in . . . Timbuktu for that matter. Important only is the basic truth: we, human beings, are all the same, and as such, we should be equals. We should foster friendships, and work together, despite any cultural differences, despite different backgrounds . . ."

He rose to light his pipe with a wooden chip from the fireplace. Perhaps it was an excuse to hide his nervousness. Still looking into the fire he gave a short laugh,

"If only we could see our likenesses and stop harping on about the superficial differences . . . Well, perhaps in the next fifty years we will achieve this . . ."

His deep-rooted anger, or was it despair, unexpected in a man otherwise so calm and restrained, moved her beyond reason. Her heart beat quickly; it was curious that suddenly she could see his point of view so clearly. His last words had struck her. She remembered only too well the ill feeling caused by Thea's marriage, and indeed her own, if the truth were known. Never before had she been made to question her own identity, her belonging to a particular class, her roots or her hatred for the Russians in general. Anthony's way of thinking meant a revision of everything she knew, and for the first time in her life she felt so uncertain and confused. Her head began to ache violently and she leaned her forehead on her hand. Sensing her turmoil, Anthony rose.

"I think you need time to digest all this. It has been a long day. Shall we go upstairs?."

Grateful for his understanding Josy followed him silently.

During the next few weeks, Anthony seemed preoccupied with some important business, the nature of which he would not divulge. This made Josy even more curious, but to no avail since Anthony would not be drawn. She sighed unhappily. Warsaw in late autumn seemed quite horrible. There was nothing but the rain and mud. No burnished gold trees, no steaming fields or wood-scented bonfires from the potato-digging days. No dogs to race across the wet grass of the misty orchard, and no end to this slowly evolving strange feeling of being trapped in a city she did not love and did not belong to. Embarrassed, she remembered her naive curiosity and enchantment with the tales of life in the bright lights, which Robert used to describe so vividly during his visits to the Lodge. "He can keep all the big cities to himself!" she thought. Oh! What she would give now to be able live in the country again! But alas! Anthony had to stay where his business was, and she wanted to be with him...

Sometime towards the beginning of December, Anthony brought home some news.

"I have to go away on business somewhere not far from the Lodge, and I am sure you would like to come too. We could take Prakseda with us, and..."

Josy sprang to her feet and threw her arms around Anthony's neck.

"Don't say another word! You're simply wonderful! I was just sitting here, all alone and feeling thoroughly homesick, when you strolled in and made everything alright again!"

Anthony laughed and she could tell he was well pleased. They departed two days later with only one travelling trunk.

"We don't need too much luggage for a week or two." Anthony's face seemed as usual but there was something different in his eyes. A glimmer of anticipation? Well, if he had any surprises up his sleeve, she could wait. Surely it couldn't be anything more exciting than her going back to the Lodge? As on the original journey, they stopped at country inns and little auberges, eating hurriedly and sleeping in the coach rather than slow down the journey. The weather was not obliging at all, and Josy couldn't see much through the rain lashed windows. But they were moving at good speed, and the prospect of seeing Aunt Cornelia and everyone else at the Lodge made her regain her spirits.

At the end of the second week of their travelling, Josy noticed changes in the landscape passed. The scenery had become richer, the fields more fertile and the villages affluent with their larger houses and well-dressed people. There was no mistake – she was coming home.

Night drew on early over the heavy sky, and Josy settled down comfortably in the corner of the coach seat. Opposite her, Prakseda was asleep already, but Anthony seemed alert and gazed frequently out through the misty window.

"You cannot possibly see anything there! We shan't reach the Lodge before morning, so you might as well have some rest now," said Josy with a smile.

Anthony turned and looked her fully in the face.

"I think we may arrive at our destination any moment now."

"Now? What is it? It isn't the Lodge's driveway, is it?"

Josy stared at her husband, wide-eyed. The coach made a half-circle and trundled to a halt. Anthony jumped out and held out his hand, saying, "Take care you don't fall, it's quite dark out here."

The coachman carried the lantern on ahead as they walked slowly up some steps leading onto the verandah of a large house. Josy tried to see around her but there were no stars to lighten the darkness, and the lantern made visible only a step or two ahead of them. Another foot forward and then she found herself in front of a massive oak door. In the dim light, just at eye level, the snarling beak and ferocious eyes of a wrought-iron eagle stared at her from the past. Her heart gave a sudden thud against her ribs. With a gasp of apprehension, she realised that this could only be one place on earth, her father's ancestral home, Vronovo.

Behind her, Anthony gave a little laugh in which Josy could discern excitement and a good deal of affection. She turned and entwined her arms around his neck.

"I would have not guessed in a million years that this was to be my surprise!"

"That's quite evident by the pounding of your . . . ah . . . bosom! Weren't you aware that I know all the secret desires of your heart?"

Suddenly the lights came on in the house, and the door opened quietly. Enthralled, Josy stepped into a stone-flagged hall. An open fire was burning noisily at the foot of a large chimney breast, and a young groom stood to one side holding a lamp.

"Welcome home!" Voices came from within the doorway of the drawing-room, and suddenly Josy saw Miss Apolonia's slim silhouette next to the rotund shape of Martha. Amid the laughter and with everyone talking at once, Josy was led in. Behind her, Anthony enlightened in whispers Prakseda, who blankly looked around, seemingly not yet fully awake.

"Where is Auntie?" Josy asked anxiously.

"Oh, she is right here, waiting for you!"

Martha pointed to the back of a large sofa, one of a pair, which stood opposite each other on either side of the massive hearth. Josy walked round it, and without saying a word, she found herself in the comforting arms of her aunt. They held each other closely, both overwhelmed with joy. Martha beckoned to Prakseda,"Supper is ready, do give me a hand with serving." They left the room quietly.

The next morning, Josy jumped out of bed at first light, unable to wait any longer. She wanted to see the house in daylight, and she tiptoed out of the bedroom, hoping to be alone at such an early hour. Quite unexpectedly and all of a sudden before she could reach the stairs, she was seized by an awful spasm of feeling desperately sick. She staggered to the bathroom and opened wide the narrow window. Her head was swimming, and as nausea overwhelmed her, she leaned over the china bowl and vomited. A rush of icy air brought her back to reality, so she dabbed her temples with cold water and sat for a while by the window, trying to control her shaking knees. And that was how Prakseda found her. On seeing the maid, Josy stretched out her hand and Prakseda helped her to her feet. "I will take you downstairs – the fire there is already going strong, and you can have a cup of tea."

They negotiated the stairs slowly, and then Prakseda settled Josy in the kitchen. She sank exhausted into the chair and watched the maid hurriedly making the tea.

"I don't know what came over me. I must have over-exerted myself during the journey, and then yesterday's excitement brought all this on . . . Mind you, I don't remember ever having been sick before."

Prakseda put a wide, steaming cup on the table, and stood looking at her reflectively.

"I think that you are going to have a baby", she said at last with a smile.

Josy looked at her in huge amazement.

"But that's not possible! I have only been married for a little while. Only six months or so . . ."

Prakseda gave a little chuckle.

"I know of a girl who's been married much, much less than six months and already has a baby".

Josy sat frowning. She could not collect her

thoughts clearly. So much had happened in the last few hours that she felt confused and weak. She tried some quick mental calculations and concluded that the maid was right. Why she hadn't thought of it herself, she couldn't think. She wasn't sure whether she was delighted with the latest news or not. She had so many plans – to restore the house to its former splendour, to help Anthony with the running of the estate . . . And now this . . . She would have to take it easy and become almost an invalid for the next few months. She shrugged her shoulders. The very thought of being careful and cautious was making her feel ill again.

As Josy had known he would be, Anthony was overwhelmed with joy. And as she had also feared, he insisted that she do nothing strenuous or tiring. Nevertheless, she was touched by the emotion in his eyes and voice. She had not thought it possible, but at that moment, she felt drawn to him even more.

Together, holding hands, they went from room to room, and Josy was surprised at her almost eidetic memory.

"I can see my mother playing the piano in here, just before tea was served in the afternoon. She really could play quite beautifully – she had the right type of hands, long, slender fingers, but strong too."

They passed the study and Josy pulled Anthony in.

"I used to hide here! My father worked in this room almost every day."

They stood silently looking round the room with its white- washed walls and simple furnishings: an old desk, two leather armchairs and rows of books and old boxes full of lead-shot on the strongly built oak shelves. On one wall hung two hunting shot-guns crossed in Eastern fashion. A tall brass lamp with a green glass shade stood at one side of the desk. Josy led Anthony to it.

"Oh, just look here! I would recognise this lamp anywhere! It has a figure of Napoleon standing next to his cannon! Father often let me play with the cannon – it's free-standing. I knew all about Napoleon's campaigns before I even learned about the history of Poland."

Suddenly she saw something on the other side of the room and ran there.

"Oh, look! Even Henryk's picture still hangs here."

She pointed to a large portrait over the fire place. It depicted a young nobleman dressed in hunting clothes and sitting upright on a chestnut horse, which seemed to dance under the rider. Curiously enough, on his arm sat a large, web-eyed crow ruffled up. The young master had a bold handsome face, and the slightly upturned corners of his generous mouth gave a good indication of his high spirits. Clear, grey eyes, so similar to Josy's, looked out from the portrait with laughing insolence.

"That's Josy's great-great-great grandfather . . ." said a voice behind them. The Duchess came quietly into the room and, unobserved, looked with lingering, smiling eyes at Josy's face, now flushed with excitement.

Anthony turned to her. "Did he live here?"

"Yes, for a while, around 1650 and in later years. He was a knight in King Kazimir's army during the Swedish War, but the portrait tells the story of his youth. It was then that this place got its name – Vronovo.* Apparently he was out hunting one day in the fields and woods surrounding the estate when he spotted a hawk fighting with a crow. The crow fought so pluckily that, impressed, Henryk shot the hawk and took the injured bird home. To everyone's surprise the crow survived and fully recovered except for the blind eye.

It was said that it never left Henryk's side and he loved that bird quite extraordinarily, for he named his home after the crow and also ordered a signet ring."

Josy's eyes gleamed and she clasped her hands. "Do we still have it?"

The Duchess smiled affectionately at her.

"This is a memorable day for our family, my dear girl. The estate is back in Horaim hands, and you are with your first child. And I can say so now, it's all because you were so fortunate in your life partner."

Her eyes rested on Anthony for a short while. It was easy to see that he was moved and delighted.

"Come with me. I have been waiting a long time for this moment. There is something I want to give you."

She left the room and Josy managed to kiss Anthony before they followed Cornelia into the

* *Vrono* (Polish) – a crow

drawing room. She opened her travelling bag, took out a small box and snapped open the lid.

"This is the ring, which is given in our family to the eldest child." She held out the open box. "Take it, for it is rightfully yours now."

Both Josy and Anthony looked with awe and wonder at the gold signet ring mounted on black velvet. Its face showed a web-eyed crow, standing in a blue enamel field.

Anthony took his wife's hand and drew it into the crook of his arm. Smiling softly, Josy gave him a sidelong glance from beneath her dark lashes. She felt him squeeze her hand and understood his prompting.

"It is wonderful," she said in a low, tremulous voice, "to see the continuity of one's family in such a tangible way. Anthony and I will do everything possible to pass on to our children the same determination to continue . . ."

Amused and strangely moved, Cornelia smiled, her eyes resting on the young couple.

"I know you will, my child. Seeing you two so happy and in this house gives me peace of mind. I know that I can now rest at last".

As December was approaching, it was decided that it would be more convenient for Josy and Anthony to spend Christmas at the Lodge. The workmen, who had been engaged by Anthony to do various repairs and alterations, thus would be able to finish the job quicker without interruptions. To her surprise, Josy felt restless and only Martha was able to distract her with a hand-written book of her best recipes.

"Here is something to start you off with your own collection."

"Oh, Martha, do you know that you are an angel?"

Impulsively, Josy took her in her arms. Over her shoulder Martha's kind face bore an expression of real concern.

"I have watched you very carefully during the past few days and you don't seem to be as fond of the Lodge as you were once. What is the matter?"

Josy looked down.

"I don't really know, except that I only seem to be happy when I am at Vronovo. We have so much to do there. There is something else – I feel ashamed, but you know, I don't like our administrator. I cannot help it, but I find him dreadfully insincere, if not sinister. I think, I think I am a little afraid . . ."

"Oh, come now, your imagination really has got the better of you!"

"I wish that were the case . . ."

"Do you believe Anthony has been taken in by that man?"

"I haven't had a chance to speak to him as yet. I feel reluctant to meddle in what, after all, is Anthony's department."

Martha smiled.

"You have a different marriage to most. It is somehow unusual to see two people able to talk so freely with each other. You have nothing to fear."

"No, no, it's not that. I am only concerned that

perhaps he isn't used to dealing with country folk, and might be a little too straight-forward. He doesn't know their cunning ways."

Josy paused and looked at Martha. The old woman thought for a while.

"What is going to happen to Anthony's business in Warsaw?"

"Didn't you know? He sold most of it to buy Vronovo back. When the Russians confiscated everything, they sold the estate to a wood-merchant from Smolensk. He only kept it for the yearly income, which is why nothing inside the house perished. But he drove a fierce bargain and now I suppose we really must run Vronovo well and properly if we are to survive."

"I think you are worrying unnecessarily – it seems to me that God's will is with you."

On the day of their departure, Josy took a long walk with Kuba among the snow-bound fields. But when she looked for him just before leaving to return home, the dog was nowhere to be found. Finally Anthony and Josy climbed inside their coach. This time nobody cried since Vronovo was only a day's drive away. Josy sat down and lowered the window to say thank-you once more when her foot caught against something soft and warm under her seat. She looked down and saw a pair of anxious eyes, full of devotion – it was Kuba. Martha could not prevent a smile, and then everyone laughed.

"My, that dog really knows where you are going, no mistake. You brought him with you from the estate as a youngster. He used to be your father's dog, didn't he?

"Yes, he used to be Papa's companion."

"There, what did I tell you! You will need a good deal of care and attention, and I dare say he is determined that you will get it. Take him with you, otherwise he will only pine for you all day long."

And that was how Kuba came home.

Josy settled down at Vronovo with remarkable ease and found the work of creating a home for Anthony and the baby she was carrying a refreshment to her spirit. She felt much better and much stronger. It pleased her that Anthony spent long hours every evening reading agricultural magazines and books, since he wanted to be able to have a reasonable amount of knowledge during his meetings with the administrator. The man still worried her, but . . . there was nothing really that she could say now, was there? It would be quite silly to talk about a bad feeling or a sixth sense, as if she were a superstitious peasant girl. Anthony would only laugh. Yet, somehow she was quite convinced that the man's unpleasant, pale, darting eyes, deep-set in his massive, well-fed face were hiding something. She could sense his unease and something akin to hostile restraint, and she resolved to be alert.

In the meantime, the house needed a good clean and the furniture brought from Warsaw had to be correctly placed in their new home. She loved rearranging the old order to suit her taste and mood. She wanted a less formal home – a home filled to the brim with the colourful, rough textures of hand-woven kilims and tapestries, bold flower arrangments and above all the freshness and golden tinge of light and air streaming through the uncluttered windows. In place of the heavy brocade curtains, she hung laces and tulles, beautifully executed in the unusual design of a silvery web. So much like a spider's real web, which she often admired, on seeing it stretched between low branches or on the orchard gates, luminous after the rain and breathtaking in its intricate perfection.

In the hall, she draped a richly coloured, floral rug over the bow-fronted chest, while another similar rug was placed at an angle on the marble-slabbed floor. On one side of the chest stood an old urn-lamp and on the other, an arrangement of dark-green leaves and fruits raised on an antique stand. A large oil painting of flowers and fruit in the Flemish style, above the chest, augmented this ambience. The combination of the chest, rugs, painting and real fruit gave an impression of three-dimensional still life and was Josy's manifestation of her love and understanding of beauty found in common, everyday things.

Sometimes Josy wondered where her ideas came from. It must be due to her affinity with everything she saw and absorbed on her walks. It excited the senses within her and evoked an instinctive, irresistible need to reflect and merge the vivid, mellow hues of the fields, the woodlands and the orchards. Startled visitors would suddenly stop at the sight of a triumphantly magnificent display (or was it a sculpture?) of glossy red apples, interwoven with green leaves in perfect symmetry raised on a crystal cake-stand, or on seeing a huge silver platter bearing squat, flame-coloured pumpkins stuck together in a soaring pyramid against the coarsely-woven threads of a black and white tapestry. The effect was striking but so unusual that it seldom met with any genuine approval from the visiting neighbours. The ladies' pursed lips would be heard whispering to each other,"Shouldn't she keep the food rather in the pantry?"

As Josy's good breeding could not be questioned, there could be only one acceptable explanation, and it was seized upon with relief – she was an eccentric. It was quite fortunate, thought Josy with wry amusement, that Anthony shared her views and liked the natural, unpretentious tranquillity of their home. But then he loved everything about his wife.

The next few months passed so quickly that Josy realised one day with shocked surprise that they had been living on the estate for six months already. It had seemed more like an eternity to her, as if she had never left there and her past at the Lodge and in Warsaw had been nothing but a dream. She sometimes thought about the future but made no plans. The only thing she knew now was that she wanted her baby to be safe and healthy and that she had found her place at last. The rest could take care of itself.

Josy was awakened one night by a strange feeling. She knew that the time had come and she woke Anthony. He was ready in an instant and left to wake Prakseda. Josy put on a dressing-gown and combed her hair. Her heart began to beat quickly, and she realised she was a little frightened, but before she had time to grow even more apprehensive, someone walked down the corridor and knocked at her bedroom door. She opened it and, astonished, saw the familiar figure of the village midwife.

"Mrs. Gorny? How did you manage to be so quick?"

"Your husband asked me a few days back to stay on the estate, in that cottage by the main gate, until your confinement."

"Oh, how good of you! Anthony has just left to fetch a doctor and Prakseda should be up already."

"You seem well enough. I will go and give Prakseda a hand with the hot water and towels. It will be a long wait; it always is with the first born. Just relax, but don't lie down. You will feel better if you walk around. I won't be long."

Reassured, Josy decided to prepare the room in the way the midwife had previously taught her, "You won't find peasant women giving birth on a bed. They usually find squatting is the most comfortable and the quickest way to have a baby . . ." She pulled a linen sheet from the chest and spread it on the floor beside the bed. She then tied to the bed pillar a long scarf, twisting the ends to form a strong handle. To her surprise, the hurting now came in quick succession. She had rather expected to be in labour for quite some time so this didn't seem right. Without understanding how, she just knew that she was going to have her baby soon, now . . . Oh, God, no, no . . .

An unknown, alien pain seized her and she fell to her knees onto the sheet. With each spasm, her body rolled itself involuntarily into a tight ball. She heard a scream and realised in panic it must have been her own . . . Stuffing a handkerchief in her mouth, she bit hard each time she felt pain approaching, feeling there was no point in making a spectacle of herself. The pain left her as suddenly as it had come. Quickly Josy discarded the now uncomfortably heavy dressing-gown. Just as she relaxed for a second, the pain returned with terrifying force. She felt ripped apart and at the same time her teeth bit right through the folds of the handkerchief. Independent of her will, her body pushed with an inhuman strength, her hands gripping the twisted scarf so tightly that her knuckles became white knobs. As she seemed to have no control over her body, she tried in desperation to find at least a more comfortable position. In the end it didn't seem to matter what she did and, unable to think clearly, she concentrated only on counting each spasm of pain, on surviving another one, and another . . .

The room around her grew horribly hot and stuffy. She was squatting now. Sweat pouring down her arched back drenched her long hair and made her hands and then the rope slippery and difficult to hold. Without warning an almighty convulsion twisted and shook her body as a gush of something like hot blood threw her down on her knees. She gave a strangled gasp but then almost immediately she felt an infinite, joyful relief. She looked down.

Among the folds of the crumpled and stained sheet lay a baby boy. His first strong cries came as the midwife carried in the jugs of hot water. Behind her, Prakseda was swaying white-faced, her stiff lips trying in vain to say a prayer. The midwife put down the jugs with a clatter.

"God's mercy! You could have knocked me down with a feather!"

Josy, pale and drawn, gave the ghost of a smile and pointed urgently at the maid. Mrs.Gorny spun round just in time.

"There, there, Prakseda, you cannot faint now. I need your help and fast. Here, have a sip of water."

She left Prakseda to recover and bent over Josy.

"Don't worry about anything. If you feel cold and shiverish, that's quite natural."

She covered the exhausted girl with a blanket and separated the baby from her, talking soothingly all the time.

"What a big, strong boy, you are, eh? Your father is going to be so proud, and your mother needs a lot of rest right now so you'd better go to sleep. Be a good boy . . . Here, Prakseda will wash you and then it will all be alright . . ."

Having recovered, Prakseda cleaned and dressed the baby, while the midwife washed Josy skilfully and helped her onto the bed. The sheet together with any other remainders of the birth was removed from the room. As Prakseda with shaking hands lit the logs in the grate, Mrs. Gorna turned to her.

"Have you any herbs in the kitchen? Aromatic ones would be best."

"Yes, there are quite a few bunches hanging in the pantry. What do you need them for?"

"To freshen the room before the master's return. Get a bunch or two and throw them onto the fire. At the double, girl, or the men will get here first!"

When a frantic Anthony arrived with the doctor moments later, they both stopped still in the doorway, astonished at the unexpected scene. Josy lay in bed peacefully asleep with the baby at her side. The room had the fresh smell of the woodlands, causing Anthony to glance around for the source of the scent, but the lights had been dimmed well, and only the small fire threw a dancing red glow across the ceiling. From an armchair, obscure in the shadows, rose the smiling midwife.

"Congratulations! You have a boy, sir." she said in a whisper, at the same time steering both men outside. The doctor asked her a few questions, and obviously satisfied, he then left, promising to come back in the morning. Anthony turned to the midwife.

"How is she? I could never have imagined that it would be so quick."

"You have got a marvel of a wife, sir. She surprised me too and nearly frightened Prakseda to death! I'd better go and check that she is alright. A good cup of tea should revive her. Would you like anything?"

"No, thank you. Get some sleep now – I shall sit

with my wife myself until morning. And, Mrs. Gorny, thank you very much."

He took the woman's hand and held it between his own. He then shook it warmly before disappearing inside the room. The midwife stood for a second looking at her hand as if it were a strange object. Finally, she turned and slowly descended the stairs, which led to the kitchen.

Prakseda put down the cup she was holding.

"Good God, Matriona! What's happened? You look as if someone has given you a crock of gold!"

"You can laugh, but that master of yours surely has winning ways about him. Shook my hand as if I were a lady, and looking me straight in the eye, said 'Thank you very much . . .' As if it were a natural thing. Mind you, the way he said it . . ."

"You haven't seen anything yet. He is quite strange sometimes. Talks to everyone alike. The other day, he asked the workmen in the barns whether they liked their work! They thought he had flipped. Have you ever heard such nonsense! It wouldn't even have crossed our old master's mind to give a moment's thought to the likes of peasants!"

"Well, I don't know. I quite like it . . . could get used to it, quick enough. And it warms your heart to see how fond he really is of his wife. I wish mine were like him even only once a year . . ."

Prakseda gave her a quick glance but said nothing, blushing at the memory of some of the village gossip, which the kitchen girls had used to laugh about. Quickly she got up to pour more tea and as if just remembering, she suddenly exclaimed,

"Oh, what have I got in that head of mine! I meant to ask you last week! With the new baby now, we will need for sure another girl from the village. Not for the kitchen, mind, but to help around the house. I thought you would be the best person to ask, on account of your knowing everyone in the neighbourhood and being god-mother to half the village."

Matriona rose to her feet.

"It is very kind of you to ask me. I think that I can find someone suitable. Perhaps tomorrow even, I shall have a word with Agnes's mother. I am sure she will be very pleased. The girl is a bit slow, but very keen and unspoiled. I dare say that you will train her in no time. When would you want her to start?"

"Now, or rather yesterday!"

"That's settled then. I shall tell her to come here first thing in the morning the day after tomorrow."

Just after sunrise on the day that Matriona had indicated, a tall, big-boned girl, carrying a bundle, knocked on the back door just as Prakseda came down to the kitchen. Matriona had been right, the girl looked clean and wholesome, her round face scrubbed shiny and pink. However, the china blue eyes held a slightly glazed, vacant expression. 'Never mind, thought Prakseda, holding her in close scrutiny, before deciding, 'I will have her running around in no time.' She motioned the girl in.

"Come in quickly and shut the door. It's still nippy at this time of day. Get the fire going while I set on the samovar. I bet you haven't had a chance to breakfast yet?"

Agnes gave her a slow, grateful smile.

"I haven't. My god-mother said to be sure to come here with the first light, and it must be close to three miles from our house . . ."

Her voice faltered and she cast down her eyes, reddening a little. It was obvious that she was worried that she might be talking too much. She busied herself with the range and, gathering dry sticks of wood into a light stake, lit the fire quickly. Prakseda gave her a shrewd glance.

"I don't mind you talking to me at all. And you have got that fire going very well, my dear."

Agnes' dim face beamed all over.

"My mother taught me."

"I am sure your mother would be glad to know how well you are doing here."

For the next few weeks Prakseda put Agnes through her paces with such speed that the girl's starched skirts positively whirled around the house and garden. Every time she made new progress, Prakseda praised her generously and the girl in turn would talk about the maid's kindness to anyone willing to listen. Matriona, who called by unexpectedly one day, couldn't have been more pleased.

"Just look at her now! Even her eyes are different – I don't know how to describe it . . . They are no longer dull, but bright as two buttons."

Prakseda was both touched and pleased by this praise and the interest, which she had aroused with her clever methods.

"I am very glad I was able to do something for her."

A sudden thought struck her, and smiling, she turned to Matriona and asked.

"Have you ever seen Agnes eating?"

"I don't recall, but probably . . . Why?"

"Well, it is both puzzling and funny. The first time that she had her dinner here, I was quite amazed. She was sitting at the table and in front of her had this big bowl that I use for making dough in. This looked so strange that I glanced at what was in it. You won't believe it, but it was full of all the courses; soup, meat, vegetables, and wait for it . . . also a great helping of apple pie and cream!"

"What?! All in the same bowl?"

Matriona was laughing helplessly now.

"Yes, all in the same bowl! And do you know what she said when I asked her why she didn't eat on separate plates?"

"Go on, I have no idea!"

"She said that, since all this food goes to the same stomach, it would get mixed well there anyway, and that it also saved on washing up!"

"What perfect reasoning!" Matriona chuckled, wiping her eyes, but her handsome face was strained and pale. Prakseda sighed in her heart. It had to be that good-for-nothing husband of hers playing up again.

The baby slept. He was now a healthy, robust three weeks old, but to Josy, as with most young mothers, her son was not just a baby, her own flesh and blood, but also a unique, unimaginable miracle. She would look at him for hours, filled with wonder and disbelief. How was it possible that she could have produced another human being with such ease, and one who was so perfect and beautiful?

The new addition certainly changed their lives. Anthony almost had to force himself to leave Josy and their new baby each morning to go and supervise the running of the estate. Josy spent most of her time looking after her son, insisting on feeding the baby herself, so it was left to Prakseda to pacify and get rid of the previously engaged wet-nurse.

"I wish that you would at least go for your walk – I am quite capable of looking after the young master for a while, you know."

"And I only wish I could! But I hate to leave him even for a second. I have changed so much that it frightens me!"

Alarmed, Prakseda looked up at her. Josy's eyes shone brightly with a curious light and her face was illuminated by an invisible, inner smile. She looked quite beautiful.

"You do remind me of an inspired angel spreading the gospel."

"Ah, you are joking, but it really is beyond my understanding. Just look at him! He sleeps so much. What is he dreaming about? How can a mere human child have such translucent eyelids, such a small, unaware mouth? I want his first conscious smile to be for me only. That will be my reward and I shall wait."

The maid gazed at her with frank affection.

"I think that you are completely besotted with that son of yours, and you have a right to be for he is gorgeous, but someone has to run this house and I guess it has to be me . . ."

She rose and walked lightly to the door. With her hand on the door handle, she turned and looked back, suddenly remembering a question. Bent over the cot, already unaware of Prakseda's existence, Josy was softly repeating soothing murmurs in her low, breathless voice. She was looking for something of Anthony in the boy's features as well as of her. Perhaps that tiny little frown between his brows was his father's, but his mouth was definitely hers . . . He was the perfect result of a very happy marriage and suddenly she felt infinitely grateful and humble. Shaking her head, Prakseda left the room quietly.

Her son's dependence on her made Josy fiercely protective. She wanted perfection in everything, which was for him. He seemed unusually alert and Josy spent hours showing him around the house: the pictures, the flowers, the gleaming silver, which made him laugh, the different rooms and then the gardens. He would gurgle happily, and the maids marvelled at his sunny disposition.

The months passed and the boy was trying his first steps. At the opposite end of the drawing room, Josy knelt with her arms outstretched, calling to him softly. The child tottered forward, his sturdy legs spread wide. From behind Josy, Prakseda cooed,

"Come here, my darling. Come to Prakseda."

But avoiding her outstretched arms, the little boy turned abruptly towards the open door and disappeared into the adjoining room. Both women jumped to their feet and hurried after him. They stopped at the sight of the little boy standing by a chair. His eyes seemed almost round with curiosity as he gazed solemnly around in a strange orderly manner at everything surrounding him in the room.

Prakseda clasped her hands together.

"Good Lord, just look at him! He seems so . . . so . . . grown up. It is quite amazing!"

Josy observed her son reflectively, her heart still trembling within her.

"I can't even begin to guess how he learned to walk without us noticing anything. Anthony will be so pleased!"

A few months later, Anthony had to travel to Warsaw to collect some new seed catalogues and to place some orders at a large agricultural company. When he came back, he brought with him a box of presents for Richard. The little boy was ecstatic. He could speak quite well now and he walked around the box, touching each package and asking, "What's this? What's this?" Amongst sheets of coloured paper, packets of crayons and wooden bricks lay a beautiful book. It had green leather binding, and from the front cover a Wise Cat looked up with an enigmatic smile. In the evening, Josy made her little son comfortable in bed and sat beside him. She opened his new book and read aloud,

"On the shore there stands an ancient oak.
Around the gnarled oak a golden chain
Is wound round and round.
And night and day on that chain the Wise Cat
Walks in timeless circles:
He turns to the right and sings a song,
He turns to the left – he tells a story . . ."

The words of Pushkin's poem preceded the collection of fairy tales. This newly published book had its title printed in large ornate letters – 'Tales Of The Wise Cat'. Intrigued, Josy turned the first page. Something made her look up. Two pairs of impatient eyes were watching her intently. Josy laughed at the thought of her husband listening to a bedtime story. Absorbed in the book, she hadn't noticed when Anthony had come in quietly and sat down by the bed.

"Are you sure you won't be bored with a child's story?" she asked Anthony with a smile in her beautiful eyes.

"I am sure I shall find your reading most enchanting", he returned mockingly. His boyish face had the look of a naughty schoolboy's. Their eyes turned to the child. Richard sat against the pillows, excited and wide-eyed.

"Tonight," started Josy, "I shall read you the

first story. It is called Little Mukh. Are you both comfortable?"

The man's and the child's voices cried together, "We are, we are. Do read the story, please!"

A smile flickered in Josy's eyes, but she turned the page obediently.

"A long, long time ago", read Josy in a low soft voice, "There lived a very little man whose name was Mukrah, but everyone called him Little Mukh. This nickname was extremely suitable because, despite being quite mature in years, Mukrah had never grown more than four feet tall. He had a very large head, which rested awkwardly on a very short body. Mukh lived comfortably on his own in a large house in the city of Baghdad.

To tell the truth, no one would have known or cared whether he lived or died, were it not for the fact that he would only leave his house once a month and always on the same day. That day soon became a source of excitement for a crowd of small boys from the neighbouring streets. The youngsters would gather outside Mukh's house from early morning on the day of his monthly excursion and would wait impatiently for him to appear.

When the door at last opened, there first emerged an enormous head, swathed in an even larger turban, while behind it followed a tiny figure dressed in wide pantaloons and what had been once a blue caftan. Around his waist was wrapped a sash-belt, made of several feet of cloth, and behind which he carried an enormous kindgaw, a double-edged dagger."

Josy stopped and turned the book round so the

pages faced Richard.

"This is what he looked like." She pointed to a large picture, and slowly outlined the various items of clothing.

"This is a turban, which is a long, long scarf which is worn around the head by some people. And a kindgaw is like a curved knife and it would be hung at the belt. And pantaloons are simply very wide trousers, gathered at the ankle . . ."

The child listened carefully, two little brows knitted together over thoughtful eyes.

"Can we proceed again? Have you seen everything?"

"Oh, yes, please!" he replied.

"Looking at Mukh," read Josy, putting incredulity in her voice, "one could never decide whether he was carrying the dagger or the dagger carrying him. At last, he emerged fully from the dark doorway, and the noise and cries of the boys rose sharply above the normally sleepy street. Some youngsters threw their caps in the air, others did headstands and somersaults, while still more clapped their hands, singing,-

"Little Mukh, Little Mukh,
Comes out on to the street
And click-clacks with his
Shoes! We don't see you
For a whole month, but
Now is the time to catch us!
Do try harder this time
You could be invisible,
Were it not for your head,

Which is as big as a cauldron.
Little Mukh, Little Mukh
Knock-knocks with his shoes
Come and catch us
Little Mukh!"

They were naughty little boys but they didn't know any better for they all belonged to the streets of Baghdad, and they did not mean any harm, of course. Little Mukh was not upset by their song or their cries. He would not chase them as they expected, for he was far too good natured. Instead he would acknowledge them all with a nod of his large head and move on without delay, knock-knocking in his very big pointed shoes. Happy with this little performance, the boys dispersed, not returning until the same day of the next month. Despite it being common knowledge that Mukh was very wealthy, he never wore any different clothes to those described – why this was so, I will tell you now:

Mukh's father had kept his son at home all these years because he was so embarrassed by his son's small stature and did not want to see him ridiculed. Little Mukh's clothes were the only inheritance he had been left by his father on the day of his death, which had happened not long after Mukh's sixteenth birthday. His father had been a tall man and so his clothes were well over-sized for his little dwarf son. This did not worry young Mukh at all, since he could now throw away his rags, and after cutting off several lengths of the caftan, he became attired in an imposing outfit, complete with large pantaloons and an enormous turban. The cut off bit of the caftan became a wrap-around belt, behind which he then put in sword fashion an enormous dagger, picked up a small stick and left home to seek his fortune in the strange wide world.

Mukh travelled unhurriedly, happily and with no problems. Those who saw him passing by, laughed at his comical appearance, but again that did not upset him. Little Mukh was happy to be free at last to come and go as he pleased. He discovered with delight that just being able to see the woods, fields and people in nearby towns, was in itself a very exciting experience. He especially liked to feel the warmth of sunshine on his face and the songs of the birds made him happy and carefree.

Alas, all good things tend to come to an end and so Little Mukh had to look for a town as he increasingly became very hungry indeed. For the previous two days, he had lived on wild berries and other fruit, sleeping on a warm, fragrant bed of leaves under the trees. However, on the third day of his journey, he spotted a large town in the distance and suddenly realised how tired he had become. Around midday, he managed to enter through the town's massive gates, and walked in, hoping for the citizens to welcome him and ask him into their homes. He could almost hear them saying:

"Little Mukh, come on in.
Eat, sing and rest your
Weary bones!"

He soon learned disappointment as no one paid any attention to him neither welcoming him nor inviting him for a meal. As he wandered around the town more and more hungry and tired, he noticed a large, beautiful house in one of the side streets. As he passed it, one of its windows opened and an old woman looked out and started half-calling, half-singing, in a strange, high voice:

"Come in, come in quickly,
You are wanted and expected.
The table is laid and the food
Is ready. Lunch is waiting, so
Hurry in to gorge yourself on the
Best food, in the gay company of
Your friends."

The door of the house opened and inside Mukh saw a large group of cats and dogs being directed towards a long table. Encouraged by this welcoming sight, he followed the animals inside the house. The old woman spotted him among the diners and asked what it was that he wanted.

"I heard you calling every one to Lunch," answered Mukh, "and since I am very hungry, I walked in."

The old woman burst out laughing and exclaimed,

"Where have you come from, you funny little man? This whole town knows that I cook lunch only for my cats, and for ages and ages, I have also invited their friends in!"

"A stifled giggle made Josy look up again just in time to catch Anthony's impression of the old woman. Delighted, the little boy clapped his hands.

"Read some more! Read some more!"

"You are going to be very tired tomorrow. It is well past your bed-time, you know."

"But I am not sleepy, not a bit! Please, please, finish this story!"

Josy couldn't help a little smile.

"Just this once then. But I bet you are both going to be asleep before the story is finished."

"I bet we won't, eh, son?" Anthony shifted himself into a more comfortable position. Solemnly Richard followed his father's movement and sat in the same way, legs outstreched, arms folded, eyes alert in anticipation.

There was nothing more to say, thought an amused Josy, but continue . . .

"Crestfallen, Little Mukh told the old woman all about his dead father, and how he had set out to see the world, but felt very lonely and tired in this strange town."

Another suppressed giggle took Josy by surprise and caused her look up. Anthony's face had assumed a new expression, looking suitably crestfallen, lonely, hungry. and very tired in quick succession, to the little boy's delight.

"Aren't you a little sleepy?"

The boy gave his father a quick glance. It was obvious they understood each other.

"Oh, no. You read with such feeling that we

won't be able to sleep a wink, if we don't find out what happens!"

Josy shifted her glance from her son's pleading face to Anthony's amiably smiling eyes.

"You could have fooled me, you two. It is a long story and I can bet you won't hear the end."

"Read the story! Read the story!"

"Very well then."

"The old woman", continued Josy,"whose name was Axavia, felt sorry for Mukh and she decided to offer him board and lodging in exchange for some help with cleaning and looking after the animals. Little Mukh soon found out that his work, although not very heavy, was not too pleasant either. Axavia had six cats, and every morning, Mukh had to brush them thoroughly (while they protested!) and apply some aromatic scents to their fur coats. Every evening he had to find them and put them for the night on large cushions in their beds and then cover them with colourfulyl embroidered eiderdowns. His duties also included looking after a little dog, but the dog was very friendly and never added to his worries.

Little Mukh ate well and life seemed to be happy – that is, until Axavia took to going out. Every time she was absent, the cats became impossible to control – they would leap and run about all the rooms, and they would push each other and play crazy games. While they played, they would break expensive vases or crystal jugs. As soon as they heard Axavia returning, the cats would pretend to have been asleep all the time and innocent of all the mayhem in the house. The old woman believed this and was very angry with Mukh, who would appear to be the culprit. She would tell him off strongly and sometimes gave him a good hiding, deaf to all his explanations.

Little Mukh sadly had to admit that it would be better for him to seek his fortune elsewhere, but not before he found out what was hidden in one of the chambers, which was always kept locked by the old woman, and which would remain locked whether she was at home or not.

One day, when Axavia went out and was not due back for a few hours, Little Mukh stood outside the locked chamber and racked his brains as to how to get in. Suddenly, he felt somebody tugging at his pantaloons – it was the little dog who liked Mukh very much. He opened a hidden panel in the wall next to the chamber and looked at Mukh as if saying, "Come with me." Mukh did not need a second invitation and followed his friend in eagerly. After looking around the room for sometime, Mukh decided he had seen nothing of interest there except for a beautiful jug, painted with figures in a strange design. He picked up the jug to look at the figures more closely, when it slipped from his fingers and broke into a thousand pieces.

This frightened him so much that he stood rooted to the floor for several seconds before rushing to the door. The little dog grabbed his pantaloons again and whispered, "Take with you this fine pair of mules and this lion's head walking stick, as they will bring you both happiness and wealth."

Without hesitation, Mukh removed his shoes and put on the enormous mules with curved toes, grabbed the stick and then ran from the house and from the town. He ran ahead without stopping, as if some force were mercilessly pushing him. After some time, he understood that the force was contained in the mules. He tried to stop, but could not as the mules kept dragging and pushing him forward. In the end he cried out in desperation,

"Oh! Oh! stop it!" The mules stood still.

Mukh dropped down where he stood in utter exhaustion and fell into a deep sleep. In a dream he heard the little dog whispering in his ear,

"Dearest Mukh, twist on the heel of your right mule three times and you will be able to go wherever you want. Your stick can find any buried treasure – it will knock on the ground three times for gold and twice for silver."

When Mukh woke up, he remembered his friend's instructions clearly. He tried to twist on his right heel without any support, but fell and grazed his nose. Luckily, he remembered the stick and with its help he managed to twist round on the heel three times, with no further problems. At the same time he wished to find himself in a far away, famous city. The mules picked him up and carried him away at the speed of lightning. However, before he could gather his wits, the mules stopped on the pavement outside the imposing gates at the front of the King's palace. The head of the guards came forward and asked Mukh, what it was he wanted. Little Mukh drew himself up to his full height and answered with pride,

"I would like to obtain the position of the King's First Runner."

"What?" exclaimed the guardsman, looking down at Mukh, "Are you joking? With your little body and short legs, you want to be a King's runner? Off with you, before I lose my temper! I am not in the mood for silly jokes today!"

Mukh stood his ground and insisted that the guardsman present his request to the King without delay. As all this happened a long time ago, when Kings would speak to commoners, the guardsman went back into the Palace and told the King about the little man and his strange request. The King was a jolly man so he gave orders to summon all his citizens to the main square outside the Palace, where a contest would take place before the whole Court. Every one in the city rushed to the main square for the best places so that they could see the little dwarf running against the King's runners. At last the King arrived with his sons and daughters and they sat in the Royal Box, especially prepared for them. Little Mukh and the other contestants were presented to the King.

The crowd went wild with joy! Here and there people were laughing and waving, as no one in this City had ever seen such a funny-looking man. No sooner had the race started than the laughter turned into gasps of disbelief and incredulity! Mukh let all the contestants go first and after allowing them a distance of a few metres, he started running in his huge mules. In no time at all, he was at the finishing post, waiting for the others to arrive, all hot and out of breath. The crowd stamped and clapped, cheering,

"Little Mukh! Little Mukh!
Three cheers for
The King's Best Runner!"
The King called Mukh to him and said,
"Little Mukh, I pronounce you my Court Runner.

I want you to be present at my side at all times. This position carries a salary of one hundred gold coins a year and you will dine at my court every day."

Mukh thought that he had found his place and happiness at last. Unfortunately the courtiers observed with jealousy and hostility all the favours, which were bestowed on Little Mukh by the King. Mukh himself felt bitter at their resentment and thought of ways to change that. He remembered his walking stick, so one day he went for a walk in a Royal Park. As the little dog had promised him, the stick tapped the ground three times at some remote spot. Mukh made a mark with his dagger on the nearest tree and went home. He came back under cover of the night and started digging at the spot. Soon he had unearthed an iron box, which was full of gold coins. Little Mukh took as much gold as he could carry, covered the rest with earth and, on returning home, placed the money under the pillows on his bed. The next day he started giving the money to various courtiers, foolishly hoping to buy their friendship. Alas to no avail! They became even more jealous of him and they whispered behind his back to each other,

"He is an idiot," one of them would say.

"Not only an idiot but also a thief," another would say another.

"He is probably the one who stole the money from the King's purse," they said, remembering the theft, which had occurred not long previously. When the King heard the gossip, he sent two of his servants to spy on Mukh, as he wanted to catch him red-handed. They followed Mukh one night to the place where he had his pot of gold hidden, and as Mukh was putting some of the coins in his caftan, they grabbed him and brought him before the King. The servants told the hushed court what had happened and the King asked Little Mukh whether it was true. Mukh tried to explain that he had found the gold by chance, but all the courtiers burst out laughing and the king became annoyed at the little man's naivete.

"How dare you offer such a feeble story as an excuse," the King thundered.

He called in the Keeper of the Royal Purse and asked him whether he recognised the gold as that missing from the Purse. Of course, the Keeper was pleased to confirm that the gold coins were indeed the same. The King ordered Mukh to be put in an iron cage, which was to be locked in one of the Palace towers. Shortly after the jailing, servants emptied the iron box in front of the King in order to count the money when suddenly they all saw a script at the very bottom of the box. It read briefly, "My son must reward the person who finds this treasure. King Kaid."

King Kaid had been the father of the present

King and it was obvious he had buried the gold during the war and had never had the chance to tell anyone about it before he died. The King felt guilty as it was apparent that Little Mukh was innocent. The Purse Keeper confessed to the theft and was executed. Then the King had an idea and said to Mukh,

"I shall set you free, if you tell me the secret of your gift for running."

Little Mukh explained that his powers were contained in the mules he wore, provided that he twisted three times on his right heel. The King put the mules on to see for himself how it could possibly work and then ran to the Royal Park. But while he knew how to start, he could not stop the mules. He ran and he ran and he ran until he collapsed with exhaustion. When he came round, he was furious and this is what he said to Mukh,

"I promised to free you, so be gone, because if you are still here when the twelfth hour strikes on the Palace Clock, I shall hang you alongside the Purse Keeper, as sure as can be!"

Little Mukh left the Palace poorer than ever; the mules and the stick had been taken by the King and confiscated. He chose for safety to walk through a thick forest, following the path of a small, crystal-clear brook. On both sides of the shimmering water grew tall fig-trees, and having walked for a whole day, Little Mukh settled wearily for the night under a tree. As he gazed up, he saw magnificent clusters of ripe figs. Happily, he picked some fruit and on giving a thankful prayer to Heaven, ate his supper. After a delicious meal, he went to the brook to have a drink of water. However, as soon as he bent down to drink he stepped back in fright at his image in the water. His head was crowned with two foot-long donkeys' ears, and in the middle of his face stuck out a long fat nose!

"I deserve donkeys' ears; for only a donkey could have stamped on his fortune with his feet!" thought Mukh.

Deep in his thoughts, he went back to sit under the tree and still feeling hungry, he picked some figs from a neighbouring tree and ate them absent-mindedly. All his thoughts were centred on how to hide those hateful long ears. He decided to conceal them under his large turban and as he went to push them under the turban, he realised that they had become small again! He checked his nose, and to his delight, both nose and ears were back to normal. He then understood that there were two types of magic figs – those which made people more handsome, and others which made them very ugly. An interesting idea came to his mind and he gathered as many figs from both trees as he could carry.

Then he went to a small town and changed his appearance with the help of an artificial beard and moustache. Completely transformed, he then headed back to the big city where the King lived. He made straight for the Palace kitchens and sold the figs to the junior chef. The fruit was much admired and was sent to the King's table the same day. The King was particularly pleased with his dinner that day, so he called the chef to congratulate him on his expertise. This tickled the chef pink, and remembering that he had especially beautiful figs in the fruit basket for the end of the meal, he smiled and said, "All's well that ends well." At that, everybody at the table wanted to know the surprise finish to their excellent meal. When at last the fruit basket arrived, all the diners exclaimed,

"Ah, what beautiful fruit!"

"How enormous and what a glossy purple colour!" said the King. "Truly, the chef deserves a reward!"

He then proceeded to give his sons and daughters two figs each, while the courtiers received one each, and the rest of the figs the King ate himself with gusto.

"My dearest father," exclaimed Princess Amazia, "You look so strange!"

Everybody turned to look at the King, who had enormous foot-long ears on his head and a long fat nose in the middle of his face. As they looked at each other stupefied, they realised in horror that they also shared the same affliction. The King called all his doctors, who tried everything, even cutting the ears off, but nothing helped. They would just grow back even longer than before. At that moment Mukh appeared again, this time disguised as a foreign doctor: a nose and ear specialist. To prove his ability he gave to one of the princesses a special fig, and as she ate the fruit, her face changed back to normal. The King summoned him and said, "Take all my wealth, but get rid of this awful illness!"

Mukh went from chamber to chamber until he found his mules and walking stick. He put on the mules, placed the stick under his arm, and then after pulling off his artificial beard and moustache, he returned to the anxious King.

"Oh, powerful King," said Mukh, "You have treated me very badly and most unjustly. I am leaving you with your ears and nose as a reminder of me."

He then twisted three times on his right heel, and before the King had a chance to call for help, he was gone. No one from the Court ever found out where he had gone. One thing is certain, however – that with the help of the lion's head walking stick, Mukh became a very wealthy man indeed. He later returned to the town of his birth and lived there happily ever after in a beautiful house.

As I told you at the beginning of this story, he would leave his house only once a month, and the joy of the little boys was indescribable! They loved his stature and his clothes, but
he did not mind their joy a bit. Not a bit!"

Josy looked up from the book. The little boy lay on his stomach, his face turned towards her. Pink hands folded into tiny fists rested next to the pouting, half-open mouth. He was fast asleep. In the armchair, Anthony slept too, his long legs stretched onto the edge of the blankets. Quietly Josy closed the book and bent over the bed listening to her son's even breathing. Satisfied, she sat for a while, smiling a happy little smile.

She felt light of heart and breathless with happiness. Yet, the feeling was almost painful for she realised with a sudden certainty that she was no longer a free spirit. The intense love, which she felt for her son bound her a prisoner. It was him and her – two beings united together infinitely. She could not know what the future held in store for him, but she hoped with all her heart that he would grow up to be a very special man, like her father and her husband had been. In his small face and constantly curious eyes she could see already the familiar imprint of generations of Horaims and she felt at peace, the uncertainty in her heart assuaged. The sudden realisation that her whole life had altered irrevocably forever overwhelmed her and filled her with excitement, and at the same time, fear.

Chapter Five

Above the heather-flowering, purple steppe, against the brilliant light of the sun, a lonely hawk glided menacingly on wings spread wide like a spirit of darkness.

Below, among the fruit-heavy brambles, a fat field-mouse scampered away, sensing imminent danger in the sinister, black shape circling the cloudless sky.

The hot, dry summer was coming to an end.

Just across the stubble fields, on the other side of the hedgerows, lay the busy Cossack stanitza. The harvest was already a thing of the past in the village life. All the wheat and rye from the rich fields rested safely in barns, and the dull, rhythmical thud of grain threshing filled the air with the joyful noise of prosperity.

Shading the narrow path, a long line of rowan trees, sagging beneath clusters of scarlet berries, led down to the slow-moving brook. Where the water took a turn to the left, a wooden foot-bridge clasped the grassy banks.

Under the bridge, a girl spread her washing out on the enormous, flat stones. Strong arms, dark from the summer sun, pummelled and squeezed until the linen became dazzling white.

Satisfied, Katriona sat back and rested for a while. At this time of day, the path was deserted, and she could remain unseen among the undergrowth, and do her thinking in peace.

The recent news brought to the remote village by a travelling wood merchant was already several months old, but to her it spelled disaster just the same. For the past few days she had lived in the hope that nobody would mention the rumour, as she considered it, to Henryk.

It had been such a long time . . . She had hoped so much that in his heart he had finally settled here, and that their lives would be linked together for good.

Involuntarily she clenched her hands into defensive fists.

"I have earned him, I really have earned him," she murmured, her face sullen, and a frown between her straight, black brows. Her thoughts on the past, she absent-mindedly picked up a handful of small stones from the path and threw them one by one into the brook, as far as she could, as if they were the obstacles to her happiness.

But the pebbles splashed sharply, only to come back to her bare feet in soft, rippling circles. These merged to form more of the new, silvery rings and then the whole surface of the water shivered and trembled, disturbed for ever it seemed. Just like my life, since the death of . . . she didn't dare bring back his name from the past. "Nobody knows, nobody could have guessed. Best left forgotten . . ."

But her eyes followed the moving circles and the dark water within them. Close to the clump of rushes, the ripples rapidly decreased towards the centre, pulled and sucked down by the hidden current. Katriona felt her eyes drawn towards the swirling pit. It had been like this before . . . she couldn't . . . oh, why couldn't she forget . . .

Her heart beat wildly as she leaned forward over the water and suddenly recognised that awful, pointed face disappearing into the sinking mud, a silent scream contorting the already blueish lips, and those evil, unblinking eyes still and fixed on her, cursing her from even beyond the grave. She gave a startled cry, and drew back.

Blind wrath arose within her, driving out fear. Flushed with anger, Katriona jumped to her feet, carelessly gathering the washing together. She wasn't going to be defeated by a dead man. Too much was at stake, and anyhow, there had been no other way. He had been a sly, sinister toad. He had deserved what he had got. Well-buried in the marshes, he couldn't harm anyone now. "It must be the damn heat making me see things. There is nothing in the water, and nothing to fear. But the news . . ."

The nagging thought came back. What if Henryk already knew it? He couldn't just get up and leave, could he? The elders would not allow him to go. It was too dangerous for the whole village . . . Thank God they were so far from anywhere.

She felt more like herself now. It was silly to worry so much. He depended on her for everything, and she would kill anyone who wanted to harm him. He might guess, but he didn't know how much she really loved him. But did he love her? He had never, ever told her. Not even now, not even when at long last he had taken her as his own . . . not even then . . . At least he wanted her, the way Vassilisa had promised he would, when she had given her the potion, but she would have to wait for his love . . . One day, one day soon, he would love her, with all his heart and soul, as passionately as she loved him. But for now she had to be patient, and thank God, over the years she had learned how to be just that . . .

She slowly climbed up the steep path. The wet washing in the two baskets weighed her arms down heavily, but the recollection of that summer's day came back with such force and sweetness that, feeling oddly weak, she put the baskets down under a tree, overwhelmed by memories. Slowly she stretched her tired back, and suddenly, without her understanding why, her whole body grew hot, remembering and began to tremble in unexpected coming. She felt herself blush, and, with her face burning and her eyes closed, she felt again his silent, hard mouth melting her skin, brushing her breasts until they felt tight and rigid; touching and stroking until her body, usually so strong and capable, was rendered weak, soft and yielding . . .

His hands learned her first and, having been brought to ecstasy, she arched her back in an urgent desire to be at one with him, to merge their heart-beats, to exist only through him, to have him, and be taken, now, now, now . . .

Their breathless sighing, his wild hands tugging away her skirts, exposing smooth legs . . . Her strong thighs held him within, guiding and urging . . . This was the moment she had awaited for so long. When triumphantly it came, in the lightning that exploded the darkness from under her tightly shut eyelids, it uncoiled through her like a burning spiral of ecstasy, and then she knew no more . . . She moaned faintly in her abandon, and forced her reluctant eyes to open. His face, just above hers, though strangely darkened and taut, was changed, and despite his silence, she knew then that she had pleased him . . .

Somewhere close by, a girl's high voice broke into a song, and then laughter. Trembling, Katriona came back to reality. It was late.

The village girls were coming back with the water needed for the evening meal, and as usual, one or two lads would tag along. The sound of their bantering seemed very close now, and Katriona hid behind the trees on the bank, not wanting to be seen. She could recognise the cheerful voice of one of her cousins, Jura.

"Hey, Dimitri, you have got close to a pound of lard on your hair! And it shines! It must be so that Duniashka can see herself while she gives you a kiss!"

"Off with you, Jura, or I shall wash your hair right now."

"Don't splash, Aniuta, you are going to need that water, and it is a long walk to the river."

"I don't mind, I might want to go back again, especially after dark . . ."

"Are you hoping, perhaps, to find someone

there . . . in the dark?"

"Oh, Tonia, Toniechka! I wish you wouldn't! Fiedia might think . . ."

"Fiedia might think . . . Why, I haven't even mentioned his name!"

One of the boys, a strongly built youth, with a shaggy, sandy mop of hair and almost white eyebrows in his sun-scorched face, jumped onto a big stone and then, turning to face the slowly approaching girls, broke into a sorrowful tune, drawing out each syllable,

Eh, you beautiful apple-tree,
When will your apples be ready?
Eh, my dearest mama, I want so much
To marrrryyy . . .

Blushing deeply, Aniuta dropped her eyes and answered in a strong, high soprano,

Coachman, don't you speed the horses so,
For I am in no particular hurry today . . .

Amidst playful scuffling and bantering, the laughing group passed, their voices slowly fading into the distance. Katriona, glad that they hadn't noticed her crouching behind the trees, hastily grabbed her baskets.

"I must be mad to waste time on such sinful thoughts. Away with me! Henryk will soon be back from the fields, tired and hungry, and I haven't even peeled a single potato yet!"

He watched her without word or gesture. Katriona set the table as she had many times before: with a white, heavily-embroidered table-cloth, thick clay dishes, a wooden board with a large, round loaf of bread on one side, and a bowl of steaming hot potatoes on the other. She slowly turned from the stove with a pot of fish stew. Fish was plentiful in their river, and the stew was Henryk's favourite. She knew how to cook it well – plenty of herbs, big chunks of fat wel*, and thick with dumplings. "You couldn't go wrong with that, eh? It would make any man mellow and . . ." She caught Henryk's eyes, and it gave her a funny little turn to see him watching her silently.

Henryk smiled.

"It smells wonderful. Won't you sit down?"

She shook her smooth head, her eyes downcast under the straight, black brows. It never failed to amuse him that she should prefer to serve him first, and would not sit down with him at the table, not even now . . .

All his life he had been used to authority, but here it was insignificant. He was kept a prisoner in the village, despite their elaborate efforts to make him feel welcome. At first, he had thought that he would only have to bide his time, and sooner or later, an opportunity would arise. He turned crazy plans of escape over and over in his mind. If only he could get away . . . He smiled. There wasn't much chance of that – being miles from anywhere, without a horse and with his leg weakened. And now Katriona . . .

Having finished supper, he rose from the table.

At dusk, he liked to sit outside on the porch and smoke his pipe. The summer days were long, and his leg still troubled him now and then. Behind him, in the house, he could hear the noise of plates and pots being washed, and Katriona's sorrowful voice softly singing:

Over the river, over the shore,
Give me your hand, my lovely!
Give me your hand or I shall die,
Tell me the truth, whom do you love?
I won't give my hand, and you won't die,
I won't tell a word, whom I really love!

Henryk listened, and thought how it seemed that music was inseparably woven into the life of these people. They sang almost every moment of the day; when they were happy, when thcy were sad, to ease their work and on the way home, when courting or just "speaking" in a song to each other across the river . . .

For a moment he tried to imagine what life would be like at this time of day at Vronovo . . . Dinner would be served by Mikhail, his old servant, and there would often be at least two guests at the table. The conversation would touch on many topics: politics, the ever-rising price of wheat, the amazing qualities of the foals born the previous year, the laziness of the tenants, news from abroad, Polish society in Paris, the theatre season in Warsaw . . . Joanna sometimes liked to go and stay for a week with their friends to see a celebrated play. It made her so happy . . .

Somewhere from within his mind, he could recall the sweet melody that she had often used to play just to amuse the girls, but it would draw him from his office, and he would watch the merriment and his "little women", as he called them, with an indulgent smile and a quiet joy in his heart.

He tried to imagine Joanna's face, delicately chiselled, framed by silky blonde hair, her very blue eyes . . . She had such translucently pale skin; with a sudden longing, he remembered the tiny blue vein pulsating in her smooth, white temple . . . She was so fragile, like a little china doll . . .

The girls would be grown up now. Would they remember him? Probably not. They didn't even know he was alive. At the very beginning Vassilisa had told him that to the outside world, as well as to his family, he was officially dead. For the thousandth time he asked himself the same question,

"Would he have joined the underground army again, had he known then what he knew now?" Looking back calmly, he could see that they had all been so elated. It was noble, the only thing to do for their country . . . Family ties had to come second. If only he could be sure that Joanna was coping on her own . . . As it was, he could only hope that her elder sister, Cornelia, the late Count Chodkievich's wife, had been able to help her with the estate. But was there anything left? Had there been any reprisals against his family?

Not knowing their fate was by far the worst. Often there were nights when he would wake up in a cold sweat, convinced that he had heard their voices calling to him for help. And damn it all, he was here, alive and well – although as good as dead to them. Then there was something else that Vassilisa had said, but he hadn't believed her. Oh, what nonsense! He was still angry with her for saying those things.

It had happened one evening before he had been able to walk. She came in and sat by his bed, making him feel uneasy under her long look of appraisal. He tried to smile at her, encouragingly he hoped. Evidently she wanted to say something and, as it happened, he was ready to ask her a few questions himself. She looked at him with lingering, friendly eyes for a moment longer.

"It's God's mercy that you are almost completely recovered. It was touch and go for a good while, and you wouldn't be here, if it weren't for my god-daughter, you know."

"I am most grateful to Katriona for her care and . . ."

"I don't think you understand", interrupted Vassilisa gently, "It wasn't only her care. She has a special gift, a certain strength, that girl. She dragged you back from the beyond, and to us, it means that you owe her your very being, your life . . ."

"You are absolutely right. When it becomes possible for me to go back, I shall send Katriona anything she wants, she only need say, I promise you."

The old woman gazed at him reflectively, an ironical look in her shiny, jet-black eyes. He felt uneasy again, as if there were something she knew, and he didn't. She said softly,

"You silly fool. You will never leave here, don't

you know? And Katriona is neither after your money nor gold."

Henryk stared at her in amazement.

"What is it that you people want?"

The old woman smiled as if he were a small child to be coaxed.

"Think again."

Slowly an incredulous realisation made him stammer,

"If, if . . . I understand your meaning correctly . . . I think you should know . . . I have a wife and family . . . and, and . . . Katriona is no more than a child. Why, she is hardly much older than my own daughter!"

Vassilisa leaned back, her thin, work-worn hands folded in her lap, and stared vacantly at the little window on the far side. Henryk watched her anxiously. It would be fatal to offend these people since he would need all their help in getting back to civilization, and of course, he assented with gratitude he owed them his life.

"I know you were married," she said at last, "but you no longer are. You wife is dead."

Henryk smothered a gasp. This was lunacy. She was quite crazy, the old witch. Vassilisa gave him a searching look.

"I am not mad, you know. And she is dead, God's mercy on her soul. As to Katriona's age, that's neither here nor there. Girls marry earlier here, that way the men have less chance to tire of their women."

Henryk was talking to himself now rather than to her. "It is you who don't understand – I don't belong here. I have my family, my children, my home and my land. I am not . . . I am not a peasant there but a squire. I could not . . ."

The old woman rose, her eyes angry, her face growing heavy and stern.

"I think you would do better to remember that we are free people here. We are Cossacks, no one's serfs! And as for your high and mighty ways, well, I shall say only one thing: you will get used to our ways. In time."

Without looking at Henryk she left the room.

Many months passed and he had to admit that she was right, the old woman. He had got used to their ways, he had even begun to understand these people and to like them. They were brave and bold, handsome and sensitive, and full of life and passion . . . He shared their deep love for the land and for thoroughbred horses, the very symbol of a Cossack man. But to be truly one of them? He would always be a stranger here. You could only be a Cossack by having been born one, Katriona's cousin had said once, and Henryk had been glad to agree. But now Katriona . . .

He had tried hard to blot that day out of his mind but he couldn't. It seemed as if it had happened in another world. It was as if . . . he had been in a trance, bewitched by the dangerously passionate creature, who was not at all like the shy, evasive Katriona he knew. He felt ashamed at the things, which his mind remembered so vividly, that he had done when he wasn't himself. Most of all, he feared that somehow by this moment of madness he had endangered the life of his wife, as if at long last, he had acknowledged her death. If only he could understand his sudden obsession, perhaps then he could regain his self-respect, even if it meant that his life would have to change and be even more difficult than it already was.

He frowned, perplexed. What was it that had seized him so that despite his love for Joanna, he had passionately yielded to another woman's caresses? He thought of Katriona's love for him, and could not quite understand why he should be an object of such devastating passion to a girl so young and beautiful.

It was strange but he couldn't help being conscious that he would never entirely escape her. He had been her first man, and judging by the intensity of her emotions, he could well be her last . . .

He had a passing thought that, perhaps, if he was very honest, he had somehow been, at least on that day, in love with her, but he quickly dismissed the idea. It would be very wrong to even allow himself such foolish thoughts, after all he was a married man. But then suddenly he remembered her arms pressing him close, the taste of her fresh lips, and the ecstasy of that moment when he finally . . .

. . . It was a fine, clear summer's day. He had been working from early morning to avoid the oppressive heat, which would rise after midday, but by eleven o'clock he already felt hot and thirsty. The small field to the east was done, but the larger one, the one on the west side, still untouched, spread in front of him like a golden ocean, calm and majestic. The sun was almost right over the field when from behind the hedgerows appeared the girl in a dazzling white blouse and blue skirt.

Katriona had brought him his lunch. Glad of the interruption, Henryk put down his scythe and wiped the hot sweat from his face. Exhausted, he dropped down onto the large, field marking stone with relief. Katriona untied the linen bundle, and carefully took out the clay double-pot. There was also a dark bottle, a wooden spoon and a loaf of bread in the shawl. He looked at her, and smiled at such devotion to his comfort.

She kept his house clean and cooked his supper before going back to Vassilisa's. One of these days she would make an excellent wife for one of the hot-blooded youths who constantly lurked about. But every time he jokingly asked when her wedding would be, she would get angry and he could not make her out. Whom could she be waiting for? He thought that he had made his position clear to the old woman. She must have said something surly.

Katriona handed him a bottle filled with kwas. It felt very cold, and he appreciated the effort she must have made in keeping his drink so cool. By now he had grown to like this peasant's draught very much, which was made by fermenting slices of stale rye bread in water. The kwas tasted differently that day, stronger, almost like wine, if he still could remember what wine tasted like. He threw his head back and drank it in long, thirsty gulps, squinting against the sun. The girl watched him intently.

Revived and hungry now, Henryk put the bottle down, and breaking a chunk of freshly baked bread, he ate it slowly, almost solemnly. The double-pot contained a well-set, yoghurt like, milk in one side, and in the other parched buckwheat, well-flavoured with chopped, crisply fried bacon. He felt much better now after the drink, and he dipped the wooden spoon into the set milk. It was deliciously cool, the thick cream on the top tasting fresh and smooth. He alternated between eating the buckwheat and the set milk, in peasant fashion, surprised at being so ravenous.

Sitting at his side, Katriona nibbled at a crust. She looked at him with a little smile.

"If I were you, I wouldn't try to do anything today. You'd better take it easy."

"Why, I feel very strong after your lunch. I shall be quite alright."

He paused for a second as though he were undecided, and then he abruptly picked up his scythe, ready to start anew. The girl looked up at him. His eyes were almost black now, the pupils enlarged and luminous. Katriona got up and standing close to Henryk gave him another, searching look. He felt his eyes drawn to hers, and suddenly in an instant, he recognised . . . he remembered those huge, liquid eyes as those of the wild creature in his dream. He felt strong, elated and generous.

"Do you know, Katriona, that you are by far the most beautiful girl in the village?"

She looked him full in the face.

"Do you think you could love me?"

Her voice was hoarse and low. For a moment,

Henryk thought he must have heard amiss, and startled he gazed at her blankly. It had never occurred to him before to seriously ask himself what the feelings of this beautiful girl were, and embarrassed, he had to admit in his heart that he had taken it for granted that she should want to help him unconditionally. Not wishing to hurt her feelings, Henryk hesitated, trying to find the right words. His voice was strained and not quite steady when he finally said,

"Had I met you before I was married, it would be different . . ."

"It would?"

Tears welled up in Katriona's eyes as she gazed at him, her hands clasped at her breast, with a sweet, shy smile. He wanted to say something to reassure her, but the strange feeling overwhelmed him again. His head swam, and the sun seemed unbearably bright. He closed his eyes to rest them, but when he looked up a second or two later, he noticed with surprise how everything around him had taken on an oddly singular dimension, become sharper, more defined and intense. He looked at the girl. She seemed different too, and somehow very special. Without knowing it, he raised his hand and stroked her silky black hair.

Gazing at him with her huge, lustrous eyes, Katriona held his hand to her face for a second before turning it over. She began to kiss the palm of his hand as lightly as a butterfly would, then slowly each finger tip and then, without taking her lips away, she moved them up his arm until her mouth found the opening of his shirt and slowly,

very slowly, in tiny, shiver-inducing kisses, her parted lips and the tip of her tongue descended unceasingly down, and down . . .
Henryk stood very still, and only the slight pressure of his hands resting on her head seemed to encourage her intentions.

He was in a different world now. The past was finished. He had been without any physical comfort for so long . . . He had denied himself this basic human need until now. He could see a new life spreading before him, and at last after all these years, happiness and freedom. He was sure that he could achieve absolutely anything – why, if he wanted to, he could soar into the air like a bird . . .

He had no doubt that the girl at his side was a sorceress. He frowned a little catching the intoxicating scent flowing towards him with every movement of her loose, black hair. She looked up at him, her beautiful eyes gleaming with specks of gold. Gently Henryk lifted her up and kissed her full on the lips, lips that were fresh, full and surprisingly tasted of wild berries. She put her arms round his neck.

"Will you come with me now?"

"Do you want me to? Do you really want me to?" A shiver of anticipation made his voice tremble slightly.

"Yes, yes, oh yes!"

The last struggle within him had been short, and he surrendered to this bewitching creature. Slowly, he followed her into the golden sea. She led the way, drawing aside the wheat as she went. He would have followed her to the ends of the earth now, and knowing her magic powers so well, he wasn't in the least surprised that, without his noticing when or how, she had shed her clothes. He could see her ahead of him, weaving through the wheat. Her slender body, pale but tinged with the pink of sea shells, seemed to glow even in the bright sunlight. He felt the veins throbbing in his temples; he couldn't reach her and desperate, he called out her name,

"Katriona!"

The girl stopped and stood still for a moment before she turned, breathtaking in her beauty, and waited for him . . .

He was shaking but the pressure of her arms was strangely comforting. He longed to feel them around him forever, and the touch of her breasts against his skin made him tremble with wanting. She sought his lips and united in a passionate kiss, they slowly knelt down together as if taking part in an ancient ritual. There was nothing around them but the golden wilderness, and he solemnly laid her down among the crushed grasses. His hands found her body, and hesitantly at first learned its curvaceous shape and the delightful smoothness of her skin. The tenderness of her response excited a passion within him beyond his endurance . . .

The sunlight seemed to affect him. Through narrowed eyes, he saw her face transformed by pure love to the utmost loveliness, and, unable to control his desire any longer, amongst her broken sighs and sweet words, he found the moist triangle, and in one fierce and passionate movement, entered . . .

With her eyes closed and her face wet with tears of happiness, she gave herself to him with such urgent willingness that he did not realise until later that she hadn't been with a man before. He was held within, taken as well as taking, wanted, touched and exhilarated until in frenzied ecstasy, he felt his spirit rise like a golden flame, and they became one . . .

Lost in reflection, Henryk stared at the wooden boards of the porch for a while. From the evening of that day when it had happened, Katriona had started behaving in an odd manner. To his surprise and no little confusion, she had reverted to being a shy evasive stranger. He had a queer feeling that if he weren't so sure of his vivid memories, he could almost accept that the whole episode had been a figment of his imagination. He could not understand her.

For a moment, he thought of the future. He didn't know what plans, if any, Katriona had in mind. He had told her the truth – he was a married man, and even at the height of their passion, he had neither declared nor promised anything. It worried him that she would not talk to him. She was silent, obliging and polite, but also darkly worried, he noticed. It was a curious feeling to know that everything he said or did seemed to affect her so much. It frightened him a little because with this knowledge came the realisation that he was no longer free. He couldn't simply leave here for it would destroy her, of that he was totally convinced.

The night came late, but the warmth of the Indian summer days lasted well into the evenings. Vassilisa sat by the window tying bunches of herbs for drying when at last Katriona came in. Her eyes were red and heavy with crying but she seemed calm.

"I thought you would already be asleep", she said as she walked to the table.

"I am too old to sleep so much. Are you all right?"

Katriona's face took on a look of defiance, and she gave a little shudder.

"I've never felt better in my life."

"You could have fooled me. I am not that blind yet, you know. I was thinking about you this afternoon . . ."

"You don't need to bother about me. I shall be alright." There was just the shadow of a tremor in her voice. Vassilisa gazed softly at the girl. It wasn't right for a young girl to be so miserable.

"Have you tried any more of that potion?"

Katriona stared down at her feet and said nothing.

"Well?"

She felt the girl stiffen. Quite suddenly, her face fell and trembling, she clasped her hands,

"I want him to love me! Me! Oh, Mother, you just don't understand how badly I want him to love me!"

She began to weep. She just couldn't lie to Henryk again. How was she to explain the terrible longing in her heart for him to have her as his own but truly, as a lover would, and not because of potions and scheming and dark secrets and . . .

The tears streamed down her face now, and she bit her lip to prevent the sobs, which were choking her, from escaping. The old woman put her hand on Katriona's arm, but the girl turned away.

"I thought it would work, but it didn't, and what can I do now? I cannot use the potion every time, can I? I wish you could give me something to make me stop loving him! And now this wretched news! When he finds out that he is free to go . . . I don't think I can stand this waiting. It hurts so much, and the only thing I know is that I shall die if he leaves here . . ."

Vassilisa thought for a while.

"Perhaps, if you were to give him a little of that potion every week, he might get very used to the wonderful feeling it gives, and then, after some time, relate this to your being with him closely . . ."

"But I want him to love and want me! I thought that after . . . after that day he would, but he gazes at me as if I were a stranger, who surprised him, amused him, even pleased him a lot, but there is no love for me in his eyes."

Katriona wiped her tears away but her voice still trembled. "I just don't know why I have to love him so . . . I hate myself for it, but I still do . . ."

Her face, even when distraught with pain, still remained hauntingly beautiful. The old woman listened calmly, but she felt cold in her heart, which was heavy with foreboding. All her plans, her ambitious dreams seemed to be even further away than they had been at the very beginning. The very beginning . . . it had been so long ago. She put her protecting arms around Katriona and rocked her gently as though she were a child.

"Hush, girl. He is going to love you – he will, never fear; I should know."

A soft, muffled noise outside the window made them both look up. Katriona went to the window, and opening the shutter a little, looked out. It was dark but she just caught a glimpse of a shadow disappearing rapidly into the blackness of the trees.

"What is it?"

Katriona turned slowly, a frown darkening her brow, but in an instant she smiled with irony.

"I think someone was listening out there. Probably one of the boys. Tomorrow the whole village will know of my infatuation – that should give them something to laugh about."

"That's not very likely, you know. He'd have to admit to listening at my window and then reckon with my wrath. I wouldn't worry, if I were you. As you said, it must have been one of those silly youths, who hanker after you."

"I don't care very much, as long as Henryk doesn't know," said Katriona with a soft smile.

"It is good to see you smiling again, my girl."

"Oh, Mother, don't you fret about me, I shall be alright".

There was a little catch in Katriona's voice, and despite her effort at gaiety, in her heart she felt pain.

The village inn was crowded, noisy and hot. In a corner sat two men at a table. One of them, a wood merchant, said, "I say, have another drink, Vassyl."

"I don't mind if I do, Thimotiey Andrieyevich – thanks ."

He gave a watery smile, his blood shot eyes disappearing into the rough, dark folds of his weather-beaten skin. The innkeeper brought them two more vodkas, but the man, who had ordered the drinks, motioned to him again.

"Bring a whole bottle here, landlord – we are celebrating a good business deal, eh, Vassyl?"

They clinked glasses, and downed the contents in one go. Vassyl wiped the hot sweat from his face and looked at his companion.

"You are doing well then? I take it that wood prices are high right now?"

"Can't complain. I have changed my route a bit and this village is handy for taking a break, and doing . . . a little business, perhaps."

Vassyl pushed back his stool and looked at the wood merchant with puzzled eyes.

"And what business might that be?"

"Oh, nothing much, just a bit of information here and there . . ." His tone changed ever so slightly. "I hear that you have a man here with a strange name for a Cossack, eh?"

"Do we now?", frowned Vassyl, looking into his glass.

"You must know who I am talking about. I have never seen the man but I have heard people talking, you know, mentioning his name – I think it sounded like . . . what was it now? Something like Henry. Would that be right?"

He poured more vodka into the man's glass, this time right to the brim. Vassyl moved unsteadily on his stool. He jabbed a finger at the merchant.

"Eh, Thimotiey Andrieyevich, you are a jester! There is no one here of that name."

"And even if there were, you wouldn't tell me, right?"

Vassyl burst into shouts of laughter.

"Oh, dear me, you are a funny man, you really are!"

The words were slightly slurred and he looked down at his glass again. The wood merchant topped up his glass readily. Changing the subject, he remarked amiably,

"I say, you have good-looking girls here. Only yesterday I saw one. A real queen she was; long in leg, her back as straight as a wood-sapling, and what an expression on that haughty, angelic face! I reckon it would be well worth my while getting slapped hard in exchange . . . for, perhaps, a little kiss, eh?"

Vassyl leaned dangerously forward, his face, shining with sweat, suddenly alert.

"And which girl might that be?"

"I think they called her Katriona . . ."

"Did she have hair as black as a raven's wing?"

"She had the blackest and smoothest hair I have ever seen . . ."

The lecherous smile vanished from Vassyl's drunken lips.

"Ugh! You would be a damn fool to even think of

trying anything with that old witch Vassilisa's god-daughter", he exclaimed in a low, hoarse voice.

"Why, that girl won't let any of the local lads even walk her home after church on Sunday, let alone the usual bit in the hay on a Saturday night! If you ask me, she must be waiting for a prince, the stupid girl. Her face, I would agree, may be as beautiful as those angels's faces – you know, the ones you see painted in those pictures you can buy from the travelling man, but she is too skinny, almost sickly-looking, and that damn arrogance of hers! Why, I wouldn't want her if she were the only girl in the village. Now, consider my Dunia,"

He put two huge fists to his chest to make his point,

"Breasts raised like two warm loaves of bread, and her hips! Oh, like a barrel of good beer, strong and round, but soft too, mind . . ."

Vassyl's watery eyes took on the dreamy expression of a hungry man, confronted suddenly by a plate full of his favourite food. He shook his head slowly,

"Eh, Thimotiey Andrieyevich, I do like my women to be good- natured like, accomodating, if you know what I mean? Take my advice, forget about that scrawny, nervy Katriona and look for someone like my Dunia; good for work, and good in bed."

The wood merchant gazed at him reflectively, and then gave the ghost of a chuckle,

"Just my luck, eh?"

He drank his vodka and then put the glass back on the table with a thud.

"Drink up, Vassyl, it is getting late."

"I don't think I should . . . I think I am really done . . ."

"Oh, you must have the last one," insisted the wood-merchant in his easy, cordial manner. "It will do you no harm, and there is no more than a sip left in the bottle anyway," he said as he poured the vodka into Vassyl's glass.

They left, and after the stuffiness of the inn, the air outside seemed cold and pleasantly sharp. Within a minute, Vassyl's massive frame seemed to crumple and he leaned heavily on his companion. They walked slowly on, wavering a little, Vassyl mumbling and humming something. They had just left the main path when he suddenly burst into a tearful song,

"Koly my sia poberem,
Koly my sia poberem, poberem, poberem?
Poberem sia na wesni,
Kak zacwitut czereszni, czereszni, czereszni!"*

After a short while, they found a lane. Vassyl's house stood dark and only the dogs barked lazily somewhere in the back yard. The wood-merchant led Vassyl to a wooden bench inside the porch and let him slump down. He loosened the top button of the man's shirt, and bending down with his mouth close to Vassyl's ear, asked suddenly in a hoarse whisper,

"That Henry fellow, where did you say he was from . . . ?"

Vassyl clumsily pushed him away,

* "When are we going to marry, we'll be married when the cherry trees flower"

"He is ours, you hear, ours. Get lost, man. We saved him and now he is ours for good. Nobody will find him down in the . . . eh, Vassylisa knew, she always knows, the witch. Perhaps, . . . perhaps, she is saving Katriona for him, who knows . . "

Loud snoring muffled the rest of his words. The wood merchant found an old rug by the door, and draped it over the sleeping man before going out into the night.

A loud knocking at the door roused Vassilisa, who had been dozing by the window. At that hour, she never expected a visitor. She went to the door, and opened it. A man stood outside, and in an instant, she recognized the broad-shouldered figure of the wood-merchant.

"Come in."

"Did I wake you?" he asked, bending his head down in the doorway as he entered the house.

"Not really – I was only resting after a meal. A privilege of my old age, I suppose . . ."

She looked at him with a smile. He was a tall, well built man with strong, clean-cut features and a head of well-kept, brown hair. His eyes, under thick brows, were a surprisingly light-grey against their dark lashes.

"Won't you sit down?"

The man took a chair. Vassilisa sat down at the table and waited. The wood merchant seemed hesitant. His eyes wandered restlessly around the whitewashed room as if he were waiting for someone to appear.

"Is there anything that I can do for you?"

"I thought that, perhaps, you could give me some of your herbal remedy for my indigestion", he said at last.

"Well now," the old woman got up and opened the chest standing under the window. It was full of little bunches and packages. "What kind of indigestion is it? The heart or the stomach kind?"

"I thought there was only one kind . . ."

"Not so. If a man is not happy, his ailment comes from the heart, Mind you, it feels very similar though. Are you a contented man?"

There was a silence, and he seemed to have some difficulty in answering her question.

"Everyone says that you are a wise old woman, Vassilisa," he said slowly, "so there would be no point in my being anything other than truthful with you. I hear you can see into the past and you know about the future. You must have guessed why I am here."

The old woman gazed at him reflectively.

"You are not so young. You spent your earlier years travelling most of the time, building up your timber business. Now you are a wealthy man, with a comfortable house and plenty of money, but no one to come home to. You lead a lonely life, sir. What you want is not a potion for your stomach, but advice on affairs of the heart, perhaps?"

He did not look at her, but spoke in a low, tense voice.

"You are right, old woman. I have everything and yet it means nothing to me without the only girl I want."

Suddenly he looked full at Vassilisa and to her concern, he spoke again with strange agitation,

"Help me, old woman! I shall give you anything you want – gold, money . . . anything."

His eyes, filled with a painful anxiety, were fixed on her face, and she could easily read his expression – he was desperately lovelorn.

"You must give me time to think."

She sat motionless and thought for a short while. It was quite unexpected, and she didn't know why, but his desperation oddly touched her. She gave him a long, searching look,

"I am not so sure that I can help. You are a wealthy man, your features are very good and you seem good-natured – why then, do you think that you need my potions?"

He looked impassively at the wooden floor-boards, and said nothing. Vassilisa waited patiently. She felt that in some way his mysterious love had to have something to do with her. Finally he said,

"I want to say something to you, but I find it extremely difficult . . ."

The old woman smiled softly,

"I am quite old, you know. I very much doubt that anything would surprise me."

He seemed to make up his mind, and without looking at her, said in a calm voice,

"As you know, I have been in the habit of stopping here for quite some time. The people are friendly and the village is on my way to Rostock. About six months ago, I unexpectedly saw a beautiful girl here. I watched her as she passed, and for want of a better word, I experienced a sensation akin to a sudden bolt of lightning striking me down." He gave a bitter laugh.

"I could neither sleep nor eat. I had to leave the next day and I didn't even know her name. For the first time in my life, I felt clumsy, awkward and stupid. I didn't dare ask anyone who she was, and then I hoped sincerely that I would be able to forget her in a short time. I was a fool. Both my soul and my body burned for her, and so I came back as soon as I could."

Vassilisa's kind eyes rested on him.

"How many times have you been back since?"

"Three times, but it's no good. I cannot bring myself to tell her how I feel. I don't think that she is even aware of my existence."

The old woman smiled,

"A fine-looking man like you? And how do you feel about her now?"

"I love her more than anything in the world. If you don't, if you won't help me, I fear what I might do in my desperation."

There was an odd catch in his voice and Vassilisa knew for certain that ignoring this man's plea would only bring trouble in future.

"I take it that you now know the girl's name?"

The man hesitated, and then gave her a quick look,

"Her name is Katriona."

The old woman said nothing. Her face was deadly pale, but her black eyes burned among the folds of her skin, like two shining pieces of jet.

Her silence disconcerted him, but he waited silently. With an effort she spoke.

"That is not saying very much, you know."

"She is your god-daughter."

"You mean my Katriona?", she sounded incredulous, but he sensed that she had known that all along, and so he only bowed slightly in affirmation.

She seemed to gather her thoughts from a distance, and it was a little while before she answered.

"I think you have to give me a little time. I don't feel that Katriona is quite ready . . ."

"I know.", the man interrupted gravely, with a little ironic smile, "She loves another man. No matter, I don't mind for now . . . When she marries me, I will surround her with such comfort, luxury and devotion that the memory of her life in this village as well as everything else will seem like a bad dream. You see, to me she is the love of my heart, life itself . . . not like she is to this, to this . . .", he stopped as if unsure of his voice. When he spoke again, it was in an abrupt manner,

"That prisoner, the one that the villagers are holding, it's him, isn't it? You are all aware, of course, that an amnesty was announced a few months back, and I am sure that he must be very anxious to go back home, or doesn't he know about it? It would be a criminal offence to force him to stay – you know that, don't you?"

Vassilisa stared at her guest silently. A sudden tremor of fear made the palms of her hands come out in an icy cold sweat. A thought came to her and she shuddered remembering the muffled sound outside her window. After all these years, she had made the mistake of becoming complacent. Damn this stranger! Prudently she kept her eyes averted. She forced a thin smile, saying,

"You have nothing to worry about. I must ask you to come back in three months time, by then everything will be resolved. I promise you that."

She thought she heard him give a disappointed sigh, but then, as he evidently thought it would be foolish to prolong his visit, he bowed low to her and quietly left.

All the next day, Vassilisa thought of her visitor. The situation was dangerous and had to be resolved quickly. But how? It was comforting to know that she had a few months in which to deal with it, but then she remembered Katriona's tear-stained face, the grim passion of the wood merchant, and she shuddered again as a cold shiver ran down her back. And then there was Henryk . . .

All her dreams and ambitions had been shattered, and she looked to the future with dark foreboding. It suddenly seemed full of pitfalls and lurking, hidden dangers, dangers which she could not foresee. It was all so unexpected. A good many years had passed, and she had thought that now she was close to her aim. No matter what, she wasn't going to give up her dream without a fight, not yet anyway. She had to make sure that Katriona would be happy . . .

That was her priority; after all, Katriona was all she had – her family, her past and her future. Throughout her whole life, she had never loved anyone but that child. If only Henryk would marry her . . . If that could be achieved, she was certain, she could find a satisfactory way of dealing with Thimotiey Andrieyevich.

Chapter Six

October approached slowly, changing with each step the faded colouring of the woodlands and fields into autumn shades – from sun-bleached fawns, golden-yellows, beiges and flaxen straw-hues to vivid reds, russets, plum-purples and rich, velvety browns.

After months of hot, dry weather, the rains came down with a vengeance, adding a rejuvenating sparkle to fruits, leaves and grasses alike. The village river swelled rapidly. At dawn, just after the rain, the freshly ploughed earth of the furrowed fields, which were now sodden with water, but still warm from the stored heat of the summer, exuded mystic clouds of chalk-blue steam. In the village, noisy groups of swallows swooped gracefully above the dusk-etched rooftops of the barns, preparing for their winter migration.

The girls and older children, divided into small groups, were busy at this time of the year gathering fruits and wild mushrooms.

Some, carrying wide baskets and small, sharp knives, went into the woods at the onset of the grey dawn to cut down wild mushrooms, which were often hidden among the wet grasses, in the undergrowth or between tree roots. After the rain, there was a glorious abundance of shiny ceps, sticky fawn-coloured fungi, known as "butter cups", and best of all, rusty-yellow, oddly funnel-shaped agarics. The woodland harvest was brought back, and the old women sat companionably in small circles on the wooden porches, sorting through the heaped baskets. The ceps were strung onto cotton thread, and then hung up to dry in the attics. They would be used to flavour and season stews, all cabbage dishes and borshch.

To the kitchen were sent the "butter cups" which, true to their name, tasted meltingly of fresh butter when cooked as a stew with rings of sweet onions, herbs and finally soured cream. This dish would be served at every table in the village at supper time, together with a bowl of steaming potatoes and a plate of bread and butter.

The agarics could last a day or two in a cool place, and so they were eaten for lunch or even breakfast the next day. They were peculiar mushrooms – crisp and dry, they needed only a few seconds of tossing and frying in hot butter to bring out their wonderful flavour. Again, their name reflected their taste; they were often called "little chickens".

The orchards were busy too, with people climbing the apple, pear and plum trees, gathering in the last of the fruit-harvest, amidst laughter and singing. It was a time of storing the fruit in the straw, of cooking and baking. It was a time of enormous apple pies, made with rich soured cream pastry, platefuls of steamed plum dumplings with sugar and cream, the frantic bottling of thick fruit juices and jam preserves, and mixing of potent tipples, which were so agreeable during the long winter months.

The mushroom pickers were back in the woods, again at the crack of dawn, this time gathering blueberries. These grew in sunny clearings on dense, short bushes, hidden amongst a multitude of tiny, dark-green leaves. The scattered group of girls and children would move methodically on their knees from one clump to another. It would take a long time not only because the bushes were laden with blueberries, but also since purple-stained hands would often stray to fruit-inked mouths. Whatever fruit was safely brought back to the village would be served in deep bowls as a pudding, sprinkled with coarse sugar and with cold, creamy milk, or as a dessert of steaming-hot blueberry dumplings with a good dollop of thick cream. The bulk of the fruit, however, would be made into a confiture, which was a preserve of the whole fruit in their own juice-syrup. The remainder was dried, to be used as fragrant blueberry tea, a much liked cold remedy in the winter-time.

In obscure corners of barns or in dark cellars, a furtive activity was being solemnly carried out. This secret distilling process would involve the men only, and consisted of an elaborate, if somewhat primitive, collection of jars, clay pots and bottles, inter-connected ingeniously by a haphazard maze of ropes and tubes, and, depending on the basic resources, either potatoes or sugar.

The end result, however, would be a reasonably clear, though unrefined, spirit. This substance was poured carefully through sheets of blotting paper into stone jars and then heaved out into the kitchens for the women to take over. During the following few evenings, they would infuse some of the previously-gathered berries, fruits and herbs, and the bottled tinctures, sealed with beeswax, were then stored on wide shelves somewhere in a cool, dry place.

There was no one in the village, who could surpass Vassilisa in this art. She had the best knowledge and collection of every herb, from simple mint and unique woodland grasses to deadly-poisonous belladonna. Her potions and tinctures of herbs or berries steeped in alcohol, some bitter, some sweet, but all fiery and aromatic, were sought by many. She guarded her recipes with a respected and understood secrecy, and only Katriona was allowed to help with their preparation.

It was the busiest time of the year for the village. After the harvest of the fields came the harvesting of the woods and orchards. It was a time of potato digging in wet trenches, a time of huge bonfires, with their languid, wet smoke lumbering low over the fields and hedgerows, scenting the air with a smell most welcome to the cold and tired workers: the incomparable aroma of field-baked potatoes. At midday, the diggers would sit around a fire on upturned, sturdy potato baskets or piles of sacks, warming their cold hands. One of the women would carefully hand out the blackened, blistered potatoes. A pot of salt, and often butter too, would appear, and . . . oh! the sheer bliss of inhaling the hot, smoky scent of the tubers, the joy of tossing the skin-burning potatoes from one hand to another before squeezing them open, and then, seasoned with coarse salt and oozing with butter, they would disappear, almost unaided, into the rumbling stomachs . . .

Both at this time of the year and later on, during windy, rain-soaked October, the newly-dug potatoes would often be served to cheer oneself up. Two dishes were particularly comforting: "Little Jacob" and Potato Latkis.

The first time that Henryk saw Katriona serving "Little Jacob" straight from the oven, he felt slightly apprehensive. He was to quickly change his mind. The potatoes, grated into foaming, hot butter, well seasoned and then covered with a thick layer of double cream, were baked in the oven in a large oblong dish until golden and crunchy on top, and soft, mellow and ambrosial inside. Never mind the rain beating at the windows or the wind crying in the chimney; when this dish was placed on the table, it seemed as if the sun had come out, and nobody minded anymore what the weather was like outside.

Potato Latkis Henryk knew well. His mother, Victoria, had used to ask Agnes, her maid, to indulge them with potato-cakes during many a grey, wintry evening. At Vronovo, they would be served on a huge tray, with a whole array of accompanying dishes, and would be devoured in front of a roaring fire, usually during a game of cards. He would have his Latkis with a dollop of soured cream and spring onions or grated cheese or sauerkraut salad or chopped pickled herring or . . . , the list was endless. Oddly enough, they even tasted wonderful just sprinkled with sugar.

The Potato Latkis served here were every bit as good as those prepared by Agnes during his childhood and they never failed to bring back happy memories. Having noticed his good mood whenever she prepared the Latkis, Katriona served them often, taking care to use the right potatoes, the freshest eggs and only a very small amount of flour. She knew that their unique taste was only satisfactory if the Latkis were feather-light and crisp, without even the merest hint of the oil, in which they had been fried. But it was well worth the effort, if it only brought a smile to Henryk's face.

Finally, with everything gathered in, preserved and stored, the time would come for killing the pig. There was always a man or two in the village, who would specialise in this skilful task, every autumn moving from one farm to another, hired to slaughter the big black pigs, which had been fattened especially for the oncoming Christmas.

While one of the men let the pig into the courtyard, the other would chase the unsuspecting animal around. Then during this "game", the pig would suddenly be rendered unconscious, always from behind, by a powerful blow to the back of his head. Within seconds his throat was cut and the swiftly-killed animal was then hung above a small straw fire in one corner of the yard to remove the bristle. After that, the men would skin the pig, and divide the meat up into various portions. The solid pork fat, often ten fingers thick, was hung for a few weeks in the cellar, or was smoked, to be eaten, raw and sliced on black bread, or used to fry the eggs together with large slices of onion.

Giant hams, shaped from the best-back, were already turning slowly in the herbal or aromatic wood smoke inside the purpose-built little smoke-house. All the neighbours joined in the event. The meat had to be processed quickly, and the next day, the same activity would be repeated in some-body else's yard until the whole village had been covered.

On long wooden tables, the men and women made mountains of herb sausages, coils of shining black-puddings, pink-and-white speckled heads of brawn, lengths of liver-sausage as well as white sausages, which were indispensable when cooking white borshch, as anyone, who was clever enough, would know.

Most of the sausages would be strongly smoked, and hanging in a dry attic, they could last for as long as a year, never going bad, but becoming drier and drier, until in the end one could chew them like candy.

The long slabs of bacon, pink and pearly, were either smoked or hung for a while, and then roas-ted with marjoram, to be eaten, sweet and tender, in thick slices, between two pieces of rye bread.

Evening descended slowly over the smoke-filled yard, and the work having been completed, all the workers had been invited for the traditional, pig-killing supper. At the long table, covered with a heavy, linen cloth, everyone would be seated in comfort on wide wooden benches. Out would come the dark bottles of the previous year's vodka, which was mainly absinthe-flavoured and bitter in taste, but the revellers sat stiffly, solemnly drinking the strong tipple, served at least twice, in thick, green glasses. This ritual was absolutely essential for the welfare of their unaccustomed stomachs, which were about to be assaulted with masses of very fresh, fatty meats. Without the protection of the burning spirit, the participants would have ended up gravely ill the next day, as some unwise outsiders had discovered in the past.

The gaily painted bowls, piled with hot, boiled whole potatoes, were placed in front of the diners, together with bowls of smoking-hot, melted pork-fat, in which to dip the potatoes. Pickled in brine and dill, gherkins accompanied the platters of boiled or fried pork, which were brought in next. The supper had begun in earnest.

As she had done every October over the past few years, Vassilisa spent the "pig-killing" evening together with her god-daughter Katriona, their cousin Fiodor Yakimovich and his family. As before in the past, Henryk felt obliged to sit down to supper with them, despite usually being put off by the heavy drinking, the too-fresh fatty meat and the coarse conversation of the tipsy diners.

He sat quietly, drinking very little, nibbling politely at the food, lost in his thoughts. Frowning, Katriona gave him a concerned glance every now and then across the table. He never looked at her. He kept his eyes averted and his face seemed to her set and stern. What was it he was thinking of? She turned her glance once more on him. Her eyes were filled with infinite sadness and yet he wasn't aware of her at all.

He had grown accustomed to being an outsider and found his refuge and sanity in farming the rich, responsive land, given to him by the village. It was the land he loved. Late each spring, after he had sown the wheat, barley and rye, and tended the vegetable patches, he would stand amongst the expanses of green sprouting fields, and ask aloud the same question,

"Will I be here in the autumn to tend and harvest you?"

But there was never an answer.

It seemed to Henryk that to the nightingale suspended in the blue skies, singing her first song, and to the fertile earth spread as far as his eyes could see, and even to the ancient apple tree growing alone, wide and gnarled, by the sandy path among the fields, he was no more than a temporary speck, a dot on the horizon, placed there entirely for nature's comfort and convenience.

He could still remember, but only just, the feeling of being a man of some standing and power, in control of his own destiny as well as that of those depending upon him. Amused at the memory, he had to concede that he hadn't been a better man then. His hands were those of a peasant now, but after years of rebellion, he finally felt more at peace both with nature and people. The memory of his previous life, leisurely by comparison, and his former arrogant misapprehension of his peasants' harsh conditions filled him with remorse. He had to get back, not only for the sake of his family, but also to put matters right to make them right and just. It was his mission and it had now become his obsession.

He felt surprised too that his deep faith remained undiminished, despite a tormenting disquiet in moments of depression that God had forsaken him. There had to be a lesson somewhere, but he couldn't be sure of what it was. Perhaps his life had been arranged in such a way in order to bend his hard back, to make him humble . . . He smiled a little, for if this were the reason, hopefully he had achieved the degree of humility required of him.

Cries of laughter and ribald songs brought him back to reality. Uncle Fiodor stood up unsteadily, and waving his glass above Henryk's head, intoned in a deep baritone, looking at a blushing Katriona,

"Ej, jabloczka, kuda ty kotiszsia?
Ej, mamienka, da-zamuz choczetsia!"*

"Hey, Uncle Fiodor, to whom are you singing?", smiled Masha, a sly twinkle in her blue, slightly protruding eyes.

"Never you mind, I know you girls, you are all the same. You will see a good-looking boy and then you lick your lips! Like this, eh! And you look like a cat that's seen a bowl of cream."

The girls blushed and giggled, nudging each other.

Henryk got up and walked round the table to

* "Eh apple tree when will you have apples!, mother, I long to be married

where Vassilisa was seated. He was about to excuse himself when, on seeing him approaching, the old woman rose,

"I will walk with you, if you don't mind. I need a bit of fresh air . . ."

The evening was mild with only a very faint breeze, and the early dusk softened the contours of the farm buildings. They walked along the main path in silence. But by the old willow on the left, there was a narrow footpath leading towards the fields on the hill. They turned into the path, taking the hill slowly because of Henryk's leg. They slithered up the pebbles, wet with the evening dew, and when Vassilisa stumbled, Henryk gave her his hand to steady her up.

Suddenly Vassilisa stopped.

"There is a scat under that tree, over there. I think we should have a little talk, you and I . . ."

Henryk followed her eyes.

"Let us sit down then", he said with a smile.

The tree and the old wooden bench, made of a halved tree trunk, stood alone amongst the open fields, and at once Henryk understood what she really meant; their conversation could not be overheard.

It had to be something very serious. His heart sank. At this time of day, standing among the restful expanse of the furrowed fields, he felt happily tired and pensive, and a dramatic, as he suspected, conversation was the last thing he desired.

But when they were both seated, Vassilisa seemed strangely quiet and to Henryk's surprise, for a moment she looked away.

When was she going to speak?

Suddenly she turned and faced him. Even in the dim light of the evening, he could see that her face was haggard and full of anxiety. Astonished, he put his hand on her arm.

"Whatever is the matter? Are you unwell?"

"You will have to marry Katriona and leave with her at once, or there will be trouble . . ."

Henryk looked at her quickly. He had not an inkling of what was in her mind. What was it that frightened her so terribly?

"Could you start from the beginning, please? I really don't know what is it that worries you so much, but if it is at all possible, I shall help in any way I can."

"But you must marry Katriona, you must!"

She stared at him with burning eyes. Henryk's first thought was that perhaps that would be the only way for him to escape, be finally free. Embarrassed and ashamed, he looked away. He couldn't marry Katriona, no matter what the old woman said. He tried to gain some time.

"Is that really necessary? Why?"

"There was an amnesty given to political prisoners by the Tsar, and as such, you could go free now and I couldn't stop you, but if you do, Katriona will die of a broken heart. I could not bear that . . ."

Her voice faltered, and Henryk was afraid that she would cry. He touched her hand quickly.

"I think that you do me an injustice.", he said, "You know I would never leave here just like that. I owe you and Katriona my life, and I will never forget that. It is a question of honour. Believe me, you have nothing to fear on that account. But, as I am already married, you have to persuade Katriona that she must release me, at least for now. If, if the situation should transpire to be ... as you have said ... I shall then be honour-bound to send for Katriona straight away. I cannot promise more than that."

The old woman sat motionless. Henryk could see that this wasn't the end of their conversation, and he began to feel a trifle impatient with her. It was a little while before she said quietly,

"There is something else. Officially, you are a dead man, and as such you are in grave danger. If anyone wished you ill, and if you were to disappear, nobody could prove that you have been alive and well for the past few years, in fact from the very moment that your death certificate was issued ..."

"But who could want me dead?", Henryk interrupted nonchalantly, his voice weary.

"Thimotiey Andrieyevich, to start with."

He stared at her blankly.

"And who is he?"

"The wood merchant. He passes through the village three or four times a year. He saw Katriona once and fell quite desperately in love with her. Somehow he has found out about you and that Katriona loves you. I don't think he would hesitate, given half a chance, to remove you from her life one way or another."

"But surely he could not seriously want ..."

"You really have made up your mind not to

understand!", Vassilisa exploded angrily. "You have been living here for years and still you don't seem to grasp how differently people think and behave. These are steppe people. They live, love and hate passionately, not in your wishy-washy squire's way! It would be nothing for them to put a knife or an axe through your thick skull, don't you know?! Tphoo!"

She spat in front of her in sheer frustration at his apparent lack of understanding of the gravity of his situation. Henryk watched her aghast. She calmed down and continued.

"Then, of course, there are the village elders. They had certain expectations, we all had, and they will not see any reason to let you go now, unless . . . unless you were to escape secretly."

"How on earth could I escape without a horse and with all those people, whom you mentioned, gunning for me?", he was sarcastic now, but Vassilisa took no notice of his interruption.

"Now you know it all, I think together we should be able to devise a plan to keep everyone, well almost everyone, happy. My main concern is for Katriona, and indirectly for you – I hope you understand that."

She laughed, and to Henryk's surprise, her voice was tinged with something like a soft affection.

The next morning broke overcast and heavy, and Henryk woke up with a headache. He got up and padded bare-foot to the window, throwing open the shutters.

The sky, low and tinted gold with reflected light,

hung over the fields in craggy skeins of clouds. Bulging with rain, and whirling in slow motion across the navy-blue horizon, they looked like a fleece of floating, giant mushrooms. The air, charged with electricity, had a faintly metallic taste, and a sinister, unearthly glow was upon all things.

A storm was coming.

Henryk closed the window and lit the range, then washing and dressing quickly. But before he had a chance to get his breakfast going, the door swung open and Vassilisa and Katriona came in. It was most unusual for the old woman to visit him at this hour, and Henryk felt unaccountably nervous. Katriona took over the range and the serving of the breakfast so that there was nothing left for Henryk but to sit down and face Vassilisa.

"It looks like thunder is close", she said, turning to him from the window.

He nodded, and waited for her to go on, fearful of what she was going to say, for he had a good idea of her shrewdness, and was now fully aware that she would not hesitate to speak her mind. It was not for himself that he was worried, but for the girl's sake. Now that he knew the reason for her recent dark moods, he would have preferred to talk to her alone. With odd detachment, he could feel himself struggling not to allow a certain conscious thought to cross his mind, but then in his heart he knew instinctively that he felt deeply for her. Unhappily he stared with an abstracted gaze out of the window at the rosy glow behind the line of swaying tree-tops.

A sudden gust of the howling wind swept the porch, and clouds of dust and sand billowed around the yard, sending clattering across the cobbles milk-pails, left carelessly outside the barn. The whirling wind gathered force and went up into the purply branches of the old birch trees, framing the house. Hissing angrily among the boughs, it bent their tangled tops right down, almost to the ground, it seemed.

The heavy clouds sped wildly, pushed by the enormous, pent-up power of the storm, across the now dark firmament. Lightning illuminated the world for just one eerie second, before a ball of thunder rolled grindingly across the zenith. For a short while, the skies reverberated with the heavy sound, sending birds squealing with fright into the sanctuary of the hedgerows, and then an ominous hush fell upon the fields.

The tension in the air was almost palpable.

Immediately, heavy rain drops pelted the window frame.

Henryk glanced quickly at Katriona. The girl was hurriedly lighting the candles and in their flickering, pale light, he was able to watch her at his ease. Absorbed in her task, she didn't realise that the candlelight threw her expression into relief. Her silky, black lashes under downcast, translucent lids hid her eyes well, but her beautiful face looked severe.

He felt weak and disloyal. What would she do if he were to escape? He could not bear to hurt her, but his fate had been sealed by the amnesty and he should be rejoicing. But now he wasn't so sure . . .

Vassilisa smiled as if reading his thoughts.

"It is not nearly so risky as you think . . ."

"What isn't?"

"The escape, of course."

Before he had a chance to answer her, there came a muffled sound of annoyance from the other side of the range. Katriona let go of a hot pan-handle and came to the table.

"Whose escape are you talking about?"

"Well, it is about time we sorted out Henryk here's situation, don't you think?"

"He isn't going anywhere." Katriona's voice was calm, but there was more than a hint of steely determination in her grave eyes. Recognising the hidden emotion in her voice, Henryk smiled at her softly.

"If I were to leave, it would only be with your blessing, Katriona, and your help."

"I would never help you! I would stop from you taking even one step out of here, do you understand, even one miserly step!"

"Katriona, you have misunderstood! Wait until we have explained the plan. The whole village will be in danger if Henryk stays here, because an outsider knows about him . . ."

Vassilisa stood up and tried to put her hand on the girl's shoulder, but Katriona jerked away from her.

"Oh, stop it, stop it! You betrayed me! You, my own god-mother! You had no right to say anything to him. You'd better do something now, or else I will . . ."

She broke off, tears welling in her eyes.

Henryk looked at her, oddly moved by her despair and her beauty. He took her hand, but she snatched it away from him. She swallowed hard, and calmed, faced them,

"What stranger are you talking about?" she asked bitterly.

The rattling of individual rain-drops now changed into the monotonous sound of a curtain of water coming down with a vengeance. The room grew oppressively hot. Vassilisa sat down wearily.

"You'd better listen carefully Katriona. Nobody, least of all me, wants to hurt you. The plan is simple, but it needs a calm mind and your help . . ."

"Oh, what nonsense! Just tell me who the man is. I dealt with Mikhail well enough, and I can kill again if necessary!"

The old woman smothered a gasp.

"You killed Mikhail? How? When?"

"It was an accident – well, partly. I led him into the marshes, stupid old goat . . . Thought he was on to something good, the toad!"

"But why, in God's name, why?"

"Well, this was by accident too . . . I overheard him talking to his friend, Gregory, about denouncing Henryk to the authorities. He was planning to ride into town the next day: well, he didn't get the chance. Gregory knew that something sinister must have happened to his friend but he said nothing, the coward. He let everyone assume that Mikhail must have been blind-drunk, and having lost his way, blundered into the marshes."

She stared at Henryk for a moment.

"I did this for you, and I would do it again . . ."

Tears filled her eyes again and she began to cry. "Now you know, and I don't care! I will kill again! I won't let you go", she was sobbing hysterically now.

Vassilisa held her in her arms, her old face suddenly tired and distorted with pain. The girl was shaking and crying, struggling to get away from her. The sorrow she had felt for herself shifted into anger and despair.

"How could you do this to me! Let me go, damn you! Let me go!"

Suddenly, before a bewildered Henryk could stop her, she freed herself from the pressure of Vassilisa's comforting arms and ran out into the rainstorm.

"Stop her! Quickly, before she does something stupid!"

Vassilisa sprang to her feet. With one hand Henryk grabbed a long coat to wrap around the girl, who would be soaked to the skin, and with the other, he hastily pulled his boots on.

"Hurry, hurry!" Vassilisa was beside herself with worry. He ran outside into the blinding rain, and shielding his eyes, he looked around.

There wasn't a soul to be seen. Splashing across deep puddles, he reached the gate, and turned towards the path leading to the fields. He was glad that he had had the good sense to pull his boots on, since both the yard and the path now resembled a fast-moving brook.

He was sure that he would find Katriona somewhere among the fields, perhaps on the old bench under the ancient tree. Tree? He tried to run faster. It was madness to shelter under a tree during a thunderstorm. He had to get to her before something dreadful befell her . . .

Katriona stood on top of the hill, breathless, drenched and utterly exhausted.

Down in the valley, the frequent strips of passing lightning lit the soaked fields, spread in dark patches, picking out the white ribbons of the footpaths, which halved them here and there.

It looked so calm and peaceful, and yet there was a storm raging around her, and a pain in her heart. The deafening sound of the receding thunder made the earth tremble under her feet.

Frightened, she looked up to the divided, dark skies, trembling in every limb together with the sodden earth. The heavy rain kept washing away the tears streaming down her face. She was at the end of her endurance and in total despair. Seized by an anguished frenzy, she held her arms to the distant sky, and called through the noise of thunder, her voice hoarse with emotion,

"Lord, help me! Help me, Lord! If I cannot have him, take my life away. Now! I don't want to live without him. I can't, I can't . . ."

Her face was distraught with grief, and tears ran from her wide eyes without any restraint. She had an urgent need for help and consolation and sympathy. She felt completely alone in the whole world, without a single soul out there caring sincerely for her happiness. More than ever, she craved Henryk's arms around her and his love, directed truly at her, and without any intervention.

She longed to go to him, but he did not want her. Their relationship had led to nothing. It was always his family, his estate, his peasants . . . first. The sky was silent.

Katriona sank to her knees. She was shivering with cold. The wet blouse clung to her breasts and her skirts, weighed down with rain, seemed unbearably heavy.

What was left for her to do now?

If he wanted to go, could she help him? Was her love deep enough to think only of him and his happiness? To forsake everything dear to her?

Astounded, Katriona looked around. Whose was this voice in her heart? Was it the Devil's or the voice of God?

Stubbornly, she clenched her hands,

"I can't, I can't!"

"Yes you can, and you will do it. Set him free. It is the only way he will love you, don't you understand?"

"I can't" she said aloud.

"You will, if you really love him, you will."

As if by magic, at that moment, she had the sensation of infinite calmness around her. In an instant, it freed her from anger, freed her from herself, and bewildered, she stood up, gazing all around her, overwhelmed by an inexplicable feeling. She felt curiously breathless and light of heart. This was the solution, and all she had to do was to seize upon it with both hands, and truly, truly believe it.

The thunder had gone. Sunlight seeped through the few remaining clouds, and the dazzling blue of emerging sky and the freshness of the air were quite exhilarating. Standing on top of the familiar hill, she felt as if on the top of the world, the pure spirit around her, and in her elated heart, she knew she had conquered her fears at last, and that all was not lost.

It was just the beginning.

Somewhere from below, an urgent, anxious voice called her. It was Henryk. To hear him calling her name like that gave her a little twist of the heart strings. No matter, she was ready for anything now. Henryk ran the last few yards, his face white and drawn with worry.

"Are you all right?"

His arms held her firmly as if she were his lost child. Feeling terribly weak and tired, she buried her tear-stained face in his wet shirt and closed her eyes.

She was safe at last.

Sometime towards the end of the month, the wood merchant's coach stopped in front of Vassilisa's house. Thimotiey Andrieyevich, dressed in a long coat with a wide beaver fur collar, stepped out, looking anxiously around the yard. He needn't have worried. The old woman opened the door, smiling broadly.

"God's welcome to you! Good to see you again."

The room smelled of herbs, and a strong fire burned noisily in the range. The merchant rubbed his hands in front of the range, and then fetched two parcels from the coach.

"I thought you might like this as winter is coming fast" he said, handing her one of them.

"You should not have troubled yourself, Thimotiey Andrieyevich. But thank you all the same."

She set the parcel aside, to show propriety and restraint, and continued to lay the table for tea as was customary. Guest visiting, God visiting so went the proverb, and only the best would do. A thin, linen table-cloth, embroidered and stiffly starched, already covered the table on which Vassilisa put glass dishes with cherry confiture and blueberry jam. Thinly-sliced bread framed a round dish full of creamy butter, while apple cake nestled in a bright teacloth, right next to the fluted bowl of thick cream. To one side, a plate-sized loaf of special bread cradled in its centre a small amount of salt.

Vassilisa poured steaming tea from an old samovar into tall glasses, held for safety within ornate holders. She sat opposite the merchant at the table and offered him the bread and salt as a sign of her genuine hospitality. Only after they had ceremonially shared the bread and then toasted each other's health with small glasses of vodka, did they slowly and solemnly drink the strong, sweet tea.

The merchant observed quietly that the old woman looked very tired, her finely-boned face drawn and pale. The jet-black eyes seemed to have lost their fire. She wondered vaguely when he was going to mention Katriona's name. When he did, as she knew he would, she would be ready, and so would her story. She tried to read his expression, but she felt anxious, and she could only discern an odd disquiet. Why was he watching her so steadily? Did he know something?

"The harvest has been good, and we hope for a mild winter", she ventured calmly.

"Oh, I am sure it will be one of those. I had a word with the lumberjacks up north, regarding my journey next January, and they assured me that I shall have no problems with the roads. Apparently they have their own very accurate ways of knowing what the weather will be like months ahead."

"You will do a lot of travelling then?"

He gave her an enquiring glance and he seemed to reflect.

"That depends on many other plans I have in mind."

Vassilisa was silent. She knew what he was thinking. The merchant leaned back in his chair and looked at her with a smile.

"And how is everything with you?"

She watched him anxiously. His jovial manner was somewhat disconcerting, since she vividly remembered their last meeting. Any minute now, she expected him to ask an awkward question.

"Everything is going very well, thank you. And what are your plans?".

There, she had managed to be the first. She gave him a smile, even if it was a trifle forced.

"You know what some of them are. Have you arranged everything to our mutual satisfaction?"

Vassilisa could hardly find her voice. She gave a sudden cough, and then proceeded to clear her throat.

"It is that cold I caught during the storm we had here a few weeks back. Don't seem to be able to shake it off . . . I shall have to look inside my chest of potions, but there is never time. You know the saying 'A cobbler walks barefoot'."

His face grew heavy.

"But what about the arrangements, old woman?"

"I have taken your advice seriously, Thimotiey Andrieyevich. The stranger has gone, as he should have, and I spoke to my god-daughter at length about you."

"And? What did she say, in God's name, what did she say?!"

The merchant could not conceal his impatience.

Vassilisa wondered, half smiling, why a little while before she had been so terrified at the thought of this man. Between them, they would be able to manage him all right, she was sure.

"Katriona has agreed to your courtship, but she doesn't want you to hurry her. It needs to be a proper courtship, you understand . . ."

When the man suddenly stood up, she stared at him startled. He took her hand and shook it warmly.

"You won't regret this, old woman. I shall drench you both in gold, I promise! When can I see her?"

"She should be here soon. But be very gentle with her. I don't think you could get far with my Katriona by being pushy."

She lowered her eyes. She wasn't sure if the merchant had understood her advice. But the man was now pacing the room, and talking aloud and fast.

"All I ask for now is to be able to come as often as

possible and present myself as her suitor. The house is ready, perhaps she could come, that is both of you, of course, and tell me what she would like changed. I wish, I wish she would give me the smallest indication as to my . . ."

"But of course, how could I not appreciate such a sincere undertaking. And we would love to see your house, wouldn't we, Mother?"

The voice from the door made them both turn. Katriona stood on the doorstep, one hand on the handle. The wood merchant stared at her as if in shock. She looked even more beautiful to him than when he had seen her last. The love he felt for her was almost a torture. He knew now that he would accept any conditions, any humiliation, if only sometime later she would let him love her, marry her and look after her for the rest of their lives.

He bowed low to her, like a serf, his hand on his heart.

"Your words give me hope and I feel alive again."

She could not help but smile. She knew how he felt, for that was how she loved Henryk.

She came to the window and sat on the chest. He watched her hungrily, taking in every little detail. The light way she walked, her small feet placed gracefully one in front of the other, the unconciously sensuous sway of her hips, the gentle movement of her high breasts, hardly disguised by the thin linen of her blouse, and her face, that sweet face of an angel, framed by the smooth black hair . . . And this woman was going to be his... He had a feeling of such joy and excitement that suddenly, unable to keep calm, he ran out of the house and into the yard. He spotted the barrel of rain water by the wall and the pail standing by. Suppressing the overwhelming desire to shout for joy he put his face into the barrel and soaked his burning head in the cold soothing water.

They arranged to go and inspect his house the next day. The chores were now minimal and Fiodor's family would look after the animals for the two weeks or so they would be away.

The merchant was beside himself with happiness and could hardly wait. Now that the stranger had gone he was sure of his chances.

The women spent the last evening packing and he wasn't to disturb them. He slept at Fiodor's but his coach was left on Vassilisa's advise outside her house.

When, the next morning he turned up quite early at her yard, fully expecting the women to be still asleep, he found to his surprise that both were dressed and ready to go. It was Katriona's first journey to the outside world and she seemed anxious to be on her way.

Before the sun warmed the chilly morning air they were aboard and moving out of the sleepy village towards the track which led, across the steppe, onto the main travelling road. The village lane was silent in its emptiness and only the dogs barked sleepily here and there on hearing the odd noise. The horses, well fed and rested, galloped without encouragement and soon they left behind the sign of the houtor.

As far as the eye could see the ruddy steppe stretched for miles ahead of them, seemingly without end.

"When are we going to reach the main track?" Katriona looked at the merchant with a smile. "By nightfall. I hope to be able for us to stop for the night in the travellers inn before midnight. You won't be too tired?" he asked anxiously.

"Oh, don't worry about me! I am far too excited to be asleep anyway."

The waddling, soft movement of the coach changed abruptly, and Katriona knew in an instant that they were now on the hard, beaten track. She waited for a few miles more and then suddenly bent down and took off her shoe.

"I think I have something like a pebble there..." with force she banged the shoe on the coach's floor.

"Let me see, perhaps I can check it for you." The merchant leaned forward.

She could not prevent the smile of secret amusement that crossed her face. She gave him a glance and very nearly laughed. Vassilisa tightened her lips and looked at her sternly.

"Oh no, it is all right, it's only a silly little stone. I think it has gone already." She put the shoe back on and gave the merchant one of her sweetest smiles.

Behind them, from the middle of the dark road, a man got up stiffly and moved slowly to the side of the track. He was tall, well wrapped up against the cold night and carried a small bundle.

When the sound of the coach receded he stopped at the road side and looked up to the clear and starry sky, his heart suddenly filled with exultation. His eyes were wet with tears of gratitude, and despite the exhaustion, he felt strangely at peace. He said a silent thanks to God, and then without looking back moved briskly forward. He could scarcely believe that finally he was on his way. There was only a thousand miles or so to his home and he wasn't going to waste any more time.

He walked on.

They were reaching Kiev at last. They had spent their last night on the road at the wayside inn, and had then set out at dawn to get to the wood merchant's home before dusk fell over the city. Katriona passed through the countryside with unseeing eyes, subdued and deep in her thoughts. All through the long journey she turned over and over in her mind the events of the last few weeks. It had all happened so quickly. Sometimes she almost had to pinch herself convinced she was dreaming. Her life had been set in a daily routine and the changes, forced so suddenly upon her, left her perplexed and dismayed.

A month ago she would not have believed it, not even for a second, had anyone told her that, by the time the new moon shone above the village, Henryk would be gone for good, and that she herself would have helped him to escape.

Slowly recalling what he had said to her in their last conversation, she wondered whether she could have done anything to prevent his departure. She had been taken unawares and now it was too late for any regrets. She had to trust that he would keep his word and come back for her. His wife was dead; Vassilisa was sure of this. As time had passed and her god-mother had grown older, Katriona had noticed that Vassilisa's clairvoyant ability was diminishing. But this was the one thing Vassilisa was certain of. She loved Henryk so desperately and yet, understanding now how Thimotiey felt, she had to hide her feelings and bide her time. She remembered Vassilisa's favourite saying: "All things come to those who wait."

A sigh escaped her and she quickly looked up. Across from her, the old woman snoozed in the corner of the carriage obviously tired, but the wood merchant leaned forward, instantly alert.

"Would you like anything?"

"Oh, no, no, thank you."

"We shall soon be riding through the city and you will find many things of interest, no doubt. I would be only too happy to explain anything you wish to know or find strange . . . Kiev is so different from your village. It is called 'the mother of all cities' as it used to be the capital of Old Russia . . ."

"I expect it must be very beautiful!"

"That it is for sure, and more, much more . . .", Thimotiey's voice was tinged with excitement and emotion. To Katriona it was oddly moving that a man of such self-control could hardly disguise the love he felt so deeply for his city.

She looked at him. He was pale and tired, but his eyes burned with anxiety. It filled her with consternation, for somehow she was certain that he was anxious about her, watching her as he had done, throughout their journey. She felt a little frightened , alone and very far from her village and all the people she knew and understood so well.

She bit her lip in order to prevent herself from crying.

"I dare say you would like to know something about the house," said Thimotiey, breaking the long silence.

"Yes, of course, I would like to very much . . ."

"Well, it might surprise you, but I built this house with you in mind . . ."

"But how come?"

"I used to live in an old house, but when I saw you a year ago, I knew then and there that it was a new beginning, a wholly new life and that I had to have a new house, built for the new mistress; you . . . I hope you will like it."

Katriona hesitated. Little did he know that the strongest feeling she had for him was that of sympathy and understanding.

"I am sure that your taste is excellent. What did you use to build it?"

The wood merchant gave an amused smile,

"Contrary to what you might expect it isn't made of wood.

I used stone but the interior walls are lined with wood for extra warmth."

"It sounds very grand . . ."

"Nothing, nothing is too good for you!"

"Oh, no, no, please . . .", Katriona blushed to the roots of her hair.

"It is very good of you, but I couldn't . . ."

"You will grow used to it," Thimotiey interrupted, giving her a long, searching look.

"Oh, I will do my best. You really are so kind to, to . . . us."

"I am content to hear you say that. For now I shall ask no more, I want you to understand that you are under no obligation, and of course you can do exactly as you choose. But perhaps in time . . ."

The words seemed to be issued from his lips with difficulty and Katriona could not easily meet his eyes which rested on her with dog-like devotion. Embarrassed, she looked down, suddenly filled with overwhelming pity for this big, hopelessly lovelorn man.

Despite what the wood merchant had told her, nothing prepared Katriona for the splendour of his house. It stood in a leafy square, two storeys high, its sandstone facade gleaming in the late afternoon sun. The windows, tall and heavily curtained, surrounded the massive front door made of highly polished oak.

Bewildered, Katriona and Vassilisa stepped in. The wood merchant's housekeeper, Matriona, her husband by her side, stood in the spacious hall ready to greet the master and the unexpected guests.

Thimotiey put his hand under Katriona's arm and gently, overcoming her hesitant manner, led her forward.

"This is Matriona and her husband Yvan. She is a very kind woman and you can both ask her for any help you might need."

The two servents looked at Katriona with intent interest.

Behind, Vassilisa gazed around the hall.

"This really is a very grand house that you have built yourself, Thimotiey Andrieyevich", she said with an approving smile.

The wood merchant looked well pleased, but his eyes followed Katriona's face, anxious for her verdict.

For a little while Katriona was silent. They all stood waiting, and she knew she must say something.

Thimotiey looked at her with worried, harassed eyes.

To her concern Vassilisa seemed amused,

"Come, come, my dear child! Don't keep Thimotiey Andrieyevich in suspense. What do you think?"

"It does seem a long way from our humble cottage."

Thimotiey took her hands in his,

"Why do you say that? You know it belongs to you . . . Do you like it?"

"I think it is very, very beautiful."

He gave a short laugh,

"Wait until you have seen your room! Come!"

He motioned Vassilisa to follow them and led Katriona upstairs.

The top of the stairs revealed the long, gallery-like landing with several doors leading off in all directions.

He stopped in front of one.

"Close your eyes", he commanded, and when she did, he unexpectedly lifted her up and over the threshold.

When Katriona opened her eyes, she did not know at first where she was. There was colour everywhere! The whole room was filled with exquisitely embroidered objects, from cushions and table cloths to bed covers and tapestries on the walls. It seemed that he had bought what were the best examples of the famous Ukrainian crafts and put them all in one room.

She stood transfixed.

How many winter nights had she spent with the village girls embroidering each others' trousseaux.

She felt a moment's admiration for his thoughtfulness.

The wood merchant looked at her curiously,

"Do I have your approval? I so wanted you to feel at home . . ."

He said it in such a tone of pride that she could not help but smile.

"It is truly magnificent!"

"Oh! Then you must see downstairs at once."

He pulled her along the corridor and then down the wide oak stairs. Vassilisa followed them slowly shaking her head.

"The drawing room is just to the right", he said,pushing open the door of the long, sunny room.

Katriona stood in the doorway suddenly shy. So this was what rich or well-bred people in the cities called "the drawing room". It was formal and very intimidating. The elaborate curtains, the sofas and side tables crammed with little expensive-looking objects made her feel alien again. It seemed quite strange to have so much free time that you had a room specially for just sitting and doing nothing. At home, her people were busy for most of the time and nobody, if not sick, would even think of such folly.How strange the outside world was.She suddenly felt inclined to cry.

What did Henryk's "drawing room" look like? It had to be even grander than this one. She felt devastated. To think that she had reproached Henryk in her mind for not thinking her his equal.

It was now that she began to understand.

He must have thought her so naive. Even here in the wood merchant's house, she was lost and uneasy; what would she have felt like at Vronovo? Her head was aching and, exhausted, she carefully sat, oh, no! sank into the nearest armchair. Thimotiey sat by the side of her chair and took her hand.

"You must be very tired. You must forgive my enthusiasm, but I have dreamed of this moment for months. Matriona will serve supper in a minute and after that you must rest. Tomorrow I shall be glad to show you the other parts of the house . . . and then Kiev. We must do some shopping, you know . . ."

She shuddered when suddenly the silvery bell rang and, smiling, Thimotiey helped her up.

"Supper is served, let's join Vassilisa."

The food was plentiful, but it was cooked and served simply as if their host didn't want them to feel in any way at a loss. He seemed aware that this was Katriona's very first venture outside the village; though perhaps, observed Vassilisa, he himself liked hearty food best.

After the long journey they were all ravenous and ate in silence. The simple fare included borstch with dry mushrooms, chopped cabbage, cooked with pieces of the best pork, mashed potatoes and then Upside-down cake. It was thus named because the dough, before being baked, was suspended in cold water and usually turned itself upside-down when it was raised and ready. However unusual the method – the cake was delicious.

In the middle of the table stood a large bottle of vodka and on a wooden board a loaf of bread and salt.

Thimotiey filled the womens' glasses with the ice-cold vodka, and then helped himself. He raised his large glass in a triumphant toast to his guests. They drank as was customary in one go.

Vassilisa couldn't help noticing the jubilant glint in the wood merchant's eyes. She looked at him again. The light of the lamp displayed his finely-cut features well. Who would have guessed that this tough, though often arrogant, face could be melted by passion to such tender kindness when he looked at Katriona?

He put his glass down and calmly returned her gaze. Embarrassed, Vassilisa looked away. She understood what his expression meant. It was a dangerous game and she would have to have a quiet word with Katriona.

She began to regret that the girl was so much in

love with Henryk. There wasn't any point in denying it: this man managed to impress her enormously, and she wasn't sure if she wanted Katriona to wait, moping, for a man who was who he was, simply because of being born in the right place and at the right time. If it wasn't for his title and his estate, how would he fare against the likes of the wood merchant?

Now, Thimotiey Andrieyevich on the other hand had no early advantages in life. Everything he owned, everything he had achieved, came from his natural cleverness and patience. Yes, he would always get what he wanted in the end by not rushing things; by his slow, perhaps even cunning ways. She remembered how different he had been when staying in their village. Almost one of them. Just judging by his accommodating, easy manner it wasn't possible to even imagine how wealthy he really was and how very knowledgeable . . .

She was glad to be old and wise enough to see this clearly.

He would look after Katriona well, no fear, and to hell with titles!

The two weeks after their arrival passed in such a whirl of acctivity that, looking back, Katriona couldn't remember having any time at all to stop and think. Thimotiey Andrieyevich planned her day fully, from breakfast until supper time. Bewildered and dazed, she was rushed through the ornate churches, magnificent parks, wide promenades and exclusive shops. Her simple peasants' skirts and embroidered blouses were replaced with elaborate dresses which made her uncomfortably hot and clumsy.

She protested a little, overcome by it all, but Thimotiey Andrieyevich brushed aside her objections. She wondered if he realised how hard it had been for her to adapt so suddenly to all the changes in her life. The more she saw of the big city, the more she felt a nagging despair.

She felt terribly alone and insignificant. The beautifully coiffured women, elegantly dressed and wearing magnificent hats, spilled from the landaus, (as Thimotiey called them), in front of the white-fronted shops. Liveried doormen would hold the coaches' steps and in they would go, laughing gaily, confident, and talking rapidly in tinkling, high-pitched voices.

Her heart sank. These were the women Henryk was accustomed to, and, despite her shyness, she was very curious and so she stared at every one of them, desperately trying to see and absorb every little detail of their appearance.

Once, noticing her preoccupation, Thimotiey gave her a soft, sidelong glance,

"Katriona", he said in a low voice,"you are far more beautiful than any one of them".

Ah, how good it was to hear him say that! For the first time she laughed and then, suddenly embarrassed, blushed deeply and covered her face for a second with her hands,

"Oh, how I wish I could share your confidence! But I feel so out of place here, I don't belong here . . . I must look dreadful and . . . and silly. I am sure my manners are all wrong and . . . I am all fingers and thumbs, and . . . to my . . ." Thimotiey Andrieyevich leaned towards her,

"That's where you're wrong! You are naturally intelligent and you can learn anything you want. I will help you, I will protect you, always . . . I promise you there's nothing to fear. I'm as certain as I am of anything, that within a year you will be accepted as the most beautifull, most accomplished hostess in Kiev."

His last words had struck her: perhaps if she really tried very hard, perhaps if she stayed longer here, then maybe she would be able to surprise Henryk, to become a woman of class and distinction for him.

A thrill of rising hope and excitement passed through her, and at the same time, a faint sensation of something akin to contempt for Thimotiey Andrieyevich who could love her so blindly.

There was a pause, and then the wood merchant asked quietly,

"Will you stay ?"

He was smiling, but his smile was a little set and his eyes were full of anxiety.

Katriona dropped her eyes.

"I don't know yet. I need a little more time."

"But of course. Talk to Vassilisa, I am sure she would agree to stay longer. There isn't anything really, or . . . anyone to go back to, is there?"

The more Thimotiey Andrieyevich talked, the more jovial he became. His eyes sparkled and he radiated an encouraging enthusiasm and kindness. Katriona moved uneasily. It was slightly

worrying that she had such influence upon him. What would happen if she said clearly that she didn't reciprocate his affection? The idea of what might happen disquietened her a little.
She said nothing.

It was not until Vassilisa was fairly settled at the wood merchant's house that she discovered how tired and old she really was. The new comforts and amenities she wasn't accustomed to, brought the full realisation of the true pleasures of living. It was so satisfying to take one's ease amongst the luxurious surroundings.

For the first time in her long life, she only needed to pull the sash in her room to almost instantly receive Matriona's tender attention. The housekeeper treated her with a mixture of deep respect and hidden fear, sensing her powers of knowing the past and the future. Admittedly she had lost some of her ability, but there wasn't any need for her, was there, to inform everyone about it. It would be very pleasing indeed if she could stay here longer. The servents could not fail to see that, to their master, the young girl's smallest wish was an urgent command. And she, as the girl's guardian, was regarded with similar reverence. All she had to do was to persuade Katriona to stay here indefinitely, and then to marry Thimotiey Andrieyevich. There was nothing to look forward to in the village except the displeasure of the elders, who by now must have connected Henryk's disappearance with their sudden journey.

Prudently, she had an argument at the ready for

their prolonged stay : it would be very beneficial for a young girl from a remote village to learn the well-bred ways of city folk.She smiled, content with herself. She felt mistress of the situation completely, and the future looked good at last.

Chapter Seven

The heavy sound of bare feet, hurriedly pounding the wooden boards of the verandah, roused a sleeping Josy. As usual, lunch with the children had been an untidy, noisy affair, and after waving them goodbye as they left with Anthony to go fishing, she sat down exhausted, for just a moment in the garden armchair, and in no time at all fell asleep. Last night the bedroom had seemed unbearably hot, and drenched in sweat, she had tossed on the bed. Next to her, Anthony had slept soundly on his back, snoring softly, seemingly unaffected by the oppressive heat.

This year's summer had, on the whole, been wonderfully hot, and all the rose bushes, covered in luscious, if now a little blowsy blooms, exuded a heavy, intoxicating scent.

The warmth and rich sweetness of the perfume from the nearby meadow, purple with clover at this time of the year, brought out a booming, humming swarm of bumble-bees.

Dazed by the scent, and woken up a little too suddenly, Josy sat rubbing her eyes.

From the side of the kitchen garden appeared Agnes, her bare feet splattered with mud. The front pocket of her outsized apron bulged with clumps of freshly plucked-out dill; reddish tops, lengthy, tangled twigs, roots and all. A bundle of young garlic heads dangled limply in her right hand, while under her left arm, she awkwardly carried a bunch of cherry sprigs. Flustered and hot, she hurried along, mumbling aloud:

"Rush, rush, rush, that's all, and all the time too. Not a moment's peace. Agnes do this and Agnes do that! If it weren't for me, nothing would ever get done around here, I am sure!"

Her bare feet pounded the verandah boards once more, as she disappeared from sight, without even noticing anyone or anything.

Josy smiled and shook her head amused. What a girl! Obviously the seasonal pickling of the cucumbers had got the better of her. She liked Agnes and her often dramatic ways of dealing with everyday life.

"She brightens the place up a little", she used to say to a sometimes despairing Prakseda.

She tried to remember exactly when they had first seen Agnes. She was then a stoutly built, timid, slightly backward village girl. Ah, that was just after Richard had been born.

Good God, as long ago as that!

Who could have imagined then that she would have four children by now? And big Agnes wasn't timid or backward any longer, although she was still comfortable of figure!

Just as well, she mused, since this place resembled a mad house for most of the time, what with those three boisterous boys running wildly about, and her sweet little girl . . . Sweet? Well, alright then, spoiled a little, perhaps . . .

Smiling absentmindedly, Josy pulled off a few rose heads that had already turned yellow at the edges of the wide petals, and the sudden disturbance of the bush filled the air again with the strong scent.

On the spur of the moment, she decided to have a lazy afternoon out in the garden, not doing much, just pottering about, and then have tea, served, perhaps here in this hidden corner, among the roses.

It had been a long time since she had done that, and she deserved a break. She strolled along the little paths, thinking about Anthony, and the past few months. It worried her a little that he wouldn't see a doctor. It was nothing serious for sure, but she had a feeling that something was amiss, perhaps because Anthony was so vehemently opposed to being examined, and minded the very idea of anything being wrong with him so much that she didn't dare say what she thought.

Dear darling, she laughed with soft affection, he didn't like to admit it, but perhaps it was inevitable that he would start to experience little aches and pains – after all, he was so much older than she. And the past few years had certainly been anything but easy. Oh,the efforts needed to keep the estate profitable!

And the constant struggle with the administrator to improve the conditions of the farm workers – it was really more like trying to squeeze blood out of a stone. She frowned with annoyance.

That man was still a stranger to them. She was never quite at ease with him – indeed, she was filled with a revulsion and secret fear, which was so strange that it embarrassed her, and so she coped with it the only way she could: she avoided the man at all cost. It wasn't that difficult anyway – after all, she had four small children to think of, and no time to waste.

It was Anthony, who was more affected, she thought, and that worried her a good deal.

He sometimes became a little impatient and irritable, and also more obstinate in getting his aims accomplished. It was almost as if he secretly felt (for he never spoke about it) some kind of urgency, an unavoidable running-out of time, and for a moment, she had a feeling of foreboding.

But the garden around her, still suffused with the late afternoon heat and the scent of the heavy blooms, didn't allow any dark thoughts for long. Sternly, she talked herself back to normality by remembering aloud that she should simply trust in God, and not allow any doubts or worries to enter her head.

Then an idea crossed her mind. Perhaps if an opportunity arose, she could test her diagnosis for herself.

And perhaps she should leave the administrator to his own fate, at least for now, and in the capable hands of Anthony.

From behind the trees came Agnes' voice, calling her to tea. Josy turned, and briskly walked back. She had so much to plan and arrange. The two elder boys, Richard and Henryk, the younger one named after her late father, were due to start their boarding prep school in September, in Lvov, and the thought of losing them so soon made her apprehensive. But Anthony insisted.

"There is nothing more valuable we can give our children than a good education, surely you understand that", he had said to her only last Sunday, "Priorities and values are changing quite rapidly. Every time I am away from this little backwater of ours, I am astounded at just how much industry is to the fore. This country needs good brains, and our sons will have every chance in life, even if it means that they live away from home."

Of course she understood this, after all, the estate had been lost once and could go again, but nobody could deprive you of the knowledge you had. Yet she dreaded parting with her children, who were still so young, and wished that there was something she could do to persuade Anthony to postpone it, at least for a while.

In the entire time they had been married, they had never had a serious argument. Well, there had been that disagreement about the church-going, or rather the lack of it, but she was too much in love to force her religion on him. After all, he hadn't been born into the Catholic faith, and when he admitted, a little shamefacedly, to being more of an agnostic anyway, she let him be, secretly hoping that perhaps with the passing of years, he would become encouraged by her example. But now he refused to listen to her pleas to let the boys be taught by a governess at home for a few years.

Once when she had told him that she didn't

know what she would do without the boys, he had answered, laughing:

"I should have thought that under the circumstances, you could spend more time with me. And you have the other two little horrors to spoil, haven't you?"

He just could not see that his insistence made her unhappy, and after that day, she did not mention the boys' departure again, instead hoping against hope for a miracle.

Towards the end of July, Anthony received a letter from one of his old friends. The chap was passing their way, and if they didn't mind having him for a day or two, he would break his journey to see them. There was one snag though – as he was travelling by the Post coach, would Anthony be able to collect him from Lvov?

Anthony was clearly delighted when he read the letter aloud during dinner.

"What does he do, Daddy?", asked Richard across the table.

"He is an investor."

"What's that?"

"It means, son, that he works with money, and quite often makes plenty of it without really working. You do have to be clever though."

Richard was silent for a while, but then suddenly said,

"I know what I want to do when I grow up."

Anthony looked up at him.

"What's that, son?"

"I want to be an investor, and make a lot of

money."

Everyone at the table burst out laughing, and Josy smoothed his hair lovingly.

"You can be anything you want, darling, but please, for now finish up all your greens first, or you will have to miss your favourite apple-pie."

The next day the stable boy was duly despatched to the nearest town with a letter to the post-master and a text of the telegram which was to be sent. A week later, in the early morning, Anthony left for Lvov.

After kissing him goodbye, Josy ran to the kitchen. As she opened the door, the smell of freshly baked bread made her mouth water. Prakseda sat on her heels in front of the hot oven, taking out a large loaf. In the middle of the kitchen table, on a wooden board, lay two enormous, silvery heads of garlic.

Josy clapped her hands,

"Honestly, Prakseda, you can read me like an open book!

Anthony won't be back till tomorrow morning, so we can have an orgy!"

"I gathered as much."

They both laughed at the very thought of Anthony seeing them right now, eating the offending garlic. It was one of the smells which he simply hated, and would not tolerate in his home.

Josy, on the other hand, brought up at the Lodge without many restrictions, had learned to love it during her visits to the kitchen, where all the servant girls ate it with much gusto.

How she missed her favourite childhood snack! Hot bread torn into bite-sized pieces, and mixed in a bowl with butter and freshly-chopped garlic.

Hardly able to contain herself, Josy pulled a small knife from the dresser drawer, and then placed the china bowl on the table.

"While you get the bread done, I shall peel the cloves", she said breathlessly,

"Shall we go the whole hog, and have coffee afterwards ?",

"Oh, my, yes!"

Prakseda was already putting a pot with water on the stove.

The bread, hot, crunchy and golden brown, melted and absorbed the soft, creamy butter. The pungent smell of chopped garlic made Josy's stomach rumble in anticipation.

"Quick, Prakseda, quick! Don't let it get cold! Where is the salt?"

"Just over there. Wait, I will bring the pot to the table."

"Look out, Josy! The coffee is boiling over!"

"Get the cream, I have got the cups ready."

At last, everything on the table, they could sit down, companionably sharing the same bowl of the forbidden delicacy.

Oh, the wonderful combination of the mouth-burning tang of the garlic, and the rich, mellow taste and aroma of hot bread and butter! It was sheer bliss!

For a moment, she was back in Martha's wonderful kitchen, a little girl again, thin legs dangling under the high wooden bench, and eyes squinting in concentration, carefully licking the salt crystals sprinkled on top of the butter, which used to rapidly melt on the hot, garlic bread-end . . .

Replete and smiling happily, they sat back in the roomy wooden armchairs. Mercifully, at a quarter to six in the morning, the rest of the household was soundly asleep.

Outside, it was still cool, but the kitchen, warm and cosy, made them feel at peace with the whole world, after the lovely, if somewhat unusual, breakfast. Prakseda got up first, and strained the boiled coffee before pouring it into the large, wide brimmed cups. She had hardly had time to add the cream, when the sound of wheels grinding on the gravel made them both jump up, and then run to the window.

The master's coach had just stopped outside, and the groom was holding the door open for Anthony.

Josy looked at Prakseda in a wild panic.

"What are we going to do?"

"Quick, open the windows wide. Where is that coffee? Oh, it's scalding hot! Damn! Where is the cream? Milk! Hurry!"

They gulped the coffee hurriedly, burning their lips. Prakseda threw the garlic skins into the bin, and then washed out the bowl.

Josy smoothed her dress, and then went out into the main hall.

Here was her opportunity, and she was determined to take it.

The front door opened, and Anthony walked in, holding in one hand a leather overnight bag, and in the other, like a stick, a rolled-up umbrella. He stopped abruptly, surprised to see his wife already fully dressed and waiting.

Josy advanced, smiling boldly,

"What happened, darling? Have you forgotten something?"

She put her arms lovingly around her husband's neck, and then slowly, she kissed him fully on the mouth.

Not used to such a reception so early in the morning, Anthony dropped the sackvoyage and umbrella to the floor, mumbling in delighted confusion:

"Did you really miss me so much already? The post-master caught me just in time; the trip has been cancelled. Well, I am back then, dearest. and . . . perhaps we could, I mean, if you would like to . . ."

Now he took her face in his hands, and kissed her lips, all the time steering her slowly towards the stairs and their bedroom . . .

But to his indignant disappointment, Josy burst out laughing, and then slipped from his arms. Pirouetting across the marble slabs of the hall, she gaily called,

"It would be wicked, really wicked, to stay in bed on such a fine day, don't you think? I'd better get you a pot of hot coffee . . ." Still giggling, she disappeared down the passage leading to the kitchen.

"Well?", Prakseda looked up curiously at the laughing Josy,

"Have you managed to talk your way out of it?"

"I didn't need to – Anthony loves me as I am! So there!"

"What?! Reeking of garlic and all?"

"That's just it! He simply doesn't know! As long as he doesn't see the peelings or us eating it, he won't know. We can have it every day!"

"How come?"

"Well, I suspected as much, but my poor darling would never admit it, of course. He has completely lost his sense of smell – and he minds terribly," she added, seeing Prakseda's blank expression.

"Wouldn't you?"

"Well, yes, but he should know me better than that. I don't mind anything about him. I cannot tell you how relieved I am that it isn't anything more serious!"

Josy poured the hot coffee from a height into two cups, and satisfied with the froth produced, placed them on a little tray, together with a plate of butter-cookies.

She smiled at Prakseda, who was watching her silently.

"You know, after all these years, I am still very, very fond of my husband".

Pausing only to hold the door open with her elbow, she walked out of the kitchen, balancing the tray in one hand with graceful ease.

Prakseda sat wearily at the table with a cup of fresh coffee. She didn't know why, but an unexpected feeling of regret had overwhelmed her. Why, those two still slept in the same bedroom after so many years!

Alas, it wasn't for her, this mysterious domestic bliss – Josy was simply born lucky, that was all there was to it.

As for herself? She had no family, no husband to cherish, and no children to spoil. Ah, but that was my own choice, she reminded herself quickly. No, not a choice, it was a necessity, don't you remember? Whom could I marry? One of the grooms or an estate worker?

After having lived with "them" in the main house all her life, well almost, (she had started in service as a young girl), how could she adapt to a mundane existance in a worker's cottage? How could she like or get used to the rough manners, perhaps even the odd Saturday beating, the drinking and swearing?

She shivered at the very thought.

She remembered the handsome, sad face of the midwife, often marked and bruised by her drinking, womanising brute of a husband. Poor woman, too proud to confide in anyone.

She could never put up with such a life.

No, this way was so much better. At least she was always with kind, interesting people, whether travelling or staying put, never bored. The children were almost as if her own, and Josy wasn't like a mistress to her, more of a friend or a younger sister, someone to look after . . .

She had got used to their way of thinking and way of life.

It had become her own. She had seen the young Horaim girls grow up, and now Josy's children were in her charge too. She loved them with all her heart, and yet inexplicably, she felt an outsider, sometimes all alone and unsure of her future. That was stupid! Of course she was part of the family – even if she were to become ill or frail, they would still look after her, surely?

Why then was she feeling sorry for herself and for what might have been? Why was she secretly wishing in her heart for a little human happiness, for somebody's strong arms around her, for the unknown intimacy of man and woman . . . ?

It was no use, she didn't belong out there, yet among those she loved and admired, her place was fixed, and it would be pointless to fill her heart with awe.

I must be mad, she thought, and got up abruptly; it is too late for me anyhow, and if I am not careful, I shall turn into one of those taciturn spinsters, and no mistake.

She washed out her cup, and put it away just as the kitchen girls arrived, giggling and prattling loudly. Prakseda smiled wryly, it was going to be another day, the same as usual, and if she were to put a bet on it, there wouldn't be any spare time to fret about it either.

The time of the boys' departure was only days away, and Josy felt wretched. To her painful surprise, the boys didn't seem to mind. Absorbed in checking their new books and uniforms, they were brimming with excitement.

"Make sure nobody plays with my toys", said Richard sternly.

"Or mine!" Henryk wasn't going to be left out.

"Of course. Your rooms will be kept just as they're left, ready for when you come back for

Christmas."

"Christmas? But that's such a long time away!"

"I know, I shall miss you terribly."

"We shall miss you too!"

"And the babies!" Henryk always remembered the younger two; three-year-old Marylka, and Cazimir, a year younger.

"Now that you are going, they will grow up quite quickly . . ."

Suddenly quiet, the boys looked up at her from their stack of books. Their eyes were solemn and clear, but their soft mouths quivered slightly, and Josy dropped down beside them, fighting back her tears. She must be cheerful, for their sake at least.

"You remember the stars at night – the ones we always watch?"

"Oh, the North Star! I can always recognise it – it is the brightest!"

"And I can spot it too!" said Henryk anxiously.

"That's it, then! Let's make a pact. Every evening, while you are away in Lvov, I shall look out for our bright star and then I shall think of you two, looking at the same star, at the same sky, and of course thinking of me. That way we can be together for a few minutes every night, and, I promise you, in no time at all you will be back home for the winter break!"

The boys laughed, delighted. Mother always invented good games, but this one was going to be the best.

The door opened quietly, and Prakseda walked in with two tall, round, gaily-painted tins.

"These are butter and hazelnut cookies to take

with you. Make sure you don't open the tins till Lvov, or the cookies will go soft."

"Um, you smell so nice!" Henryk held Prakseda's hand, nestling up to her.

Richard gave her a quick look, without getting up,

"I bet you've brought some for now, haven't you?"

Prakseda laughed softly, "Nothing can ever be hidden from those beady, little eyes of yours!"

She took the cookies, which were wrapped up in a tea towel, out of her apron pocket, and put them on the table.

"You really spoil them! How are they going to survive without you?" Josy's voice trembled a little.

"Oh, they are big boys now, almost men. And I have something else here."

She went out, but came back almost instantly, bearing a tray with a jug of frothy cocoa milk-shake, glasses and a large bowl of black cherries.

"Hurray! We can all have a picnic right here!" shouted the boys.

The atmosphere was joyful, as if it were a party, and all their sorrows forgotten, they toasted each other with milk- shake, ate the crunchy, melting cookies, and practised spitting cherry pips into the bowl from a distance. They laughed, happy and excited, while Josy watched over her sons with a heavy heart.

The journey was only a day away.

The morning of the departure broke wet and misty, the first real autumn day, and Prakseda took the boys' coats and caps out of their school trunk, which stood in the middle of the hall, waiting to be collected by the coachman.

Anthony, who wouldn't normally have breakfast with the boys, since at that hour he would already be working in his office, now made them laugh by eating his porridge with a huge serving spoon, and painting funny faces on the boiled eggs, while Josy, subdued and silent, had a last chance to quietly look at them across the table.

Just as well that Nanny was attending to the younger ones in the nursery – she could have the boys all to herself. She wasn't too worried about Richard. He was a bright, boisterous, strong-willed boy, and she was quite sure that he could look after himself. No, it was Henryk who gave her cause for concern. Always following his brother or her around, he was timid, quiet, and so kind. What if he couldn't settle down at the school? What if the other boys made fun of him?

Whom would he be able to turn to for help?

She resolved to write to the headmaster, and ask him to have a talk with the boys to reassure them that they could talk to him about any problems they might have. The idea made her feel better, and she even managed a pale smile at Anthony's attempts at spoon-juggling.

Finally,when breakfast was over, they all went out into the drizzling rain. The coachman had already roped the trunk onto the back of the coach, and the boys, dressed for the first time in their smart school coats, stood stiff and awkward while Josy and Prakseda hugged and kissed them.

"Time to go," Anthony helped the boys up, and then stepped into the coach, closing the door. The boys, kneeling on their seats, looked out through the pulled-down windows.

"Tally-ho!", shouted the driver from his box, and the coach slowly circled the courtyard before rolling away down the muddy driveway.

Richard, who until then had seemed unaffected by his departure, on seeing his home and mother becoming smaller and smaller with every forward lurch of the coach, suddenly uttered a piercing scream,

"Mummy, Mummy! I don't want to go! Please, oh, please . . . Mummyyy!", his words were drowned out by the sobs which almost seemed to choke him. Anthony tried to hold him, but the child was screaming hysterically now. He rocked to and fro in agony. Opposite, Henryk sat silent, tears streaming down his pale face and disappearing onto his new coat.

The coachman, muttering something under his breath, nudged the horses with the end of his whip, and sensing his mood, they broke into a gallop.

Josy dashed forward, her outstretched arms ready to snatch the boys back, ready to fight anyone or anything which threatened her children, oblivious to the reason for their going, only knowing that they needed her – but to no avail.

The coach was already disappearing between the trees.

Oh, the pain in her heart! She could have screamed then, but in an instant, she was left behind, wet and crying helplessly, standing in the middle of the rain-swept driveway.

Prakseda, eyes wet with tears, quietly came from behind, and wrapping a shawl around Josy's shaking shoulders, gently led her away, back into the house.

In the warmth of the kitchen the maid soon recovered some of her usual vigour, and set about making some strong, sweet tea, with a good dash of cherry vodka.

Josy was not crying now. She sat dry-eyed and calm, and though low, her voice was steady.

"As long as I live, I shall never forgive Anthony this betrayal".

"Oh, come on now, you don't mean that! Drink this tea quickly, it will bring colour back to your cheeks. The boys are probably already laughing at the whole thing. You know what children are like. Anyhow, they will be back in no time.

"It is really no more than a storm in a tea cup!"

She smiled at her unintended pun.

Josy did not speak. Her face wore a sullen look which until now Prakseda had never seen.

"I don't think my husband ever thought the consequences of his actions through."

"Oh, my dear girl, don't talk like that. It's too bad to put the blame on Anthony as though he actually meant to hurt you or the boys. You know he is only doing what is best for them. Tomorrow you'll feel better and see things more clearly – I am sure of it."

"He has let us down terribly, that is all there is to it."

"What are you going to do?"

"Now? I shall go for my walk, and then play with little Cazimir and Marylka to give Nanny a break."

"You know I didn't mean today."

Josy gave a bitter laugh.

"Oh, don't be afraid, Anthony will come to no harm. He will be quite safe . . ."

"For God's sake, don't talk like that, Josy! Nothing, nothing has really happened!"

Prakseda's voice rang with anxiety.

"I know," said Josy tearfully, "it's only my stupid heart that is broken".

She slowly rose to her feet, and then, feeling that she could not hold on to her self-control any longer, walked swiftly out through the door, before Prakseda even had time to move from her chair.

Josy spread her shawl out, and then sat down on a fallen tree log, moss-green with age, atrophied with lichen and half-sunken in a tussock of wild grass. Not far away, among the spreading boughs of an oak tree, a wild pidgeon warned his mate of the intruder with a high-pitched "Hoo, hoo, ghroo-hooh."

The sanctuary of the woods subsided Josy's anger, and glad of the solitude, she sought to think the whole situation out.

All around her was the magnificence of Autumn, burning with warm colours.

The late sun had partly dried the morning rain, and a fitful breeze chased the remaining flecks of cloud across the blue of the sky, now and then bringing the sharp, satisfying smell of wet, fallen leaves.

The gentle murmur of the wind swaying the tree-tops in the woods reminded Josy of the joyful, calming sound of water rushing down the falls.

There was a sense of calm and purpose about everything, but despite the soul-pleasing beauty of the nature surrounding her, her heart was full and tears kept springing to her eyes.

Somewhere from the direction of the main path came the sound of broken twigs and a horse's hoofs. A minute or two later, a rider emerged from between the pine-trees – it was a woman.

To Josy's dismay, on seeing her, the woman stopped and slid gracefully to the ground. She led her horse to a patch of grass, and slipped the reins around the end of a tree-trunk.

"Hello there! I hope you don't mind company. I think Fritz could do with a rest too . . ."

"Oh, no, of course not. Are you a stranger to these parts? I don't remember seeing you before."

"I live in Paris. By the way, I usually answer to Zuzanna . . . My uncle, Dionizy, owns the Rookery . . ."

"Oh, but that is more than ten miles from here. I live in Vronovo. Everybody calls me Josy . . . , short for Josephine . . .

"I hope you are not lost?"

"Not really – at least my horse isn't. I was told that he would bring me home if I asked him politely."

She smiled wickedly, and Josy brightened up.

"Do sit down for a while. It is ages since I heard any news from abroad."

The woman took a leather bag off her shoulder, and rummaged around in it impatiently. Finally she found a gold case, snapped it open, and held it out to Josy.

"Would you like a cigarette? I'm dying for one."

Startled, Josy took one with slightly trembling fingers.

Zuzanna watched her from under dark brows.

"I see, you don't smoke. Well, there is always a first time for everything. All my friends do. It is quite a trend in Paris."

Knowing instinctively that Anthony would not approve, Josy lit the cigarette in a gesture of defiance.

Inhaling the smoke too soon made her cough, and she blushed, annoyed with herself. She felt nervous and overwrought in the presence of this elegant, sophisticated woman, and only the satisfied realisation that, even after four children, she had still retained her trim body, not so dissimilar to the beautiful figure of the stranger, made her assume a lighter manner, and she smiled as she said,

"It gives me such a good feeling to do something a bit naughty once in a while. Be warned, though, it isn't Paris here – all our neighbours would be horrified to see us behaving in such, shall we say, an un-lady like manner."

"I thought as much. Well, I'm only here for a very short time. The wilderness does not agree with me; give me Paris anytime!"

"I quite like it here. Once, years ago, I had the chance to live in Warsaw, but after a few weeks, I could not wait to come back to my beloved fields and woods . . .", she broke off, embarrassed.

Zuzanna gave her a reassuring smile,

"Oh, but you are a Romantic, I can see that. I love the country too, but only in very small doses."

She indicated the smallest pinch with her long, manicured fingers.

Josy laughed. It was good to be able to talk to someone so different from the nice, but older and oh, so boring neighbourhood ladies.

"Perhaps, you would like to look us up if you have nothing better to do this week."

"I should be delighted. We could talk much longer then . . . Here, keep these, I bet you won't have much chance to get them on the quiet."

She put the cigarettes in Josy's lap and rose with an easy dignity. Her movements had the smoothness and grace of a wild cat, and it was easy to see that men must find her bewitching, and that she was well aware of the fact.

"I must start back or Uncle Dionizy will fret. I shall come to Vronovo, if I may, sometime at the end of the week."

"Oh, good! Goodbye then, and thank you. See you soon."

She watched Zuzanna disappearing through the trees, confident and at one with her horse. It was obvious that she was an excellent horsewoman. She must go riding in the famous Bois de Boulogne in Paris every day . . .

Josy walked home slowly. Her annoyance with Anthony had almost evaporated; indeed, she could not prevent a smile of frank amusement from crossing her face at the memory of herself running towards the disappearing coach. I must have looked a perfect fool, and I probably not only frightened the children, but the horses too.

Well, it was always better to laugh at the bad incidents in life than to cry – that's what Martha used to say.

This changed feeling surprised her; there was a certain acceptance in it, but also a slight regret.

She thought over what she had so carelessly said to Prakseda.

It wasn't in her nature to sulk, and she decided to have a word with Anthony. Perhaps it would be possible for her to go to Lvov and visit the boys at half-term?

In an odd way, she felt that the unexpected meeting with the attractive stranger had helped her to regain her sense of proportion and good-humour.

She very nearly laughed. It was time to get back and take over from Nanny. Cazimir and Marylka liked to have their tea with her and, with the boys now gone, it was important that she should be there for them.

She had almost reached the orchard gate, when suddenly from the direction of the stables came the protracted, blood-curdling yelping of a dog. Josy rushed forward without a moment's hesitation. Even as she ran, she could hear the sound of voices, and within seconds, saw people surrounding someone or something.

Her heart was pounding wildly as she reached the yard.

She was frightened now. What on earth could have happened?

The stable lads moved aside to let her pass through.

And there, in the middle of the human circle, she saw a hunched, ragged beggar sitting on an upturned water-bucket.

He looked utterly exhausted.

Kuba, her old dog, half-blind with age, who had been brought with her from the Lodge, danced around the man in a crazed frenzy, seemingly forgetting his stiff legs. He kept on leaping up at the man's chest, desperate to lick his face, and then, finally threw himself at the man's feet, his hoarse barking rising into ecstatic, triumphant whining.

The man bent down to hold the whimpering dog, and stroking his old body, whispered something in a soft, low voice.

Around him, the young grooms were all talking at once:

"I was going to send him off . . . he seemed a bit touched, or something. But the dog went beserk . . . You don't know what he might have . . . the plague or measles or even cholera . . . Where did he say he came from? ... Who knows? I still say he seems strange-like ... Ugh, don't say it, he is human like us, and surely it isn't right to let a Christian perish for want of food and water... But he might not even be a Christian soul ... One thing though is for sure – the dog does know him, ... It's uncanny, he could be someone who used to know the dog at the Lodge ... Hush! Hush! The mistress is here!. She might know..."

The beggar must have seen the edge of a woman's dress, for slowly, without stretching, he looked up from under a wild mop of dark, tangled strands of hair, straight into Josy's eyes.

Wearily he tried to stand up. One of the softer-hearted lads helped him. With a hand on the whimpering dog's head, he straightened up his tall, gaunt body and took a small step towards her. His eyes were fixed on Josy and she could not avoid his steadfast gaze.

"What's your name?" asked the man in a low, hoarse voice, still without taking his eyes off her. Without thinking, she answered as if she were a child,

"I am Josy".

"Jo-sy" ... The man drew out her name, savouring each syllable. He gazed at her reflectively, a soft look in his tear-filled eyes mingling with an expression of singular kindness and something akin to love.

Josy stepped back, staring at the beggar in astonishment. She waited for him to go on, and yet she was fearful of what he was about to say.

And then from the side of the house Prakseda

came running, flushed, tearful, and shouting wildly at the gaping men:

"It has to be the old master! I tell you, it is him, it is the master! Oh, Lord have mercy on us for fools! Only the dog could tell!"

Josy was trembling so violently now that she could not stir, tears streaming from her eyes. Yet something within her still fought, still refused to believe it.

Gently, the man held her as if she were a little girl.

At first, distracted by his dirty, fetid rags, she could not comprehend his muffled words, but then slowly their meaning reached her, and the realisation made her heart lurch wildly against her ribs, for the stranger repeated over and over again:

"Josy, Josy, my dearest child!"

Then pandemonium broke loose. Some of the grooms ran to find the administrator, others moved around the yard as though in a daze. The maids rushed about the kitchen getting a bath of hot water ready. Prakseda brought Anthony's clothes into the guest room, together with his spare soaps and shaving-brushes.

After the long, hot bath, the smartest of the lads was summoned into the house to shave the master and cut his hair. From this ordeal, Henryk emerged a new man. Of similar height to Anthony, he could wear his clothes with ease, except that they hung on his gaunt body as though upon a scarecrow.

The normally placid, Prakseda was adamant that day:

The master will have his meal in bed and after that he must have total rest. Tomorrow will be soon enough for all his news.
She was right. Henryk could hardly eat, and with the tray pushed aside, he fell into a deep sleep before Prakseda had even brought his tea. Across his feet lay the watchful Kuba. And when Prakseda, on leaving the room, wanted to take the dog downstairs, he growled at her for the first time ever.

Josy came in, and stood at the foot of the bed, watching Henryk for a while with a strange, unreal feeling.

She had a sudden glimpse of that afternoon at the Lodge when she had sat alone with her thoughts in the summer room. The shady faces of her loved ones, which she had seen in the silvery depths of the mirror, had not included her father's, and she remembered being disturbed and upset by his absence for days after.

Henryk stirred, and Josy turned to go. She gave him one last lingering look. With a pain in her heart, she noticed how thin his folded hands were. They had once been so slender and fine, but now they were nothing but rough skin and bone.

And yet, now clean and shaven, without his long hair, and sleeping soundly in the safety of his own house, his strong, still- handsome face was at last relaxed, the ravages of the past few years seeming less apparent, and he looked again like the man she once knew, her own beloved father.

A few days later, just after dinner-time, Anthony approached the last stretch of Vronovo's drive with some trepidation.

Would Josy still be upset? She had never been emotional like this before, and not having had any experience of serious quarrels, he felt at a loss.

He could now see the grey contours of the house, emerging from behind the trees. To his astonishment, instead of the expected darkness, since the dining-room was situated at the back, all the windows were ablaze with lights, the main door stood wide-open, and there were many coaches in the drive, which he recognised, on getting closer, as those of his neighbours.

A young groom hurried from around the back of the house to open the coach-door; Anthony stepped down, and went in.

The drawing room was full of people. Anthony stood on the threshold for an instant, and unobserved, looked around the room. He could see the back of Josy's smooth head as she sat facing her companion, a tall, dark man, who was talking to her.

Slowly advancing towards them, Anthony suddenly realised that the man was wearing one of his own suits.

Taken aback and uncomprehending, he stood, a little behind Josy, looking at the stranger for a short moment. The man noticed him and rose. His dark eyes held Anthony in an unembarrassed look of appraisal.

The voices around them suddenly quietened down, and Anthony could almost feel all eyes scanning his face with disconcerting, if amiable attention.

"Oh, Anthony, Anthony", Josy jumped to her feet. She took his arm, and her voice trembling with excitement, led her startled husband forward, "This, this is my lost father . . . Captain Henryk Horaim".

The man looked at Anthony with smiling eyes, and held out his hand.

"I am sorry if I don't do justice to your excellent clothes, which I have been forced to borrow . . ."

He gave an easy chuckle,

"I am delighted to meet you at last. Over the past few days, Josy has told me so much about you that I already feel as if I have known you for ages. I cannot find the words to express my gratitude for the way you have looked after my daughter, and also for retrieving Vronovo from the Russians."

He had a light manner of speaking, and Anthony, dazed as he was, liked him instantly.

"Vivat! Vivat!", shouted someone from across the room, and all the guests joined in:

"Vivat! Here's to a brave man! Vivat Horaim!"

Suddenly they were surrounded by well-wishers; the men, suspiciously moist-eyed, kept slapping Henryk's back, and muttering admiringly about his amazing come-back from the dead, about his cocking a snook at the Russians . . .

The women wept openly for his late wife who " . . . died so tragically of a broken heart, not knowing, poor little thing, that her dear husband would one day come back . . ."

The atmosphere was charged with emotion.

Slowly, Anthony and Josy prised him away from the crowd.

Smiling sweetly, Josy steered the ladies to a side-table laden with a cold buffet, which had hurriedly been prepared by the suspiciously red-eyed Prakseda.

The men refilled their glasses, and noisily drank Henryk's health.

Free at last, Anthony led his father-in-law into a peaceful corner, where they sat down on a high backed sofa, its curved wings affording them some privacy.

People around them relaxed, and looking discreetly away, resumed their conversations.

Close by, a corpulent gentleman, in a sandy jacket and similarly coloured waistcoat, which was a bit too tight over his hefty calves, and wearing check trousers, loudly continued a long, rambling story about a shooting incident concerning a bear, which had occurred last spring:

"... Just then, I stepped backwards rather awkwardly, and lost my balance. As I fell, I dropped my rifle, and at that very moment, the brute leapt forward in two huge bounds. I was terrified! But remembering some old advice, I lay absolutely still pretending to be dead. Oh, but he was huge! He nudged me a few times, and I don't mind telling you that in my fright, I had an unfortunate accident. And would you credit it! The brute sniffed me with disgust, and went away... grumbling..."

Anthony met Henryk's eyes, and they both smiled.

"I didn't realise how many people knew you, and

judging by this splendid turn-out, how very popular you must have been . . ."

"I must say, I was very surprised and touched myself. It seems that the news of my return has spread like wild-fire."

Having recovered from his initial shock, Anthony fell in easily with Henryk's affable manner,

"I know it's a silly question, but where have you been all these years?"

Henryk took a drink from the tray proferred to him by a passing servant,

"It's a very long story, and not generally intended for the ears of strangers," his eyes lightly indicated the guests.

"I shall be able to tell you more later, but for now let's just say, I survived hidden in a remote Cossack village. The villagers helped me in every possible way: they healed my wounded leg, they nursed and fed me, but up until two years ago, we hadn't known about the amnesty. When the opportunity finally arose for me to leave, unfortunately it wasn't exactly with their blessing. And so when I found myself, one starry night, on the road, with the Cossack's stanitza so far behind me that it was not even a speck on the horizon, I was far too grateful at being free at long last, to worry about not having any money or a horse – and then of course I had no papers.

However, I knew that I had to be very careful because as I was officially dead, I could have been an easy target for all those who wished me ill.

"How long have you been travelling back?"

gasped a woman who had quietly come and sat down close to their sofa.

"It will be two years next month . . ."

"Oh, you poor, brave man, no wonder you look so, so exhausted . . .", she broke off, tearfully.

Henryk's shining eyes rested on her, and he smiled,

"How kind you are. But I am fine now, rest assured. One cannot expect to look one's best after so many months on the road." Josy pressed his hand,

"Prakseda and I will get you back to your usual self in no time at all."

For a moment, Henryk looked down. He did not mean to let all these people see how deeply their concern and what they said, had affected him. He still found it so difficult to believe that he really was back home, a home that still stood solid all these years later despite the reprisals, that Joanna was dead, just as Vassilisa had said, that little Thea had gone, and that he was a grandfather four times over . . .

With a chilling clarity, he remembered the assurance he had given to Vassilisa: " . . . and I shall be honour-bound to send for Katriona, I can promise you that . . ."

He could almost see the effect that her coming here would have on his guests and his family . . . What would they say if he were to marry the peasant girl?

Well, it was too early to do anything yet.

He had looked very little into the future, and had made no plans. The only thing he knew for now was that he wanted to get to know his family again, to find Thea . . . to bring about changes for the peasants . . . but first to just get well.

The friendliness of the people around rested him and he smiled. Again he made an effort to sound jovial,

"I have a few stories to tell you, if you are interested . . ."

"Interested? Are you joking?
We are all absolutely rivetted!"

They drew closer.

"Well then, I shall begin . . . It all started when the convoy had to stop for the night in the Cossack houtor, on the edge of the Ukrainian steppe . . ."

The hours passed, but nobody seemed to notice. They all sat there, listening, talking, laughing, and drinking, late into the starlit night, which was still warm, even though it was already October.

"Where do we start?" Anthony paused and held the door open for his father-in-law.

Henryk hesitated for a moment, but Anthony, who was watching him closely, could see from his face that his mind was already made up.

"I thought," he said slowly, "that it would be a good idea to meet the farm workers first to thank them for all their good wishes".

"Do you think they will appreciate it?"

Anthony stood awkwardly in the doorway looking him straight in the face but Henryk, his eyes down, put on his outdoor jacket, meticulously doing all the buttons up. He was so long in answering that Anthony thought he had refused to hear his question.

"Why should they be happy at my return?" Henryk asked at last.

"Whilst I haven't done anything particularly bad to be fearfully remembered by, equally I haven't made their lives better in any way. It is quite embarrassing to be greeted by these people as if I were a benevolent man, who has been sorely missed. I feel that I owe them, at least for now, a hand shake and a thank you".

Anthony turned a little as though surprised, and looked at his father-in-law reflectively for a second, before, evidently unsure of himself, decideding to say nothing.

They took a short cut through the barnyards, then the wind- swept, deserted orchard, and through the soggy, already ploughed for winter fields down to the narrow lane which led towards the village.

The farm workers' cottages squatted to the left of this road, their walls discoloured and covered in dark, damp patches.

It was Sunday, just after church, and most of the men were at home. Henryk followed Anthony into a passage between the houses. The street was narrow and winding, and it was difficult to see how many people lived there. Small groups of children played outside open doors, and as the two men passed by, they could smell food being cooked in every front room. Some of the older children, mainly girls, hurried to and fro with huge buckets hanging from the kolomysla* across their shoulders. Evidently, they had just fetched water from the nearby river and as they rushed home they had splashed not only their bare feet, but the road as well so that it was wet and sticky with slimy mud. In the makeshift gutters lay piles of rotting garbage, old and new, and the stench of it, was quite nauseating. In one dark corner, two thin dogs were growling at each other over a rancid bone. The children stopped their games and stood silently, staring at the visitors from under frowning brows, their eyes hostile, like little frightened animals.

Anthony walked slowly, choosing his steps with care, a faint expression of distaste on his face. Henryk followed him grimly. He was determined not to allow himself to surrender to his instinct. Perhaps it was easier for him, he thought, because he had had to endure cold, dirt and hunger on his journey back and could thus find pity in himself for this human cesspit.

During that long, lonely journey he had thought

incessantly of the changes that he would implement, and of making amends with God for letting him live. He saw the Cossack village, prosperous, clean and cosy as a model for his dream, but faced now with this reality, he was no longer sure. It was so unexpected, as if time had stood still here, drowned in this pool of stagnant water.

The future seemed lonely and difficult. Who here would be able here to understand that these men lived like animals because they weren't free. The Cossacks were serfs to no one, Vassilisa had once said, and he finally grasped the true sense of her proud statement.

What could he achieve on his own, or even with Anthony, without the support of all his neigbours? He could almost see their astonished, uncomprehending faces. Let the peasants be free, that was a sick joke, they would say.

The administrator had already warned him that any such notions would be strenuously opposed. From the pained expression on his face Henryk could sense the man's conviction that he wasn't being quite himself and should be closely watched. There was something else too in the administrator's face, an odd watchfulness, or fear perhaps . . .

He could not stop wondering why that should be.

Anthony looked at his watch.

"I'm afraid that we must go back to the house. It is almost lunch-time and Prakseda will be cross if we are late."

"I think that you're right. There is no point in my

talking to these men unless I can present them with something better than this . . ."

They slowly walked back, watched from behind by the silent children.

Anthony gave Henryk a searching look.

"You are probably wondering right now why I haven't done anything to improve the conditions here. Well, I somewhat naively thought that I had, but the cottages were renovated five years ago and are now in need of total repaire again. They won't do anything themselves, you know. I also had set up a village school for the children, but from the very start most of the men were against it. In the end, no one would send their children, so that was that."

"But why?"

"Well, they couldn't see any reason for their children to learn to read and write only to end up working in the fields like themselves. I had to admit that they had a point there. I am not so sure that I will ever be able to understand these people, after being used to the quick-thinking, street-wise ways of the men in the factories I used to own."

"Don't you think that someone might be putting these ideas into their heads?"

"The thought had crossed my mind, and it would not surprise me to discover who that might be . . ."

"The administrator?"

"I very strongly suspect that it's him. I'm also completing a lengthy investigation into the estate's financial affairs.

I think that he has been falsifying the receipts for quite some time now.

Worse still, I also think that he is guilty of something much more serious than fraud, but I must have proof before I can confront him."

"Does he know that you suspect him?"

"I don't think so. He is a violent man and I hope we will be able to alert the police first."

"If you need my help in any way, please say so . . ."

Anthony smiled,

"I am very grateful to you, but for now I must work by myself. But maybe later."

Henryk felt disappointed but he allowed no sigh or gesture to escape him.

"As you wish."

"I knew that you would understand."

A few weeks later, just after dinner, Anthony rose from the table.

"Would you mind if I said goodnight to you both? I have some work to do in the office, and I daresay that everyone will have gone to bed by the time I've finished."

He kissed Josy and bowed to Henryk.

"Don't stay up to late". Josy followed him to the door.

"I won't." He replied as he left the room.

The office which was tucked away in the east wing of the house was quite chilly at night, and after working for a couple of hours or so, Anthony felt cold. There was an unpleasant draught coming from somewhere and he got up to check the win-

dows, hidden behind the long curtains.
As he suspected one of them was open.
Annoyed, he made a mental note to admonish the maid. A quiet movement behind him took him by surprise. He turned swifly,

"What are you doing here?"

He didn't get an answer. A muffled shot rang out and Anthony fell heavily to the floor.

Josy was awakened by a loud knocking. She turned to Anthony's side of the bed only to find it empty. Her heart began to beat quickly. Had something happened?

Before she had time to rise, the door swung open and a man burst in.

"What are you doing here? What is the matter?" she gasped.

The administrator came to the foot of her bed and held up a little lamp. The light brought out from the darkness his sinister, agitated face.

She looked at him alarmed, and pulled the bed-cloths around her bare arms. She did not trust him.

"Come with me at once"

"Why? What's going on?"

Through the partly-open door Josy could smell burning wood.

In a panic, she jumped out of bed and put her dressing gown with shaking hands.

"You must keep calm. There is no time to lose. The whole of the eastern wing is ablaze."

"My God, Anthony is in the office!"

"He is alright. He sent me to get you, because he

wanted to warn your father himself. Get the children! Quick!"

Josy ran into the room next door and within seconds came back, leading a half-asleep Marylka and Cazimir. The man looked outside into the corridor and then turned to Josy,

"Give me the boy. You'd better hang on to my hand. We must leave now."

They hurried through the passage towards the staircase which led down into the main hall. The smoke had become quite thick now and they all started coughing.

"Down! Get down, for God sake!" He pushed Josy and the children to the floor making the little one cry out in fright.

"You must keep them calm! The smoke is getting dense now but there is a small amount of air still left at floor level left. Even if we have to crawl along inch by inch, we should be . . ."

An attack of cough made him let go of the whimpering child.

Cazimir gave a little cry and Josy grabbed him with one hand.

She held the crying children in front of her, pushing them forward across the unnaturally warm floor-boards.

"Hush, darlings! Everything will be alright," she kept whispering in a choked voice. Tears began to stream down her cheeks.

Where was Anthony? Where was her father?

Why had no-one come for them, except . . . except for this horrible man.

She didn't want to hold his hand and she tried to

guess directions by herself. Somewhere in the house, through the fog of smoke, she heard the sound of voices screaming orders, but they all seemed distant and muffled by this strange, all-encompassing noise.

At last, she recognised it, it was the sound of roaring fire.

The dark tunnel seemed endless. She didn't know where they were as she pushed the children in front of her.

Faster, oh, please, move faster, she pleaded.

Smoke was filling the passage and any moment now it could be too late for them. She cried out at the thought of leaving the other two boys without a mother and her beloved husband without the wife he adored. She was shivering now, despite the stifling warmth of the passage.

The administrator was no longer with them – he must have turned in the other direction . . .

She felt a hand on her shoulder. It was an odd sensation, as the touch was light yet compelling. She could not see anyone in the darkness, and confused and tearfull she cried out, "Anthony! Is that you?"

There was no reply but the guiding hand gave her something like an impatient push forward.

She did not have the strenght to resist, and she blindly followed the directions of the hand. The children stopped whimpering and hurried too as if understanding the urgency. Suddenly they all stumbled, and then softly fell down, rolling over and over as they went. But even then, she didn't lose her tight grip on the children, and when they finally came to a gentle halt, they were still entwined together in one big heap at the bottom of the stairs. Amazed that they had no broken bones or even bruises, Josy got up slowly.

Just in front of them the big, double-fronted door stood wide-open, and smiling through her tears, Josy led the children into the safety of the fresh air.

The sound of Prakseda's and children's crying, and strange voices rising around her came and went on a wave of choking nausea. Her head swimming, she took a deep breath and without knowing it, she fell at Prakseda's feet unconscious.

The pale light seeped through the drawn curtains and skimed her eyelids. Josy made an effort to open her eyes. From the side of her bed, a soft voice called her name. She recognised the gentle tones of her aunt, the Duchess Cornelia.

"You are safe now, Dear Josy. Just rest here. Everything has been taken care of."

"Where are the children? Anthony? Father?"

Her voice sounded hoarse as if the inside of her throat had been burned. Just saying those few words exhausted her and she drifted back into oblivion. The Duchess tucked the covers around her and wearily sat down, a sigh escaping her. It was fortunate indeed that Josy couldn't ask any more questions for if she knew the truth in her frail condition, it might have killed her.

When a few days later Josy finally regained her consciousness for good, there was nothing left for

Cornelia but to tell her the truth.
Pale and tired, the Duchess braced herself for the ordeal.
Josy sat rigid against the pillows, while Cornelia softly related to her the events of the past few days.

Vronovo had been burned down completely and there wasn't much left from the vast collection of furnishings. Josy and the children were taken back by Prakseda to the Lodge.

There was a strong suspicion that the fire, which had been started deliberately, could be linked to the administrator, but as he had been found dead, lying at the foot of the staircase, which led to the east wing, the inquiry did not have much to go on. Anthony's office had been destroyed and with it all the papers, which perhaps, could have shed some light on the matter.

Until now, Josy had waited patiently, but feeling she couldn't stand the uncertainty any longer, she interrupted the Duchess,

"Where are they? Where are they all?"
She faced Cornelia, her eyes welling with tears.
The Duchess leaned forward,

"You must take care not to tire yourself, my dear girl."

She took Josy's hand and patted it affectionately.

"The children are here, but Prakseda keeps them amused, away from your room. You really need some peace and quiet.
Josy pulled her hand away,

"And Anthony? Is he here too? And my Father?"

There was a silence between them. Finally in a voice breaking with emotion, the Duchess said quietly,

"God bless you, my child, for only He can ease your sorrow."

Josy stared right in front of her, feeling a scream rise within her, and then with surprised detachment, she heard someone screaming like a wounded animal.

It wasn't until a few days later that Josy was able to take in the full enormity of the tragedy. Even when she attended Anthony's and her father's funeral, she couldn't weep.

Like a statue of stone, she stood over the gaping graves, which had been freshly dug that morning. It was only the terrible pain in her heart that made her feel alive, and yet even then she instinctively knew that she had to be strong for her children. Thankfully for now, the Duchess took control of everything. There were arrangements to be made about the sale of the estate, and sorting out the financial position of the young widow.

It was decided that Josy would have to live in a small house in town, close to the schools, and the rest of the money would be used to set up a fund for the purpose of her children education.

The duchess accompanied by Miss Apolonia spent lengthy hours on discusion with her lawyer. Josy sighed everything into Cornelia's care, seemingly indifferent to the procedure.

"Right now the children and their happiness are

more important to her than the money. But then, without resources, it would not be possible to keep up the same standard of living as they were accustomed to when Anthony . . ."

Miss Apolonia's cool, distinguished voice faltered a little.

The lawyer nodded,

"One only has to take into account the price of land and the high inflation," he scribbled something onto a pad.

"The two elder boys still have several years of fee-paying, and then there would be an university. I understand their late father wished them to study at Heidelberg. That can be provided for."

The Duchess looked up from her papers,

"I still have enough left to educate Marylka. I know she was going to be sent to my old school, Sacrē Coeur, the girls' Lycee in Lvow."

Miss Apolonia's lips tightened,

"That only leaves little Cazimir."

The lawyer consulted his papers again.

To Miss Apolonia observing him quietly, he seemed like an eagle for he was a bald, dried-up man, thin and tall, with a precised manner so essential in his profession.

"Well, now," he assumed his even tone,

"I don't think that there will be sufficient funds left for Cazimir's university years. Nevertheless, with prudent investment, it should be possible to equip him reasonably well throughout his college time."

Slightly alarmed, he had to repeat his verdict, since the Duchess seemed to have lost herself in thoughts of the past.

She sighed heavily. It could not be helped, but she felt disappointment all the same. The happy past was brutally finished. She could only hope with all her heart that the future would bring some compassion and streght, and buoyant spirit to aid those children on any path they choose to follow.

Chapter Eight

The day Cazimir saw Kamenskoye for the first time was in the early Spring of 1902. The town, tucked in a small depression, formed by the River Dnepr coiling around the rich plateau of land, was a sprawl of houses and gardens, all gravitating towards the town's nerve centre – the Steelworks. To Cazimir, the distant works' buildings, gleaming pink in the morning sun, looked like a dream contained.

He had arrived only the day before, straight after graduating from college,and three weeks after his seventeenth birthday. It was the first time that Cazimir had left home and his mother, Josy, for more than a day, and he already felt unaccountably nervous. Involuntarily, his hand touched the brown envelope, safe inside the top-pocket of his best suit. It was a letter of recommendation from the Head of the College of Technology in Dubno.

When the clock on the church tower chimed seven, Cazimir knocked on the office door of the Chief Manager of the works. He waited for a minute or two, his mouth dry, and then knocked again. This time a booming voice called him in. It was a large, dark room, with a high ceiling and walls panelled in oak, and numerous shelves and the table crouched under masses of files and papers. A giant of a man stood up from behind an enormous desk, and sweeping his arm expansively, ushered Cazimir to a leather chair. Despite his size he sounded jovial and looked approachable.

"Ah yes, Cazimir, I know, I know . . . I have already had a letter about you from the college . . . only last week . . ."

Unsuccessfully, he tried rummaging among his papers for the letter, but then thinking better of it, he straightened up to give the young man a thorough, open appraisal; obviously satisfied, he continued,

"I have known Ivan Andrejevitz for a very long time, and I trust his judgement. If he has recommended you, it means you have got a future here. I shall put you in the draughtsmen's office to start with. If you show you have mettle, you will make fast progress – we are fair here."

He rose, indicating the end of the interview, but after motioning Cazimir to stay, he then pressed the bell-button on his desk. The door of the adjoining room opened and a bespectacled young man walked in.

"Good morning, Anton. Come and meet our new employee, Cazimir Anthonovitz. It's his first day here, and I thought he could start by getting acquainted with the works first. Take him around, will you . . ."

"Very well, sir ." replied Anton as he held the door open for Cazimir.

They left the building, and turned into the wide

entrance of the steelworks. The courtyard, littered with pieces of broken slag, bits of iron and skeins of wire, led into the hubbub of the workshop. A cacophony of noise hit them. Anton pointed to the huge, high furnace. A gaunt man, in dark glasses and protective clothing, stood several feet from the open furnace doors, stirring the red-hot liquid iron with a long rod, which was shaped like a giant ladle.

"Have you noticed what the rod is made of?" shouted Anton through the noise of the huge bellows and the rhythmical beat of the hammers.

Cazimir looked closer; the blackened rod was made of wood. He turned to Anton surprised.

"Yes, it's wooden. A metal rod would melt in seconds!"

Somewhere from behind their backs, a low train of open, metal baskets, full of ore, trundled rustily towards the side of the furnace. Each basket was raised by a special lift to the open mouth of the furnace before being emptied swiftly. Cazimir looked amazed, and Anton couldn't help a smile,

"Wait until the pour – then you'll see something to talk about."

"When is the pour?"

Anton checked his fob watch. "It should be any moment now . . ."

A loud bell drowned their voices. The founder solemnly put on a hat with a wire net, covering his face. Next, went on knee-pads, a thick hide apron and finally, long, wide gloves. Only then did he slowly drill, using an oxyacetylene flame, the opening through which the fluid mass of iron would flow.

The semi-darkness around them was suddenly lit up by the flash of a thousand burning stars. From the mouth of the furnace gushed a stream of flame-coloured lava, which glided swiftly through the channels and into the waiting containers. The luminous glow, the heat and the sheer brilliance of the oscillating colours took Cazimir completely by surprise. He looked on, spellbound. He felt moved beyond reason and breathlessly light of heart; so much so that when the founder removed his hat and gloves, and came to greet them, Cazimir, without a word, shook his hand strongly.

"Would you like to see more?" Taking Cazimir's silent nod for agreement, Anton led him to the ironsmith's workshop. There, shimmering sheets of metal flowed, with a haunting, strange whining, from the rolling-mills onto the wide benches. The sound of this alien music made Cazimir come out in goose pimples, and yet he wanted to stay right here in the middle of this workshop and listen more. He turned to Anton with an embarrassed smile,

"This is as beautiful as any music. I didn't know that poetry is not only in flowers and music . . ."

"And yet this is a man's place. They say a man needs certain attributes here: skill, stamina and courage . . ."

Anton gave the young man a kind look, and was somewhat surprised when he met Cazimir's burning, excited eyes.

"Welcome to the club – you have caught the bug too." Anton gave a short laugh and pointed to a dark entrance at the far end of the rolling-mill.

"The foundry is next, over there. Shall we go?"

Reluctantly, Cazimir followed Anton across the iron-dust covered floor.

The foundry produced wrought-iron gates, fences and ornate lifts, and Cazimir couldn't help but admire the half-naked, sweat-gleaming torsos of the men, working in every part of the workshop. It was a dark place, almost pagan with its wildly leaping hearth flames, the rhythmical beat of hammers on the anvil, and dusty, narrow windows. Again, Cazimir stood watching, moved in a strange way. It was as if he was taking part in an ancient, sacrificial ritual, as old as humanity itself.

That evening Cazimir wrote the first of many letters to his mother:

" . . . I never thought I would find anything to equal university and working in research, but the steelworks are my future and my vocation now, and I only wish you could see for yourself how intoxicating this place is. It's real men's work; I love it with a passion . . ."

The next few months Cazimir spent almost entirely at the steelworks. Fiodor Yakimovich, the chief engineer, smiled under his moustache every time he caught a glimpse of the tall boy rushing past his door.

"That new boy has his head well-screwed on. Have you noticed?" Anton looked up from his plate of lamb-stew. Fiodor's eyes were following Cazimir's progress across the canteen floor, his arms full with a plate of stew, bread and books. "Like a young colt, eh? But I like him – he's quite indispensable in that eager-to-please way of his . . ." Anton nodded, his attention on the last bit of gravy he was mopping up with bread. "And another thing . . .", Fiodor continued, his gaze still on the boy. Cazimir sat at an awkward angle, engrossed in his book and eating slowly.

" . . . have you noticed how he gobbles up anything you tell him about the work?"

A smile lightened Anton's face, "Yah, he reminds me of all those days that I had to spend over the manuals, but I still think practice is the best tutor."

Just then Fiodor remembered that Anton had failed his finals, and it would be better to drop the tricky subject altogether.

Three years later, Cazimir qualified as a junior engineer. At about the same time, he met Maria, the eldest daughter of one of his colleagues at work, John Zelski. An experienced steel engineer, John came from a town situated almost two thousand miles away in the West. His family were to follow after he had settled and found a suitable house. For a short time, John shared with Cazimir boarding accomodation at Mrs. Novcova's 'Rooms To Rent' place. They often spent evenings together. The older man, touched by Cazimir's enthusiasm, didn't mind lengthy technical discussions, while in return, Cazimir listened to John's talks of his lovable, large family. In the short time it took to find a house, he learned so much about John's wife,

Melanie, and his five daughters that they could almost have been his own relations. Although their conversations were interwoven with anecdotes about every one of his children, Cazimir felt that somehow Maria, the eldest daughter, was John's favourite, since his voice would change and soften at the very mention of her kind, sunny nature and her exquisite beauty. Intrigued, Cazimir could hardly wait for their coming.

Two Sundays after the arrival of John's family, Cazimir received an invitation to tea at their new house. It was his first formal visit since his coming to Dniepropietrovsk, and he put on his best suit; the same dark suit he had worn at his first day at the steelworks. On the way out he caught a glimpse of himself in the hall mirror and felt a twinge of surprise at seeing the reflection of a tall, well-groomed stranger. However unexpected, the feeling gave him pleasure, and he quickened his pace.

The house, which had been built on an old settlement, was freshly painted white, and stood in a pleasant, mature garden. Cazimir rang the bell, and a young maid with shy, downcast eyes, led him into the drawing room, where one of two voluptuously curved crimson sofas was already occupied by the other guests. The family photographs in teak frames formed an oval pattern on the wall opposite. As Melanie, John's wife, came from an army family, the photographs showed stern-faced men, dressed in uniforms or long army coats and tall fur hats.

On a round table covered in cream lace over a crimson hand-woven cloth, steamed a silver samovar. Plates and platters heaped with hot blinis and chopped boiled eggs, soft butter-cakes, wild cherry confitures in crystal bowls, honeyed young cucumbers and whole small tomatoes with dill, stood ready to be served. Tiny, gold-rimmed glasses surrounded a crystal decanter filled with blackberry liqueur.

Mrs. Novcova, John's previous landlady, a plump blonde with hair piled high, was handing out strong Russian tea in wide china cups, chattering excitedly in her melodious, breathless voice.

"Ah, Melanie, you cannot even imagine how John missed you all! I honestly used to despair. Wouldn't eat much, the poor man. Now, of course, he seems like a new person . . ."

Melanie listened, smiling absent-mindedly, and poured yet another cup of tea for Mr. Schevchenko. The local school-teacher sat upright on the edge of the sofa in his dark sourdut and stiffly-starched shirt, and sipping tea from his saucer, as was the Russian custom, discreetly observed the four young Misses Zelski.

"Perhaps a bit shy, but their eyes are bright . . .", he thought, before being pleasantly distracted by Mrs. Novcova's plump arm offering a heaped plate of hot blinis, oozing melted butter.

"Do try these – they are simply delicious . . ."

At the window, John and Mr. Levicki discussed the latest news from the Manchurian front.

"You know, I don't think that the Russians can hold out much longer. Why, they have lost most of their troops and ships, and now even their own army is mutineering . . . I take it that you read about the Potemkin affair?"

"I did, and I am not too happy about the way things are going at the moment. It is no good for business. Only last week, I had an order cancelled, and prices are falling . . ."

Wedged between the arm of the sofa and Mrs. Levicka, the gentle, stammering wife of the wool-importer, Cazimir surveyed the table. The sumptuous array of dishes and the silver samovar brought back memories of countless Sunday teas at Vronovo, making him suddenly feel homesick. He looked discreetly at Melanie's kind but plain face, echoed in her small daughters, and wondered about the parental love, which made John see Maria as beautiful. And where was she anyway?

As usual, kind Mrs. Novcova was the first to notice his detachment.

"Ah, Cazimir, perhaps a little cucumber with honey. It's from my garden, you know."

Smiling with gratitude, Cazimir accepted the honeyed cucumber and took a bite. Just then, Mrs. Levicka asked hesitantly,

"Yyou wwork . . . at the steelworks . . . too?"

Before he could answer, the door swung open and the eldest of Zelski's daughters walked, no, glided in. Cazimir swallowed hard, and almost choked on an overly large bit of cucumber. Never in his entire life had he seen a girl so beautiful. Tall and slender, she had the perfect figure of an Amazon, a radiant face with starry, cornflower-blue eyes, but her hair was the most extraordinary. It framed her face in a golden halo, and then went down to the small of her back in a thick plait. The soft upturned corners of her well-defined mouth gave the impression that she was always ready to smile.

Introduced to everyone, she perched playfully on the arm of her father's chair and joined in the conversation as if she had known the guests all her life. Cazimir observed her from under his brows. He envied the apparent ease with which she conversed with perfect strangers, and her charming gaiety. Tongue-tied and rather silent, Cazimir listened to the sweet sound of Maria's voice, and thought that her beauty was strangely moving. To his own amazement, he realized with an utmost, painful certainty that she was the girl he was going to marry.

During the next two months, Cazimir saw a good deal of Maria, and her family began to treat him like one of their own. Melanie and the younger girls became used to the young couple talking and laughing at their evidently private jokes.

"Those two are forever engrossed in something or other . . ." observed Melanie softly.

"Do you think Maria is serious about him?"

"Oh, I do hope so – he's such a lovely boy!"

John looked at his wife,

"The boy is as dear to me as if he were ours," he sounded wistful, and Melanie couldn't help smiling.

"Don't worry, it looks as though those two were made for each other. Just give them time and don't rush things as you always do . . ."

Unconvinced, John decided to probe a little.

"It seems that he is awfully in love with you . . ." he remarked to Maria one Sunday after dinner.

"That's just as well, because he is the man I am going to marry . . .", Maria gave her father a dazzling smile as she spoke, and John couldn't tell if she was being serious.

"He is a young man of promise, clever and utterly decent, and nothing would please me more," he answered gravely.

Maria kissed his head. "Tra-la-la, Papa, there is something else I can see in Cazimir . . ." Laughing, she ran away, leaving John completely baffled.

Not long after that, Cazimir took Maria on a long-promised tour of the steelworks. She was curious to see what was so special about the place, which enticed both of the men she loved. The mysterious atmosphere of the forge, full of dark and wonderful spirits, heart-touching sounds, and the unexpected, spellbinding spectacle of the pour, had the same effect on her as it had done on Cazimir; and on impulse, she touched his arm in a gesture of understanding. Their eyes met, and in the red glow of the fires, Maria's face seemed infinitely beautiful, and solemn. Cazimir turned her to face him, and, looking intently into Maria's eyes, asked,

"Would you do me the honour of becoming my wife?"

To his surprise, Maria's answer came clear and without hesitation,

"I thought you would never ask."

Within a week, the young couple had become officially engaged, to the delight of John and Melanie. Cazimir thought himself the happiest man in the world, and he begged John to allow the wedding to take place as soon as was decently possible.

In the meantime, he searched for a house of their own, and was able to buy one straight away. His mother, on hearing about the engagement and Cazimir's yearning to give Maria "everything, the whole world if possible," wrote back a lengthy letter, which ended:

"As to the price of the property, you should be able to afford a reasonable place. I have saved quite a large sum from the sale of Vronovo, and I consider it only proper that you should use it to acquire a home; after all, you are the one who missed out on the education which your brothers received."

The letter also contained a hundred and one questions about Maria, all designed in such a way that in order to answer them, Cazimir would have to stop and think hard to see if he knew all there was to know about his future bride. He could not help smiling at the consummate skill with which Josephine elicited the information she wanted from him. Maria was perfect in every way, and even his beloved mother would have to agree with his judgement, given time.

The house, which Cazimir bought, backed, through a long garden and orchard, almost straight onto the River Dniepr; surrounded by old trees, the place was otherwise secluded.

The wedding of Cazimir and Maria made an event in the small town, and was remembered for a long time afterwards. They settled into their comfortable, large house and Maria set about creating a home for them both.

In later years, on looking back, it seemed to Cazimir as if in those days it had been summer for months on end. He would hasten home, and without changing his clothes, he would rush around the house, searching for Maria. Often he would find her somewhere in the one of the back rooms, engrossed in sorting out the masses of presents, given to them by the wedding guests. Without warning, she would find herself lifted up into Cazimir's arms, still holding a cloth of some sort, and waltzed across the spacious floors.

Sometimes she would be in the garden, tending the freshly-dug beds or planting another bush, her hands covered in earth and her cotton dress crumpled. Half-teasingly, half-serious, she would push Cazimir away,

" . . . Don't touch me now, I am hot, sweaty and dirty. Let me go!"

Cazimir breathed in the hot, moist scent of her body, a healthy mixture of soap and fresh sweat, and felt the blood throbbing in his temples. Helplessly laughing, Maria would be carried upstairs to their vast bedroom. But there were times when going up the stairs seemed such a waste of time in their urgency. Solemnly and carefully, Cazimir would lay Maria down on the long, soft grass, surrounding the apple tree. Breathless and willing, Maria would help him to unbutton her blue cotton dress, and with a strange, melting feeling, she watched, enthralled, how in the diffused light of the late afternoon sun, Cazimir's eyes, heavy with desire, turned almost black in his tense face . . .

Their devastating passion for each other was totally absorbing, and the world had decreased to a small circle, where there was no place for anyone else. Faintly alarmed, Maria's family waited patiently, sure that it would only be a matter of time before the young couple settled into a more seemly routine. Josy, Cazimir's widowed mother, remembering the wildly passionate days of her earlier married life, was relieved to see her favourite son so happily married.

Their first-born child, a little girl Elizabeth, didn't change much in their relationship. They simply included the baby in everything they did, and if anything, she enhanced their life.

Two years later Maria was pregnant again. Their happiness, sometimes almost more than they could bear, made Maria want to share it with her beloved father. On a rare occasion when the two of them were alone together, she hugged him, saying,

"Papa, I am so very happy".

John smiled, but in his heart, sighed. He belonged to the old generation, who believed that an open admission of one's happiness was unlucky, but he said nothing as he held her close.

Then quite suddenly and without warning, the last few weeks before her confinement made Maria horribly ill, and a distraught Cazimir sought help and advice from three doctors. All agreed that something was wrong, but what exactly, they could not diagnose at this stage.

The birth was prolonged and difficult. The little baby boy, born at dawn, was weak and distressed, but alive. Cazimir's relief was beyond measure. Overwhelmed with joy, he hardly noticed Melanie, who was alternately crying and laughing, or an ashen-faced John. Maria was safe and he had a baby son.

A week later, Maria's doctor unexpectedly requested to see Cazimir. A tall, ramrod-like man, the doctor came to the point without preamble.

"Your wife is not as well as would be expected. Her confinement confirmed my previous suspicion that she has a kidney problem . . ."

He hesitated as if embarrassed at being the bearer of bad news. Stunned, Cazimir said nothing, for his heart had given a sickening lurch. It seemed ages before the doctor continued.

"I am very sorry that I have to say this . . . Your wife cannot, under any circumstances, have any more children. If she were ever to become pregnant again, it would certainly necessitate an abortion. Continuation of the pregnancy would lead to one thing only for her – death."

He paused for an instant as though he were hesitant to say more, but then, without looking at Cazimir, he touched his arm in compassionate support, and left.

Alone, Cazimir could almost feel the oppressive stillness of the room, and with a strange, detached clarity, he sensed his happiness disintegrating into an elusive, already distant, past. The silence was intolerable, and he broke down and wept for the second time in his life.

After that conversation, Cazimir and Maria's life changed irrevocably. The unbounded, wild affair, which their marriage had been, had given way to a serious thoughtfulness, devoid of magic. The year was 1908, and contraception was virtually unknown. While Cazimir could still hear the doctor's impassive voice, Maria, fully recovered and well, felt the harsh verdict might have been due to the doctor's over-reaction to her difficult labour.

"I don't think there is any danger of my dying. Why, I feel as strong as a horse. The old dear is probably just fussing too much . . ."

"We cannot take any chances. I just can't bear to even think about anything happening to you . . .", Cazimir's voive quavered.

Maria gave him a look of such tenderness that all their fears forgotten for a moment, they clung and held together, strong against the menacing unknown.

On the surface everything seemed to have returned to normal. Cazimir engaged a maid, a nanny and a cook to relieve the strain of looking after the house and two young children.

The spring of 1911 was particularly beautiful. Behind their house, the orchard trees, bushes and hedges were a riot of colour and scent. Clear at last of a cold, wintry mist, the Dniepr rippled and glistened in silvery-green strands, with every breath of air.

In May, Maria became pregnant again.

"I shall speak to the doctor at once", said Cazimir.

"No, leave this to me." Maria smiled sweetly, but he knew it was her way of keeping him calm.

Not much was gained from the subsequent visit – the old doctor was adamant,

"My dear child, either you have an abortion as soon as possible or . . . well, there is no doubt about that."

Maria's eyes suddenly filled with tears. The old doctor, misunderstanding her despair for fear, patted her hand as if she were a fretful child,

"There, there now, you mustn't worry. It will be over in no time at all."

When Cazimir looked at Maria's face, outside the doctor's surgery, he knew at once that they were confronting a decision, which, either way, would affect their lives profoundly. While deeply religious, Cazimir somehow felt absolutely sure that they should not have any doubts,

"We must go back right now, and make arrangements for . . . the abortion".

At the sound of the word, Maria shivered, her face pale and uncustomarily serious. At last, she found her voice,

"I cannot decide here – please, please, let's go

home!"

Cazimir didn't argue. His mind was made up – there was no question about it – he wanted Maria safe and out of danger, however slight. He was sure of John and Melanie's full support, and he relaxed a little with this knowledge.

A family conference was called and Cazimir stated the facts calmly, his face pale and set. He looked expectantly at his in-laws. John listened, his eyes were wet with tears; Melanie sat with clasped hands, her normally contented, pink face haggard. She faced Cazimir and her husband,

"Surely something can be done?"

Cazimir spoke with calm insistence, "Yes, there is only one thing to be done – an abortion."

As he finished saying that horrible word again, he gave Maria a quick glance. She sat motionless, staring at the elaborate wallpaper opposite. Melanie cried softly,

"Is there nothing else we can do?"

Before Cazimir could answer, John interrupted,"We all hate this solution, but if it's the only way to save you, my child, then it has to be!"

The insistent voices of the men, and her mother's soft crying made Maria shudder. Why did nobody ask her? She waited for a moment, but since no one spoke, she stood up and turned to Cazimir,

"I think you ought to know . . . in two days' time I am going back to Plock to see Father Damian."

Astonished, Cazimir looked at her questioningly.

"He was my chaplain at school and gave me my faith . . ."

Cazimir felt a sudden chill in his heart, for he

already knew what she was going to say next.

"I trust him with my life; if he says that I should have . . . it, then I won't argue. But if he decides against it, I shall leave my fate in God's hands, and accept whatever may come . . ."

Tears began to stream down her cheeks, and Cazimir caught her in his arms. There was something about her expression which made him change his mind,

"If you feel that it will help you, I won't stop you going. Perhaps, Melanie could come with you . . ."

"I will pack at once," Melanie wiped her eyes, and gave a pale smile.

Frowning, John looked unconvinced and confused. However strong his family's religious beliefs, this was an exception. He didn't like the delay, uncertainty and risk involved. He decided to say nothing, but his silence was heavy with unease and despair.

Two days later, both women left for Plock as planned in good spirits and a great deal calmer. Father Damian was regarded by many as being a saint. An ascetic old man, who had turned away from the pettiness of human distractions, he had the serenity of different, distant worlds. If anyone could advise on matters of life and death, he certainly was the right person.

The long journey left Maria exhausted, so she stayed in her room at the small hotel situated conveniently near the station. Having spent several days travelling in the company of strangers, she was glad to be alone. Melanie had gone out to arrange the meeting at the monastery and would not be back before the evening meal.

The sparse impersonality of the hotel room made her feel restless. She thought incessantly about her small children and her beloved Cazimir. The times of happy love seemed thousands of years away, and however much she tried to find it, she knew there was no way back.

She thought over and over again about the way in which she had been brought up to believe, trustingly and without the slightest doubt in God's goodness and mercy, but now she could no longer understand. Only a few years back, it seemed, at her Confirmation, Father Damian had given her a picture to commemorate the day. It showed a little girl crossing a fallen tree over a busy stream. Behind the child followed a guardian angel, ready to save her from a fall or any hidden dangers . . . This was the only way she knew and understood God. Trust, she must have trust, and everything would end well . . .

But then the doubts came back, and the thought that she could be taken from her loved ones, was more than she could bear. She wanted to return to them at once. With mounting despair, she remembered the baby – what about the baby? Could she kill it in cold blood? It was her child too, and she loved it already. The dilemma was breaking her resolve, and she cried desperately at the awful feeling of impotence, of being unable to do anything, anything at all, that would not hurt someone in the end.

She decided to at least write to Cazimir and the

children every day of her absence, and this resolve brought her slight consolation. She started in earnest.

"My very dearest Cazimir, . . ."

A day later, Maria got out of the hired coach, which had taken her almost to the gates of the monastery, and slowly walked up the worn stone steps. The young monk who answered the gate, led her through a courtyard, and then down a long passage to a room on one side of it. She sat on a wooden bench under the window, which opened wide onto the sun-strewn garden, and waited.

The door opened quietly as Father Damian came in. He didn't seem to have aged much since she had seen him last. He looked at Maria with piercing blue eyes, a smile on his lips.

"How are you, my dear?"

Maria grasped his hands. She had wanted to greet him, calm and grown-up, but instead she began to cry as if she were still his young charge, asking for help with a grazed knee or cut finger. The old monk sat her down, and brought her a glass of water from the table. He looked at her kindly,

"What is the matter, my child?"

Each word, which Maria had prepared so carefully in her mind, now seemed unimportant. Between sobs, she blurted out her awful dilemma.

"Why, Father? Why? Is it because I have been so happy? How could it be wrong to love my own husband?"

The monk stroked her head and shaking shoulders,

"Hush, my child, you have done nothing wrong, nothing at all. I wish we knew all the answers, but God's judgements are inscrutable."

Maria clasped her hands in despair, and looked the old monk full in the face,

"Father, I have a husband and small children. I love them more than it's possible to say. What should I do, what in God's name should I do?"

She waited, trembling and stifling her sobs, tense and intent, to the limits of human endurance, on his answer.

Father Damian stood still, seemingly looking at the garden and beyond. At last he turned to face her,

"You mentioned your two children and husband, but the unborn one is your child too . . . Who else will protect him, if not you, his mother?"

He looked at Maria with infinite kindness, but his eyes were sad and reproachful.

Maria paled to hear him say that; her heart beating wildly, she rose to go. He didn't seem aware of her despair. His belief uncluttered by doubts, he seemed surprised that she didn't see it clearly.

"'Thou shalt not kill'," he said at last, very quietly. "Don't be down-hearted, my child. Trust in God, for there is no other way for us . . ."

Maria decided to stay at Plock for a week longer. She wanted time to think, to plan the next few months carefully, and the familiar little town of her childhood seemed to sustain the comfort she derived from it. As gently as she could, she explained her decision to her anxious mother. Melanie wasn't brave. Her cosy, secure life had never been touched by tragedy, and now faced with one, she wondered how she would cope. What if something happened to Maria? What then? She couldn't understand the calm manner which her daughter displayed outwardly, while she herself was frightened out of her wits . . .

It wasn't her fault that she wasn't cut-out to be a heroine, and now Maria's inhuman courage gave her sleepless nights and indigestion. They really ought to change the cook at this place. I will have a fit if I have to eat their sloppy food for another week! she thought fretfully. And John probably isn't eating anything. Apprehensively she wondered how John would react to the decision. It wasn't going to be easy, she sighed unhappily – he loved his daughter fiercely and there was no telling what he would do . . .

Three weeks passed before Maria saw again the dusty Kamenskoye station. It was early morning and the clear air indicated a fine day. Even before the train had stopped, Maria saw the anxious faces of Cazimir and her father, who were waiting on the platform. She stood impatiently at the open carriage door, and waved. Oh, the joy of being back home! It was the first time that she had been parted from her beloved husband, and her heart lurched at the sight of Cazimir, now running towards her. Without waiting for the slowing train to stop, she jumped into his arms.

The euphoria of her return didn't last long. Back at home, Maria had to explain again her decision. It disconcerted her to realize how much they wanted to protect her whatever the cost. Weary after the journey, she thought for a while, both men waiting patiently. Unable to hold back any longer, Cazimir put his arms around Maria, his eyes on her face.

"I have decided to have our child, and . . . and, we must trust in God . . .", she said simply.

"But the doctor is totally against such a decision!"

John was now quite angry. "And I disagree too!"

Maria faced her father solemnly, who felt his eyes drawn to hers.

"I have to listen to my conscience first, Papa – no one can make this decision for me. Father Damian reminded me only of what I should have remembered myself. I have to . . . I want to give our child a chance."

For a moment she had a picture in her mind of the kind eyes looking down at her so reproachfully. She saw that her father was about to speak again, and without waiting, she sprang to her feet and left the room, closing the door behind her.

A whole week passed before Cazimir finally accepted that Maria's decision was final. It was obvious that she believed with her whole heart that she had to protect her unborn child first, and that God would protect her. She seemed to have softened and mellowed, and yet he could not make her understand the gravity of their situation. As it was, every day made it worse, and it was simply going to be too late.

"What will happen to us if anything goes wrong? The doctor is very concerned." He tried to reason with Maria.

"If anything happens to me?" She looked up at Cazimir with her beautiful eyes, and smiled. "You will have to bring up our children properly, and help my parents, and live in this house forever, and remember me . . . and . . ."

She didn't finish, for her husband knelt down and put his arms around her, his face against her dress, feeling the warmth of her body.

"If anything happened to you, God forbid, I would go with you!"

"Hush, darling. No more of this silly morbid talk! Nothing, nothing will happen. There is nothing to fear, I am sure of that."

She stroked his head, and spoke little words of reassurance and love. He wanted to believe it so much, and her calm tenderness had at last the desired effect.

The weeks and then months that followed were filled with tranquil happiness. Elizabeth and little Boleswav spent most of their time playing with

Maria. She took strength from holding their young bodies, kissing their soft faces, talking their joyful, animated talk, or simply watching her children safely asleep: the shadow of butterfly eyelashes sweeping the flushed curve of a cheek, and the small, softly breathing, half-parted mouth . . . She felt she could watch them forever.

Sometimes, involuntarily she would hold Elizabeth too close, and the fretful child would push her away.

"It hurts, Mummy . . ."

"Oh my darling, did I hug you too hard? It's only because I love you so . . ."

Slowly, taking care not to be noticed, Maria tidied every drawer, every chest and cupboard in the house. She wrote long letters to friends and family, and when finally there was nothing more to be done, she relaxed.

Sometime around late autumn, Cazimir arranged a surprise visit to a photographer in town. Elizabeth in cream lace and Boleswav, still in a little dress as was customary for very young boys, came too. The portrait was being taken for the grandparents, and Maria put on John's favourite dark blue dress. She wanted to make amends. Her father had seemed so very quiet during the past few months, and it wrung her heart to see him so unhappy. Only now, herself a mother, could she understand how much he worried about her.

Cazimir looked at the portrait in shocked disbelief. The realisation that he was no longer a young, carefree man, came as a complete surprise;

why, he wasn't even thirty yet. From the portrait frame, a sombre family group looked out sternly into the camera. Maria's pale face seemed tragic against her dark dress, and only little Elizabeth had a mischievous sparkle in her eyes.

With a sudden chill, Cazimir realised why the picture seemed so strange – it looked as if the photograph had been taken after somebody's funeral. Terrified, he gasped in a low tone. Quickly, before Maria could notice, he tried to pull himself together.

"What nonsense. There is nothing to fear. God must be with us. I should not doubt Him, not even for a second!"

Just before Christmas, Josephine arrived, breezy and cheerful.

"I could not stay away: you know how I love babies, and perhaps, you may find something for me to do."

She hugged Maria, before crouching on the floor to kiss the children and unpack the presents. Elizabeth gave a gasp of delight when Josy pulled out a beautiful, china doll, almost as tall as the child herself. Cazimir could already hear her planning games with the children and making Maria laugh with her description of her fellow passengers on the train.

". . . and the woman sitting opposite me had to take her girdle off, she was so hot. Her eyes were popping out from her shiny red face! I thought she was going to faint! But you'll never guess what she had for breakfast in the station buffet! Sausages!

Must have been close to a good pound, and of course, those butter buns to go with them! And what do you think her husband said? 'My wife is so delicate!'"

Both Josy and Maria giggled with such carefree abandon that Cazimir breathed a sigh of relief. His mother was here and she would banish any dark terrors from the house.

Knowing of Cazimir's interest in science, Josephine had brought with her a French newspaper with the latest news.

"One can hardly believe this! Our own Maria Sklodowska has won a second Nobel Prize! Shame that she had to leave Poland to be able to study what she wanted."

Cazimir read the article slowly. For a split second, he felt a pang at not having been able to do in life what he once had wanted so much. It did not matter now – he would be blissfully happy, if only Maria would be well . . .

The Russian winter was usually at its worst in February, and that year it was as bad as ever. The snow rose half-way up the iced window-panes and the frost took one's breath away. For the past few weeks, Maria had felt sick, and from time to time she would feel an odd pain in her back. She decided to say nothing as she was able to endure it, and she would hate to worry Cazimir unnecessarily. It was natural that she should feel that way – after all, God willing, she should be having her baby quite soon. She remembered the doctor's instructions, and his concerned face. Perhaps he was a little surprised that she had come such a long way without a hint of trouble after all.

During one visit, when he and Cazimir were left alone, he said quietly,

"The worst is not now, you know, but yet to come. If her kidneys continue working during and just after the confinement, we can safely say that all is well. But if not . . . ," he frowned.

A few nights later Maria woke with a start. She recognised at once the peculiar feeling of being unwell. She had felt like that previously, moments before she had had her other two babies. Cazimir sat up the instant she moved.

"Are you alright?"

She leaned against him, braving the pain rising within her body.

"I think you had better send for the doctor – it hurts now . . ." She held him close, and then kissing him on the mouth, said solemnly, "Whatever happens, don't worry. I will be all right. I promise."

He was out of bed in a second, and she could hear him knocking on Josephine's door. Within minutes, everything was organised as planned. Maria wanted to change into a fresh nightdress but the odd pain, the old one, came back with such ferocity that she screamed. She realised in a panic that she was being torn by birth pains, and at the same time, far worse by the pain in her back. Hot and sweating, she tried to raise herself on the pillows, but before she could call for help, she was violently sick.

Josephine rushed in with water, towels and bowls. Hurriedly the bed was changed around Maria, who, by then drenched in sweat, was fighting for breath. Then she retched again. Josy cleaned the bilious substance off the floor, bending down to hide a face frozen in terror.

The doctor arrived and grimfaced, followed Cazimir up the stairs. A harsh scream made them almost run. Maria lay in a disarrayed bed, her wan face deep in the pillows. Crying softly, the maid stood by, holding the bowl with water. Cazimir knelt by the bed, and held Maria's hand, hanging down at the side. He looked at her face in desperation. Her half-closed, liquid eyes flickered and focused wearily on him. Her lips moved, but at the same time, pain seized her body again, and she cried out an awful, animal-like scream. Choking with anger and despair, his voice hoarse, Cazimir turned to the doctor washing his hands meticulously.

"For God's sake, do something, quick!"

The doctor dried his hands and leaned over Maria, checking her pulse.

"I think that it would be better if you waited downstairs," his voice betrayed little emotion.

Cazimir shook his head, without taking his eyes from Maria.

"You will only impede my work." The doctor drew a syringe, and motioned to Josephine.

Without a word, Cazimir rose and went out into the corridor. He could hear behind the closed door, quick movements, and urgent commands. Once or twice, the maid ran out to fetch something, her face pinched from crying. Cazimir stood by the door, staring straight at the wall in front of him and trembling inside in terror. Panic seized him, making him feel sick and cold in the pit of his stomach. He didn't realis that his hands were shaking, for his mind was on one thought only. His lips moved in a silent, but urgent, prayer,

"I shall not doubt You, I shall not doubt You, I shall not doubt You, merciful God!"

Downstairs, Melanie dressed with unsteady hands the sleepy children, ready to take them home, while John sat alert in the drawing room, his hands clenched.

A faint noise came quite suddenly from behind the door; it was a child crying – a pitiful sound, like a kitten mewling. Cazimir stood still. He didn't dare open the door. It seemed to him that there was nobody else there except for that fretful creature, and silently he begged God to spare his wife. He lost all sense of time. After what seemed like eternity, the door opened quietly as the doctor came forward, motioning him inside.

Cazimir rushed into the room, and leant over Maria. She lay still, a small bundle in the crook of her motionless arm. Her eyes were half-closed, and she looked asleep.

"It is the morphine. At least she is no longer in pain."

"Is there any hope?"

John, who was standing behind the doctor, looked at his daughter with vacant eyes, his face drained of colour. Cazimir turned to him. "She is only asleep, I wish you wouldn't . . ."

"I am sorry, but there is no hope. It is only a matter of time. I cannot believe myself that it had to end like this – I thought she would make it . . . And the baby . . . it is a girl."

The doctor looked worn-out, old and angry.

Cazimir was aware that Josephine held his arm, but nothing mattered now.

"Please go, all of you. I want to be alone with my wife."

The door closed behind them and Cazimir bent over Maria, urgently searching her face for any sign of recognition, desperate to make contact, even if only for a moment, even if for the very last time.

The baby slept and he looked at the red, puckered face with distaste. How could this little girl be worth his wife's life? In desperation, he leant again over Maria, his mouth directly on her ear.

"Don't leave me now! You promised, you said there was nothing to fear, didn't you? You can't leave now, not now . . . Wait! Wait for me! Do you hear me?"

Maria lay still, strange and unrecognisable. Her eyes seemed to stare somewhere into the distance. Cazimir kissed her once, and then again. She had to wake up. Impatiently, he grasped her shoulders and tried to hold her up, but her limp head fell to one side like the head of a rag doll, and with a terrifying realisation, he heard someone crying. The awful sound of harsh, broken sobs.

Josephine gently eased Maria's body from his

arms. The doctor gave him an injection and he was led from the room, unaware of the chaos left behind him.

When he woke up hours later, he felt numb. He remembered that Maria had gone. Somehow it didn't matter now. All he wanted was to go with her, and he calmly thought about it. It seemed to him that if he waited, death would come very soon. Anyway, even the effort of opening his eyes seemed too much, and so he lay in darkness, feeling nothing but infinite weariness. For some reason, he kept turning grindingly, over and over, in his mind the most important date: Friday, 2nd February, 1912, Friday, 2nd February 1912, Friday, 2nd . . .

Within hours, Cazimir had been taken away to a sanatorium. The doctor who arranged the passage, reassured a crying Josephine,

"He is very young and strong. While now he seems ill, it is because he is demented with grief. He should be better in six, perhaps eight, months, I would say. Personally, I don't know of anyone dying from a broken heart, and I am sure he will be back to normal within a few months. I am rather more worried about Mr Zelski – he seemed very unwell indeed to me . . ."

There was no time for grieving. Josephine knew that it had happened so many times before, and she had to go on. Now, not only for Cazimir's sake, but also for his motherless children and orphaned baby girl.

Just before the funeral, Josephine went to the open coffin to say a silent goodbye. Maria, dressed in black, with her hands folded on her chest, looked as if she were asleep.

"I wonder, where you are now?"

For a moment, Josephine's eyes rested on the thick plait of golden hair framing Maria's pale face, before she fetched the scissors and cut the plait off.

"This is for your baby daughter, to have something of yours to remember you by when she grows up . . ."

On that same day, Maria was buried in the snow-swept, deserted cemetery, with only her closest family present. When the grave-diggers began to throw in the frozen earth, and the coffin disappeared from sight, Josephine closed her eyes, suddenly utterly exhausted. They stood around the grave united in their grief, and yet she felt horribly alone.

The awful sound of earth rattling against the wooden coffin, brought the realisation that it was final, and she wept. It seemed only yesterday that she had been standing over Anthony's and her father's graves. She thought about the future of the little children and about their father, her beloved son, Cazimir, who was now miles away, broken with grief and guilt, and about the senseless tragedy of his love, lost forever, passing inevitably away with death . . .

On the other side of the grave, Melanie held John's arm. Despite the freezing cold, he stood with bared head, strangely calm as he listened to the priest's sonorous voice. The beautiful words seemed somehow misplaced. With a pain in her heart, Josephine thought how strangely fickle life was, and how terribly unfair.

After the funeral, Melanie led John away. Josephine drove back home alone, and once inside, she wearily took off her coat and hat. She was glad that the house wasn't empty.

A wet-nurse had been found for the baby, and the children had come back home. She could hear their voices, somewhere in the house. I have to tell them, she thought. Thank God, they aren't old enough to understand.

She walked slowly from room to room, leaving each door open. There was no sign that anything was different from the time she had arrived two months ago – as if the tragedy she had just witnessed was a figment of her imagination. Only the garden door of the room, where Maria's coffin had rested before the funeral, was wide-open, the snow covering the parquet floor, and the room stony-cold. Josephine closed the door and shivered at the memory. It was getting dark, despite being only early afternoon, so she lit the oil-lamps. The golden lights, softly reflected in the mirror, offered comfort and warmth. A loud sound of knocking at the main door brought Josephine back to reality. Melanie stood on the doorstep, her eyes red-rimmed in an oddly austere face.

"I thought I had better check with you about the children, . . . and . . . and everything else . . . I left John at home, he seems so very tired."

"Do come in – I was just going to have some tea

and warm up a bit . . ."

Josephine, glad of the distraction, sat Melanie down and set about ordering the tea. A steaming samovar was brought in, and she poured the tea, handing a cup to Melanie, before pulling a dark bottle from the depths of the sideboard. Slowly and without spilling it, she poured an amber liquid into two large glasses.

"Take this, Melanie, as medicine – it is so horribly cold today . . ."

They drank quickly in one go, the welcome, warming feeling rising slowly within them. Taking care to sound composed and almost casual, Josephine turned to Melanie.

"It is better for the children to stay in a house they know, now that they have lost their mother and temporarily their father . . . At least I am here, as is the cook and the nanny. And you will come as often as you can, I'm sure . . ."

Melanie breathed a sigh of relief. She hadn't slept for a week, and what with John ailing, and then her other children, she really didn't know where it would all end. She smiled gratefully through the tears welling again in her eyes. Josephine put her hand on Melanie's shoulder.

"I don't know whether this will be of any comfort to you, but I keep thinking that there has to be a reason. Maybe this child has a special future in front of her, who knows . . ."

Melanie wiped her eyes, and tried to smile bravely.

"Oh, thank you, I don't know what we should do

without you. I don't know about the future, and I still don't understand . . . Everything is in such confusion . . . And then there is the christening to arrange . . . What shall we call the little one?"

Josephine met Melanie's eyes,

"I think that there is only one name possible, don't you?

We shall call her after her mother – Maria."

Cazimir came into the room where Josy stood by the window, facing the door. Her hands were trembling and her heart was beating wildly. She was glad that her face was shaded from the light and his questioning gaze. His dark eyes, unnaturally large in his thin, deathly-pale face, seemed oddly immobile and sombre.

"You wanted to have a talk with me?"

"In point of fact I did", she answered in stilted tone.

She took a deep breath, but her lips trembled so much that she could hardly form the words. Twice before, she had tried talking to him, but he had brushed her off impatiently as if the subject were trivial and unimportant. It had to be this time or never. She couldn't wait any longer.

Why, it was sixteen months since Maria's death, and out of those, he had spent nine in a sanatorium.

She could see as plain as daylight that the children had suffered greatly; first both parents had disappeared, then the company of the peasant, servant-women, however well-meaning wasn't satisfactory.

And then . . . and then, oh God, how she hated to admit it, Cazimir was now a stranger to them. He had come back a withdrawn, unsmiling man, who only spoke when absolutely necessary in cold, measured tones, and who kept the time spent with the children to a minimum, and if the truth were known, seemed to be doing his best in avoiding the baby girl, Maria, altogether.

She looked at him now and saw that his eyes

were fixed on the window behind her. He was waiting for her to speak.

It was awful that she couldn't control the trembling of her lips. Determined not to allow her son to see how close to tears she was, Josy took a deep breath and motioned him to sit down. For a moment, there was silence between them, before she haltingly started to speak.

"You know that I have been far from being an interfering mother to you. But this time it's different. This time the children's, your children's, well-being and future is at stake. They are very withdrawn, Cazimir, and very disturbed.

It's not their fault that their mother . . . has gone, and that you are . . . It breaks my heart to see you so unhappy! "He droppped his eyes and said nothing. Slowly she composed herself and continued.

"I don't think that there's any point in ignoring the issue any longer. It is very hard for me to say this, since I have loved Maria too, but your obligations towards your children are the most important, far more than your own concern and . . . and your sorrow."

She couldn't bear to look at him, yet she sensed his eyes fixed on her, and a strange watchfulness sparked in the air around them. She faced him boldly,

"I have to say this aloud, however painful it may be. You must take a wife, Cazimir, someone kind-hearted who would be a mother to these poor children, and who could perhaps, bring a little light and happiness into this bleak house."

There was another silence before he answered.

"I understand and appreciate your concern, Mother. You have mentioned the subject twice before and I have given the matter some thought, but I can't see any easy solution to this problem."

She noticed a trace of irritation in his voice, and decided to say nothing to correct his conviction that the problem was entirely hers.

"I have made my decision, which is final as far as I am concerned."

She looked at him sharply – there was a frown between his brows and his mouth drooped at the corners a little, as if he swallowed something unpleasant and bitter.

"If I were to accept your solution and marry, it would be in name only, Mother. Whatever I have will belong to my wife in exchange for her looking after my children well. For myself I could not, and please understand this, offer anyone love, physical or otherwise, or even the affection expected in marriage. I wish to be left alone.

If you are confident that you can find such a girl, then please go ahead. I will comply."

There was a pause. Josy sat very still, her mind in turmoil.

Where on earth could she find a bride on those harsh conditions? She would have to go back to Dubno, and ask all her friends, or perhaps the nuns in the convent would be able to recommend someone . . . maybe an orphan.

Suddenly, she remembered a young girl, Clara, who had been a pupil a year or two ago at the convent school for young ladies in reduced circumstances. Everyone in Dubno knew her sad story well. The family had lost everything in the reprisals, after the girl's father had been killed in battle. Her mother, Ludmilla, was an Italian who had married Clara's father, a Polish landowner, after a whirlwind romance, forsaking her family for him. They had been totally opposed to her marrying a foreigner and going to live so far away.

After his death they only sent her a note saying: We told you so.

The poor woman was now earning her living by giving piano lessons, and Clara's first post after finishing school, had been with ailing, old Colonel Gordon.

Perhaps, perhaps she would be interested in having a home of her own?

The more Josy thought about it the more convinced she became. All at once, she looked up with a gleam of hope in her now sparkling eyes. Once more she was her cheerful and optimistic self.

Surprised, Cazimir looked at her. She exuded an encouraging confidence. She smiled at him, with her wicked smile of old.

"I accept your challenge, my son. I shall leave tomorrow and make my inquiries in Dubno. If everything goes the way I suspect it might," she quickly checked herself, and prudently added, "and if God's will allows it, these poor children might have a mother in time for Christmas, and you might have someone who will give you peace and comfort when you come home after work."

Cazimir winced, "Whoever you have in mind, Mother, should first know about my conditions.

You will make sure of that, won't you?"

His voice had the same constrained tone which she should have got used to by now, but still hated all the same.

His self-control was inhuman and she knew that there wasn't a moment to lose.

She had to save him from this awful illness, the illness which no doctor believed existed. But like any mother, she knew without a shadow of doubt in her mind that her son was suffering from a broken heart. It was as simple as that.

"I am sure that we shall be lucky," she replied, and she was able to smile as she spoke.

Cazimir said nothing more, but bowed, before going to his room.

He went over to the window and stood there looking out reflectively on the afternoon sunlight-suffused gardens below.

After two hot, humid summers, the rose bushes which Maria had planted in the first year after their marriage, had grown tangled, and the whole garden was now an overgrown wilderness, uncared for and neglected without its mistress.

There was a sense of dejection everywhere, the previous magnificence in ruins, and wild creepers twining themselves around the trees and garden walls.

He had to accept that Maria's spirit no longer dwelled there, and that left on his own now, he was horribly alone in everything that he had to decide and endeavour.

It was final and Maria was no more than a pain

in his heart. He wanted to cry and yet he couldn't weep. It still seemed incredible to him that God had let them down, that he and Maria had played some part for Him, without understanding it, without any meaning. Was it all a cruel joke?

Perhaps it was all nothing but a dream, and that any moment now he would suddenly awake from it with a sigh of relief.

Or perhaps Maria had just been a figment of his imagination, only a shadow against the reality of life.

But then there were the three children . . . He had to look after them for Maria, even if all he wanted to do was to stay at the steelworks all day and night, burying himself in his work. It had even begun to seem quite natural to him living such an odd existence.

An idle, curious thought passed through his mind – who was this woman, who was desperate enough to accept his conditions, as his mother believed she would? And why would she?

He frowned a little. There was no point in guessing – he was indifferent to his mother's plans, and felt so weary.

The mellow sun came down over the apple-tree, and cast strips of pale gold amongst the shadows of the long grass underneath. Even the warm and balmy air had a subdued quality.

A little butterfly, resembling an exotic flower in its beauty, floated upon the dreamy air, its shimmering wings reflecting the golden light.

Somewhere in the future, there must be happiness, at least for the children. He wished nothing for himself, except that maybe one day, the anguish in his heart, all the dreadful unhappiness which he had suffered, would be assuaged, and that perhaps, he could learn to smile again.